Longevity City

Longevity City

David Murphy

Five Star • Waterville, Maine

First Edition, Second Printing.

Published in 2005 in conjunction with Tekno Books and Ed Gorman.

Set in 11 pt. Plantin by Minnie B. Raven.

Printed in the United States on permanent paper.

ISBN 1-59414-352-8 (hc : alk. paper)

LEABHARLANNA THIOBRAID ÁRANN

TIPPERARY LIBRARIES

Castle Avenue, Thurles, Co. Tipperary; (0504) 21555

Items should be returned on or before the last date shown below. Items can be renewed by phoning your local library: give the date due back and the number on the barcode label below. Fines will be charged for overdue items at the rate of €0.25 per item per week.

DATE DUE	DATE DUE	DATE DUE
NG. 11/06 ✓ Nenagh (067) 34404		
02 DEC		
08. FEB 07.		
16. FEB 07.		
20. APR 07.		

For Barry and Claire

Acknowledgments

Eternal gratitude to Brendan Gillen, Roulof Goudriaan, John Kenny, Bob Neilson and Greg O Shaughnessy for their advice and encouragement during the writing of this novel. Thanks also to Gordon Aalborg.

Part One

Chapter One
Lee

Lee and his friend Hugo tiptoed past the womb machines and the dehumidifying plant where they knew Zenga would be dozing in an old rocking chair. No longer young, Zenga always took a nap after lunch—particularly at this time of year, when the air was dead with heat. Lunchtime over and the bulk of his day's work done, the old Polynesian was now the only stumbling block to afternoon freedom. The six other adults would be easy to avoid, too. They were all in the work or recreation areas at the far end of the labyrinthine complex that was Camp Agrina. The air-conditioning unit behind the classrooms dispensed a fair old hum, but Lee's ears were sharp. When he heard the old man's snores he gave Hugo the thumbs up and out they sneaked.

Tropical air hit them like a tsunami. It filled their senses, playing on them with its warmth and heavy moistness. Lee and Hugo kept to the shade, flitting between spears of sunlight shafting down through gaps in the canopy. When they were out of earshot of Camp Agrina, the boys laughed and shouted their way along a well-worn path. Lee and Hugo had better things to do than sit on rickety classroom chairs watching boring videos of early millennium economic wars and environmental crises. The day was hot and fish were jumping in the Ludese River. They could be there and back, with time for half an hour's fishing, before school was out. There was no tuition robot on duty for the afternoon lessons—their nine classmates had promised to cover for them and there was little danger of being discovered.

Hugo, the eldest of the two by a year, was interested in birds, fish and girls—not by any means in that order. Lee was going on fifteen and interested in everything, including the bird that swooped low over the calm surface of the Ludese.

"What was that?" Hugo pointed a finger after it, the tone of his voice demanding an immediate response.

"Oriental Darter," said Lee.

"Top marks, my man. You get the first stab."

Lee pared a razor-sharp tip to one end of a bamboo cane. Then he stepped into the river. Up to his shorts in water, he stood motionless, waiting for a passing victim. A stillness came over both boys; one on the bank, watching; the other in the water, stalking.

An unsuspecting finfish swam up close. The only thing that betrayed movement in Lee's demeanor was a subtle change in the angle of his makeshift spear. Like the hand of a clock, it seemed not to move, but did as he made tiny adjustments to its position. It was a moment when time stood still.

The fish edged within centimeters of Lee's left foot. Hugo had to fight hard to resist the impulse to laugh at the thought that the smell attracted it. In that instant Lee struck—his bamboo cleaving the dorsal fin in half.

"Wa-hoo! Sure beats learning about ozone holes!" he roared, hoisting his prey in triumph.

The cane had penetrated right through. Stepping ashore, Lee speared the sharp end of the weapon into the marshy bank, impaling the dying fish to the ground. It looked up with wild eyes, its gaping mouth pleading for mercy. Hugo put it out of its misery with a karate chop and kept the edge of his hand on the fish's head while Lee withdrew the bamboo.

"My go." Hugo sprang to his feet and stepped into the water.

"Looks like we might have time to catch a couple each."

"Right. We'll hide 'em and pretend we caught 'em after school. That way they won't know we sneaked—" Hugo's sentence remained unfinished—the excitement that gripped his face saw to that.

He was up to his knees in the river, arm sweeping in an arc toward Lee. By the time the younger boy turned around, Hugo had already identified the exotic-looking creature flying low above the water. "Wow!" he yelled, "look at the size of that kingfisher!"

The moment Lee saw it he knew there was something wrong: the unusual size; the way it flew *exactly* in midstream; the way its flight path never varied in altitude; the way it craned its neck to stare at them. Lee met its eyes only briefly. Like an angel of death, it flew around the bend and disappeared. One glance at Hugo and he knew he was not alone in thinking something was not quite right.

"Christ," said Hugo. "What the hell was that?"

"Ain't no kingfish, that's for sure." Lee stood with hands on hips, staring at the river bend.

Hugo stepped ashore, trailing the blunt end of the bamboo in the water. "Somethin' fishy about that bird," he said.

"That was no bird, Hu."

"Sure looked real."

"Naw," said Lee. "It wasn't real."

"How can you be sure?"

"Dunno. Somethin' . . . unnatural . . ." Lee let his words

11

dangle. He kept staring at the bend, as if the bird might re-appear.

All interest in fishing gone, the boys debated whether or not to report what they had seen. Hugo was sure they should but uncertain if the bird was real. Lee was certain it was not real but unsure about reporting it.

They sneaked past a still somnolent Zenga and slipped into their rickety classroom chairs with forty minutes of video-lessons left to run. Despite the air-conditioning, their classmates were dead to the world from the combination of stultifying footage and the overpowering, sleep-inducing weight of a South East Asian afternoon. They could hardly raise their eyelids, never mind their curiosity, to ask about the fishing trip. When school was out, Lee and Hugo re-turned to the river and discussed what they had seen some more. Hugo did most of the talking. By the time he had fin-ished, Lee realized he was right.

"Okay, Hu. You want me to do the reporting. Fine, as long as I tell them we saw it now—after school. Right?"

"Right."

Down by the river, time passed quickly. Back at Camp Agrina, it dragged. Seven o'clock and Lee had still not re-ported what they had seen. He was leaning against the main entrance of the underground complex—which in reality looked like little more than the mouth of a small cave. Dinner had finished half an hour previously and Lee was kicking dust, rubbing his forehead—a migraine attack ges-tating in his skull. Hugo stood some distance away, chatting up two girls beneath the shade of a palm tree. One of the girls was tall, hair shorn like five o'clock shadow across her skull. She had been top of Hugo's list for weeks now, though he hadn't made his move yet. Lee couldn't see anything attractive about her. She was too skinny and loud for his liking. He wished he were as confident as his friend when it came to dealing with girls. Right now they were a mystery to him, though these days he was beginning to take an interest. His eyes were drawn to the shorn-haired girl's companion, a fifteen year old whose strawberry blonde head reached only to the other girl's shoulder. Lee had been noticing her a lot lately and it surprised him who she was with. Sharon was anything but boisterous. Something about her pale blue eyes, freckled cheeks and quiet nature made him want to stroll down to the palm tree and say hello, but there were other things on his mind. That river bird, for instance. He took his hand from his pocket to check the time. Minutes were limping by. No point in putting it off.

Hugo was animated, all arms. The tall bareheaded girl listened, entranced, then threw back her head and laughed. The joke was lost on her small blonde companion, whose lonesome round eyes searched for the fair-haired boy loitering near the entrance, but saw only his back as he walked into the cavern in the hillside.

Camp Agrina was largely underground, consisting of tunnels hollowed out between dry stone caves. Converted to living standards by the Australians in the 2050s, it had fallen into disuse by century's end. When Zenga, the old Polynesian, discovered it sometime later, it became a womb-station for the Association. Womb machines were in batteries of twenty-four, three of them in an area between the schoolrooms and the rear entrance.

The passageways that made up the underground warren at Camp Agrina were shaped like inverted 'U's and carved so smoothly they resembled tunnels encased in metal. The only way of telling they were carved of solid rock was by touch—even then their smoothness was deceptive. In many

13

places, the brightly colored walls were decorated with murals of the pupils' own design. Lee had contributed to some of these but was too preoccupied to notice them now.

Raul and Haria Armitage had almost finished their meal of curried rice and diced banana when he knocked softly on their door.

"Come in," said Haria, putting aside her knife and fork.

"Am I disturbing you?"

"Not at all," said Raul in response to the quiet fourteen-year-old in the doorway. "Come right in, Lee. Have a seat."

The boy sat at the table, trying to look nonchalant.

"Want some sweet milk or coffee?" asked Haria.

Lee declined politely.

"Have you eaten?" she said. "You look pale. Migraine again?"

"Just a mild attack. It's going away, I think. Yeah, I've eaten." Lee's hands were on his lap, his eyes flitting from one object to another on the small cluttered table.

"We heard you caught a fish for dinner."

Sometimes Lee wondered if his foster father was psychic.

"Something bothering you, son?" Raul carefully shepherded the last grains of rice onto his fork.

Lee watched them disappear into his mouth. "Yeah—drogues."

If there was a momentary lapse in the way Raul chewed, Lee did not notice it.

"Go on," said his father.

"Me and Hugo, we think we saw one down by the river—after school."

"After school?"

"Yeah." Lee shifted uncomfortably. "At three o'clock."

Raul pushed his empty plate to the center of the table. "Okay," he said. "Tell us about it."

14

Lee described as best he could what he and Hugo had seen. Raul and Haria asked endless questions, making him repeat himself until they too had a clear picture of what had flown along the Ludese River that day. When he had related all he knew about size, flight path, altitude, and the curious way it tilted its head to view the riverbank where the boys stood—they were most interested in the realistic way it seemed to look at them—they concluded that it may well have been a fake kingfisher with a microchip for navigation and a camera for eyes. Then again, it may not.

"Doesn't matter, anyway," said Raul. "All it saw were two boys fishing. Many a bird's seen that."

When Lee had gone he turned to his wife. "More coffee, Haria? Could be a long night."

Lee hid in an alcove near his foster parents' door, settling down in the shadows to see what might happen in the wake of his revelation. He did not have long to wait. Five adults soon arrived. From his secret recess in the wall, he watched them enter the Armitage quarters. Old Zenga was last in.

With the entire adult population of Agrina in Raul and Haria's living room, Lee hurried from the alcove and scampered down the corridor to the exit. Once outside the underground complex he looked around, desperate to find Hugo, to tell him that a meeting had obviously been called on foot of the bird incident. There was no sign of his friend—no sign of the tall, bareheaded Tamara either—though the strawberry blonde girl was sitting alone under the palm tree, reading a book. Lee gathered up his courage and tried to look casual as he walked over to her.

"Hey, Sharon," he said with his hands in his pockets. "Any idea where Hugo went?"

She lifted her gaze from the pages and looked at him, her

pretty eyes squinting in the evening sun. She shielded them with one hand and pointed with the other at the jungle. "In there," she said.

Something in her smile, in the way she looked up at him, made Lee's throat go dry.

"Want me to show you exactly where?"

"No, no." Lee felt suddenly foolish. "It's all right—I'll catch him later." With that he turned, worrying that she had seen him blush.

He spent an hour in the library checking the digital files for drogues. It was difficult for him to concentrate. Sharon was pretty. She was full of secret depths, unlike Tamara. When Tamara came into Lee's mind he started to think of what Hugo might be doing at that very moment. Then it became hard for him to keep his mind on drogues. Eventually, he found the files he was looking for, studied them, and returned to the alcove to wait for the meeting to end. Time passed slowly. In its passing he thought again of Sharon and wished that she were in the alcove with him. He had never been alone with a girl. Right now he would have given anything for her to be with him in this secret place, away from prying eyes, away from the world.

At half past ten the door opened and the five visitors left Raul and Haria's quarters. When they had disappeared down the corridor, Lee knocked on his foster parents' door for the second time that evening.

"Well, well." Raul did not seem surprised to see him again. "What can we do for you now?"

"It's the bird. I know it was a drogue."

Raul glanced at Haria. "Do you now? What makes you so sure?"

"The way it looked at us. No bird would do that. Besides, I did some research."

"Research?" said Haria.

"Yeah, in the library just now. I know you called a meeting." Lee blurted out all his ammunition in one gulp.

"Want some more coffee?" Haria addressed her husband, a trace of a smile on her lips.

"No," said Raul. "Fresh air's what's needed. Come, young man, let's walk."

Ivory light shining through the canopy bore witness to a full moon. It provided enough illumination for the two figures to walk quickly to a rocky outcrop surrounded by wild garlic plants.

"Keeps the vampires out," said Raul as they sat and listened a while to the noises of the night. The air was laden with the sound of jungle wildlife—insects, mainly. Somewhere in the distance, Lee thought he heard a high-pitched squeal. Hugo and Tamara, probably.

"Okay, son. What exactly did your research tell you?"

"I checked the vidfiles and digitapes. There's a bird-drogue programmed to follow the course of a river, flying always at a constant height above the surface, keeping always in midstream—except when there's an object like a boat or a bridge. It's designed to fly over those. It keeps going until the water ends. Then it ascends to several hundred feet and flies directly back to base, keeping always well up in the air on its return flight. While it's scanning, its cam-eyes swivel from side to side, locking on to whatever it's been pre-programmed to look for." Lee paused before adding, "May I ask how you knew it was a drogue?"

Raul plucked a blade of grass and rolled it between forefinger and thumb. The boy was shrewder than he had given credit for. Well mannered, too.

"There was a flitter on the radar today."

"A what?"

Raul flicked the grass away and joined his hands around his knees. "A flitter is caused by something mechanized. The scan picked it up only briefly. It was in the vicinity of the river, around one o'clock. Your report confirmed it. Thing is there's a discrepancy of two hours between it and your reported sighting of the bird."

Lee was grateful for the darkness that swallowed up his reddening face. He cleared his throat and began, "Em, to tell the truth, we . . ."

"Don't worry about skipping off school—it's not important. The main thing is you had the gumption to report it. It could have spotted you anytime."

"Has one ever been seen here before?" Lee felt enormously relieved, and full of admiration for the way his father had fended off the time discrepancy.

"No, but we've been expecting it. Bio's wings are spreading to the third world. Though it'll be years before they come into this wilderness."

"Why have they left us alone for so long?"

Raul shrugged his shoulders. "It suits them to keep most of the world underdeveloped. They started with an elite, remember? Only the affluent were given Geminizon at first. Later, they forced it on the rest of society, but not without encountering one or two problems. They still have trouble with pockets of resistance in the north. Besides, the logistics of introducing the Geminizon drug worldwide would be too much. There's not enough womb-banks or colonies to cope with the number of twins."

"They're increasing the number of colonies, aren't they?"

"All the time. It's part of their grand plan. They'll also drastically reduce the population of the third world."

"How will they do that?"

"War and disease did it for them last century, just as President Petty came into office. Before that, back at the turn of the millennium, certain politicians led the U.S. down an isolationist, anti-environmental path. Then came the wars, the chemical crises causing widespread infertility. That provided them with an excuse, a justification for introducing Geminizon. 'Let's increase the population,' they said. 'We'll duplicate people to protect against infertility becoming a problem again.' Then they said, 'The only way a childless couple may have a baby is if they agree to take the drug that causes twins to be born'. Yes, Lee. War and disease worked for them in the northern hemisphere. Maybe it'll work here, too." Raul's body trembled, as if a chill had come from somewhere.

To Lee, his foster father seemed suddenly old. He looked Raul in the eye and said, "Petty was a bastard to start all this."

"He was just a lackey, used by forces beyond his control. If you want to know who the real culprit was during the Petty Administration, well, a man by the name of Ronald Carver Junior set himself up as a sort of benign despot—a ruler, a dictator who promises to be kind. Guess what?"

"He goes rotten."

"Right first time. What does a despot do when he's not benign any more? He installs his own son to take over when he dies, that's what. Now we're stuck with Ronald Carver III. Do you think a man who colonizes Mars is going to let parts of his own planet stay free from his influence?"

"I've heard of him," said Lee.

"Study your history if you want to fully understand the way the world's gone. In the past, especially the late twentieth century, society was friendlier toward children than it is now." Raul paused and stared into the night. He was sur-

19

prised at what he was saying—things he'd never said to a fourteen-year-old before.

"What happened to your twin?" asked Lee.

Raul smiled. The boy was nothing if not direct. "Back in '071 there was an accident in one of the New Jersey womb-banks. The life support failed—no twin."

"But they let you live?"

"They lost only one womb-battery, like the ones in there." Raul jerked his thumb over his shoulder at Camp Agrina. "If an entire womb-bank had gone kaput they would've eliminated all the twins, but twenty-four spread over a city the size of New York? Seventy-six years ago they tolerated the odd singleton. Matter of fact, they used them for propaganda—made those with twins feel how lucky they were. Having a twin became a sought-after thing among the well-off sections of society. As for the poor, the down-trodden, the government was never interested in them until they realized that by making Geminizon compulsory for ev-eryone they could weed out the undesirables, the malad-justed, the socially disaffected. Not one of the seven adults in Camp Agrina has a twin in the bank. Zenga's from Poly-nesia, a Geminizon-free zone, so he wouldn't have one anyway. As for the others, most of them died in battery fail-ures. In some cases, like your mother's, it was different. Her twin's death was solitary."

"I didn't know that. What happened?"

"No one knows. Faulty womb-unit, maybe. The fetus just died. It happens."

"How did she find out?"

"The Association accessed Bio files and discovered her twin was dead. After watching her for a while they ap-proached and asked her to work for them. That's how most volunteers are recruited—or were, I should say. Did they tell you in school that eleven years ago Bio decided that all singletons were to be eliminated—and that they made it retrospective? Know what that word means?"

"Yeah. The Purge of '136. That was the year Bio introduced a law that if someone's twin defected to the Association, or if a fetus was smuggled out of the womb machines, or even if the twin just plain died in an accident, then the surviving twin was to be terminated no matter what their age. Even if someone's twin had disappeared years before, they would still terminate the survivor, no matter who they were. They did that so there would be no more singletons among the ruling elite. Bio called it the Resolution of '136—we call it *The Purge.*"

Raul flicked at an insect crawling up his trouser leg. "Your mother gave up a life and a career to come here. It was a big wrench for her, coming from a cool climate and a cozy lifestyle. Don't you ever forget it. There are many things about Sulawesi she finds difficult to cope with."

"Yes," said Lee. Then, "Of the six adults who came from the north, all their twins are dead, right?"

Raul was getting to his feet, anticipating what might come next.

"What about my twin? If he was killed in '136, why won't you tell me about my background—my biological parents?"

"You know too many things already for a boy of your age." Raul chided himself for letting a fourteen-year-old take control of the conversation. "Come on," he spoke with a firmness that killed any further questioning. "Time to hit the sack."

Haria was in bed by the time Raul Armitage returned to his underground quarters. He undressed by the dim light

21

from the living room, not wanting to disturb his wife by turning on the bedroom lamp in case she was sleeping. Behind the mosquito net he saw their single white sheet rise and fall with the rhythm of her breathing. He switched off the outer light, padded across the room, pulled aside the net and slipped gently into bed where he lay for a time staring at the ceiling.

As his eyes accustomed themselves to the dark, so his mind began to see things with greater clarity. That boy, Lee, had the intelligence and initiative to be a born leader. On such tender young shoulders the Association might one day pin its faint and fleeting hopes. Raul turned in the bed to Haria—who was definitely asleep. She was tired these days, always tired. Inwardly, he castigated himself for saying what he had said to the boy about Haria wrenching herself away from her own life and career. What were the things he had said she had left behind—a cool climate and cozy lifestyle? That there were aspects of life on Sulawesi she found difficult to cope with? He clucked his tongue for being so loose. The last thing he needed was to make the young boy feel guilty about the sacrifice his mother had made all those years ago. Raul put his hand gently around Haria's stomach and edged closer until he felt her curly hair on his face. Fifteen years was such a long time, yet it seemed like just last week.

Chapter Two

The officer-in-charge spoke matter-of-factly to her five orderlies: "Make sure you hold the fetus in the prescribed manner—head toward you. When facing the cameras, lower your arms and un-cup your hands slightly so they get a good picture. Then turn and walk slowly to the womb-cot and carefully insert the fetus. Got it?"

Her orderlies nodded and mumbled affirmatively.

"Good. Carry out procedures as instructed. Remember who follows who."

The door to the anteroom opened. The clinic administrator poked his head in and said, "We're ready now, officer."

"Fine," she said. "Let's go."

The five orderlies marched in single file, the first in line a lot more nervous than the rest. It was not the glare of cameras that was getting to Haria. Her anxiety had more to do with the metal capsule, thirty centimeters long, ten in diameter, strapped to the back of her left thigh.

The orderlies marched slowly down the long delivery ward. Haria knew that what she was about to do had been well planned: basics such as walking normally despite the capsule stuck to her leg had been adequately dealt with in training. The Association had selected her for this task partly on account of her long legs and broad build. Yet she could not help but fear that the capsule would show through the motion of her calf-length medical gown. Her head kept telling her there was little chance of being detected—her heart refused to believe it. Smuggling a fetus out of the clinic was bad enough. Switching the empty capsule on her leg for one containing a live fetus was worse. Crazy, she told herself. Crazy.

The orderlies marched in time to the slow rhythm of the clinic's PA system. The ward they stepped into was large and L-shaped. To the right as they entered was the recess that formed the bottom bar of the L. In it the portable womb-cot awaited its five fetuses. To the orderlies' left, opposite the womb-cot, was a dais on which the administrator stood. Alongside him, running all the way down the long wall of the ward, were five tiers of student nurses and doctors rising to their feet at the administrator's command. Beneath the bottom tier were rows of cameras. Most were trained on the five beds jutting out from the wall opposite them. Some of the lenses followed the orderlies' slow progress along the floor in the middle of the ward. When the solemn beat ended Haria and the other four were in position, each standing to attention two meters from the foot of each bed. Haria carefully aligned her feet with the small 'X' on the floor opposite the last patient. As she waited for Deliverance to begin, she felt the heat of vidcams worming into her back. Behind and above the cameras, she knew there were all those student nurses and doctors, each with their eyes trained on what would happen next.

The following ten minutes were the longest in Haria's twenty-seven-year-old life. Her palms felt clammy, despite a pair of surgical gloves. She told herself that her forehead was sweaty from lights and heat, and that the other orderlies were sweating, too. Deep down she knew it was not the hot smell of cameras that was getting to her—it was her own anxiety. She thought of all the things that might give her away: the rings beneath her eyes indicating sleepless nights contemplating an act which would change her life utterly— quite possibly end it, too. Three toilet visits in the previous hour must have highlighted her nervousness. Most of all, her height: all 1.9 meters of it. Haria stood one full head above the other orderlies. The height that once brought proficiency in sport and embarrassment in school now invited scrutiny from intrusive cameras. Her face felt like a flashing beacon. Often she had wished to be at least fifteen centimeters shorter. Now she wished for it like never before.

A brief glance revealed her commanding officer peering through the anteroom door. For an instant there was eye contact. In that moment Haria was certain her CO would see into her mind and through her gown. She looked away, trying to concentrate on the bumps and hollows of the lavender bed sheet covering the anaesthetized patient before her. Concentration was no easy matter, given the background noise of a high-pitched speech glorifying long life and the power of the Geminizon drug.

After what seemed an age, the voice grew quiet. A strident fanfare heralded the act of Deliverance. Moving rhythmically to the music, the machinery around the bed furthest from Haria swung into action. Twin metallic arms reached down from the ceiling, gripped the top corners of the bed sheet, drew it up like a curtain and slowly pulled it to the foot of the bed where it fell in neat folds. The woman beneath lay in a long white gown. It looked like a regulation hospital bed gown, standard issue—with one major difference. There was a circular piece of material, roughly thirty centimeters in diameter, missing from the middle, exposing the patient's stomach. The machinery at the next bed drew down its bed sheet, too. Likewise with the next and the next; the removal of each lavender covering revealed a mother-to-be wearing the same white garb, each with that round window on the stomach. The white gowns reminded Haria of shrouds except for the circular bits missing around the midriffs.

Other mechanical devices, containing medical instruments and video equipment, descended from the metal housing above the beds. With movements small and precise, the instruments hovered over each patch of exposed skin. The music resumed, somber as before, as the operations on all five women began. In spite of the music and the blood pounding in her ears, Haria could hear the dull whirr of moving motors and cutting blades. Far enough back not to have a direct view—she thanked whoever ordained such things for that—she kept her eyes from straying to the gory close-ups on the large wall-screen above each bed. Whichever way she looked, Haria could not prevent a warm knot of nausea rising in her throat, just as she could do little about the overpowering smell of antiseptic rising from the bed before her.

Incisions were made in the lower abdominal wall and through the lower region of the uterus. The hospital scanning equipment selected which of each of the twin fetuses to remove, basing its decision solely on which could most conveniently be sucked out. The amniotic sac was pierced, the umbilical of the chosen twin sliced, cutting it off from the placenta. The fetus was removed through incisions quickly repaired with a skin-melding solvent, leaving its lucky twin to develop normally in the mother's womb.

The orderlies stepped forward to accept mechanically held offerings. Some of the students whooped and applauded, reminding Haria that every med school has its share of cretins. Most people felt guilty about the Deliverance operation. They wanted to forget that it ever took place, preferring to think of the fetus as being less than real. At twenty weeks, the lungs were unable to cope with life outside the womb—to prevent distress, this part of the operation ended almost as it began.

As the music changed to the soothing tones of a lullaby, the orderlies turned and marched quickly to the large L-shaped recess at the far end of the ward. The womb-cot contained five openings, like portholes. Each housed a transparent temperature-controlled capsule with artificial placenta. Haria placed the fetus in the womb-cot capsule and hooked up the umbilical. She looked momentarily at the creature floating in artificial waters. A fine downy growth covered its skin. Real hair was beginning to grow on its head—his head; she could see its sex now. Already there were eyebrows, though the lids were fused. She slid the capsule in, knowing the fetus would thrive in it for three weeks before growing large enough to warrant transfer to a womb-battery.

The music stopped as the three orderlies in the middle stepped back, leaving Haria and the orderly at the far end to wheel the womb-cot out of the ward. Another speech began, the administrator on his dais as boisterous and emotive as ever.

Haria's pulse raced. It was almost time.

The leader of the Chicago cell of the Association had decided that the ideal moment to strike was when the womb-cot was being wheeled out of the ward. There was a supporting pillar, a blind spot, behind which the capsule would pass. That was the moment. The problem was the orderly at the other end of the cot—it all depended on whether she

27

could be diverted. It was the best plan they could come up with. Though the cell could not get another Association member on orderly roster that day, they did succeed in infiltrating the student ranks. At least, Haria hoped they did. She had been afraid to look to check if her colleague was in the ward in case a stolen glance might give them away. She would soon know, anyway.

She pushed one end of the cot as the other orderly began to pull. Out of the corner of her eye, Haria sensed her commanding officer's gaze. Damn, they had not counted on the door to the anteroom being open. Deeper music now—a requiem for departing fetuses.

The cot looked like a child's drawing of a ship without a funnel. It was three meters long, the capsules in their portholes fifty centimeters apart. The pillar was four meters away. As far as Haria was concerned, she approached it only very slowly. *Come on,* she mumbled as she wheeled the womb-cot forward. The orderly at the other end glared at her. Realizing she was pushing too hard, Haria told herself to ease off, which was no simple matter—her adrenalin was pumping so much she could almost smell it.

The other orderly was behind the pillar now, pulling the far wheels out of sight. *Not much longer,* Haria told herself as the cot edged out of view of the cameras and the first porthole disappeared from public scrutiny. She tried to keep her head steady. Porthole number two slid into position. Haria fought to control her breathing. Number three passed behind the pillar. *Keep your head level,* she yelled inwardly. The fourth. *Concentrate on the wheels,* she told herself. *Align them with the pillar.*

As soon as the fifth porthole was wheeled behind the pillar, Haria bowed her head. This slight movement was the signal her colleague in the student ranks had been waiting for. He pressed the remote button in his pocket.

The sharp blast of rending metal was like a thunder-crack outside the delivery ward. The bomb was not large—a small amount of explosive had been used, and the clinic windows had not shattered—but the shock of the blast had the desired effect. Everybody turned to look. Some of the students screamed, others clung for comfort to the nearest available body. Cameras swiveled, hoping for a piece of the action. Haria stood rigid. For an endless instant, the orderly at the other end of the mobile womb also froze. Then, as expected, curiosity won out. 'Jeez!' she whispered, abandoning her post, walking—running—to the nearest window.

Now Haria was faced with another obstacle—her commanding officer. She stood in the anteroom doorway, eyes fixed on the backs of the gaping crowd at the windows. *Go and look!* Haria muttered in the back of her throat

Her CO refused to budge.

The orderly who was supposed to be on womb-duty at the other end of the cot brushed past her commanding officer. Oh no, thought Haria, the CO's going to order her to return to her post. To Haria's relief, it had the opposite effect. Like a magnet, the excited orderly drew the officer in her wake.

Now. The moment was now. Haria stepped behind the pillar, pulled the target capsule out of the porthole, placed it on top of the womb-cot, whipped up her white gown, plucked the empty capsule off the magnetic straps around her thigh, and inserted it into the porthole.

It stuck halfway in.

Her heart missed two beats. Cold fear sailed up her spine like a surfboard on her back. The glint of artificial light on the capsule's see-through surface convinced her that the vidcams had swiveled back to capture her treacherous act. She glanced fearfully over her shoulder, expecting to be confronted by the full glare of cameras. Instead, she saw that they were still focused on the parking lot.

To her, it seemed as though eons had passed since the whip-crack of explosives outside the clinic. In reality, it had been only seconds. She pulled the capsule back a fraction and tried again. It ran in smoothly. Muttering a silent prayer, she whipped up her gown once more, placed the target capsule on her thigh-magnets, and breathed again. She wiped the cold film of sweat from her forehead knowing the fetus could withstand such rough treatment. It was surrounded by protective fluid just like in a mother's womb. With a sigh of relief, she stepped from behind the pillar and joined the curious throng at the windows.

The ceremony resumed one minute later. The device in the parking lot had cratered just one hoverbay—sufficient to divert attention and give her the time she had needed. The downside, she knew, was that the flap in security might cause problems later. Wheeling the cot out of the ward, Haria convinced herself that the worst was over. Out in the corridor, she and the orderly who had pulled it from the other end stood to attention, backs to the wall, on either side of the womb-cot.

Six members of the Illinois State Militia formed a ceremonial guard around the fetuses. Double-doors at the corridor's end opened with a soft swish, allowing the administrator and the students to file in and join the cortege. When all was ready the honor party moved off, escorting the womb-cot to G-wing for installation in the womb-bank.

As the line of people filed by, Haria stood perfectly still, her gaze fixed on an invisible point midway across the floor.

She tried to calm her nerves by throwing passing legs out of definition with her fixed stare. It worked for all the legs— except the last pair. They came sharply into focus when they halted and turned to face her. Haria at once recognized the boots and trousers as standard militia issue that could only belong to her commanding officer.

She slowly raised her line of sight, pulse rate again in treble figures, heart pounding so loudly she could hear it as well as feel it. Her CO must have heard it, too. Their eyes met. Then the commanding officer glanced at the other orderly before looking straight ahead. "Dismissed," she barked, walking briskly after the cortege.

The changing rooms at Chicago Gemini Clinic contained enough lockers and cubicles to provide plenty of nooks and crannies for private undressing. Haria was not in the mood for taking chances. Conscious of widespread surveillance, she refused to take off her gown, opting to put her street clothes on over it. The gypsy dress she stepped into was wide and layered, of a kind briefly in vogue the previous year. She had taken to reviving the fashion in recent weeks, so people would be used to her out-of-style eccentricities and pay her no heed.

She had also taken to exiting via the militia section. Orderlies were supposed to come and go via maintenance wing, but that doorframe incorporated X-ray vision. It was the same at every exit except militia. There was a security man on duty right now. She had cultivated him with small talk, though he filled her with nothing but distaste. She picked up her racquet bag and slung it over her shoulder. The flyball arena across the street from militia was her excuse, the bag her passport, for exiting that way.

Archie Bennett's security equipment did not include

X-ray doors, but he did possess a handheld scanner to give passing personnel the once over. Haria had deliberately teased him once or twice about how he preferred using it on women, which was true. She knew Bennett fancied her. From his latest line in chat she judged he really fancied his chances. When he saw her walking toward him, he slid his pornzine under the desk.

"Hi, Archie."

"Hello, Haria. Late for your game again?" He nodded at her racquet bag and reached for his scanner.

"Yeah. Say, Archie—are you trying to sneak another peek through that thing?"

Bennett's hand was on it now, lifting it. "Fringe benefit of the job. Only shows an outline."

"Talking about your job, Archie—are you on duty later on?"

Bennett was beside her now, scanner at the ready, but he wasn't thinking security any more. "You mean tonight?"

"There's a party down Fontana Street. Lots of iso-music. You're into that, right?"

Bennett's eyes were wide and bright. "Yeah, I'd love to . . ."

"Ten o'clock in Iris's. Don't be late." Haria smiled sweetly and turned to the exit.

Bennett watched her step out onto the pavement; his beady eyes following her every move. Shame about that skirt; it hid her curves and spoiled the way she moved.

A gulp of Chicago air. Out at last. Though the day was hot and humid, and Haria was by no means a hot summer person, she inhaled the stifling air of the city as if it was the freshest, coolest, cleanest air in the world. She was definitely out. The fetus was out. That was all that mattered now. As she puffed her cheeks to blow the air gratefully from her lungs, a familiar voice behind her called, "Hey, Haria."

Oh Christ. What did the creep want now? She turned around.

Bennett stood framed by the doorway, arm extended, pointing his scanner at her. "You know how it is. I gotta do my job."

Fuck. The air in her lungs turned to ice. No, not now. Please not now. Not when she had made it all the way to the street.

"You never give up, Archie." Not a breath escaped her lips but the words came out. She did not know how, but they did. And more: "Can't you wait until tonight, Archie?"

"Aw, Haria. Gimme a break. It's not that. It's your bag—I gotta check your bag."

Haria walked one block from Chicago Gemini Clinic and turned left, a perimeter wall shielding her from Archie Bennett's leering eyes. Ignoring the flyball arena, she stepped into a hovercab parked conveniently at the sidewalk, its quenched roof-light indicating it was off-duty.

The cabbie switched on the roof-light and engaged alto-mode. When the hover was at level one, he asked, "Okay?"

His passenger let out a long low whistle. "About five heart attacks. Otherwise, I'm fine. How long have we got?"

"As soon as the second phase of the ceremony is over and the students begin to disperse, they'll check for life signals and find an empty capsule. Right about now I should think. Best insert it."

The cabbie swung the hover onto flyway five, level two. He was conscious of Haria's long legs as she lifted her dress and gown to remove the capsule. Through the sides of his eyes he saw her hitch her clothes even higher to remove the topmost magnetic strap, the one inches from her panties. It was a favorite fantasy of his, to have a customer lift her skirt in the cab. As the air-conditioning in his hover seemed suddenly inadequate, he reminded himself that he was working for the Association and that this was no ordinary pick-up. He was tempted to remark that removing the capsule like that might cause a collision. He thought better of it and kept his silence. When her legs were covered again, the capsule on her lap, he prodded an indicator stalk. A flap opened in the doorframe alongside her.

"Time we were out of this town," she said.

It was a snug fit. The flap closed again.

"Yep," he said, setting the controls to maintain the capsule at the correct temperature all the way to Oregon.

Chapter Three

Raul Armitage craned his neck and gazed at the tall-masted *pinisi* in Paotere Harbor. It constantly amazed him that schooners were still used to transport cargo, but then Ujung Pandang, capital of Sulawesi, had always been renowned for its seafaring tradition. Raul shook his head at the incongruity of a sailor shimmying up the rigging in this day and age, and looked instead at the hydrohoppers and hoveryachts that made up the bulk of vessels in the harbor. He also noted a number of patrol boats moored near the marina.

Early morning air was heavy with smells of fish and chilies. Raul walked past the schooners, the markets, and the last boy spinning for his breakfast, to where a jetty provided respite from the thronged harbor. It also afforded a vantage point for scanning incoming traffic. Raul sat on the jetty and let his feet dangle over dark ripple-free water. A glance at his watch told him it was almost time.

Stuart Mulroy's hydrohopper landed like a swan in the outer reaches of Paotere Harbor. Raul watched it touch down, knowing it would take Mulroy five minutes to guide it to its mooring buoy, another ten to punt his passenger ashore, and five more to bring her to the Celebes Hotel.

Raul sauntered back along the quayside, arriving at the Celebes with time to spare. He sat at the bar counter and ordered sweet tea. Two sips later, he sensed a shadow stalk across the floor, approaching him from behind. Bracing himself for a shoulder slap, he heard Mulroy greet him with his customary, "How are they hangin', Armo?"

"Fine." Raul winced and rubbed his shoulder blade, still smarting from the blow. "You're right on time as usual."

"You know me," Mulroy winked at the barman. "Punctuality is my only vice. Set 'em up, Sumba. A long shot for the sailor, a fresh cup for Armadillo Armitage here, and whatever you're havin' yourself, okay?"

"Looks like the fleet's in," Mulroy whispered as soon as the grateful barman was out of earshot.

"I saw the patrol boats out there. Any trouble from them en route?"

"They stayed well clear. My passenger's on her way."

"Good," said Raul.

When the drinks arrived Mulroy said, "I gotta moor myself to one of those easy chairs. Been standin' all day."

"You know how it is, at his age." Raul winked at Sumba and, wary of another slap, pretended to give Mulroy a wide berth as they moved from the counter.

They sat in the far corner away from the barman's ears. Raul had a good view of the otherwise empty saloon. From his chair he could also see the hotel lobby and the two figures walking toward them. He recognized one of Mulroy's crew. Then he looked at the passenger. Raul always was a sucker for tall women. He watched the lady walk across the floor to their corner and admired the gentle way she placed a piece of brightly woven traditional basketry on the floor. The crewman put her suitcase by the wall. Mulroy waved him away. Then he pulled over a third chair for his passenger. As she sat, her eyes met Raul's but just as quickly turned away again. "Cup of tea for the lady, Sumba,"

36

shouted Mulroy. Then, leaning in close, he introduced them with a whisper. "Raul Armitage," he hissed. "Meet Haria Roberts."

She took his hand and met his eyes again, this time with a smile so understated in its beauty Raul could hardly wait to find out more about her.

Next morning Haria Roberts stepped out of the Celebes Hotel and walked along a quayside full of smells and grease from the oils of fish and fishermen's sumps. She turned down an alley and was met by a familiar figure—the sailor who had escorted her to the hotel the previous evening. He took her suitcase—she insisted again on holding on to her souvenir basket—and led her to the unlocked rear door of a dreary-looking office building. An elevator took them to the rooftop where Raul Armitage's flyer was in take-off mode. The sailor handed Raul the suitcase and helped Haria aboard. He saluted Raul and returned to the elevator. Seconds later, the vehicle was climbing fast.

"Any problems?" asked Raul.

"No. Your directions were perfect."

"Is that it?" he jerked his thumb at the brightly colored basket on her lap.

"Yes." She held it firmly as Raul maneuvered onto flyway two, the main route north.

"It's a good idea—the basket makes you look like a tourist. Did you sleep well?" he asked as streaks of gray swept across the sky.

"Yeah, though it's kind of muggy at night in these parts."

Raul again admired her delicate smile. He was tempted to say that the interior would make a muggy night in Ujung Pandang seem like Lapland, but he wanted that smile to stay.

Dawn came quickly in the tropics. Ujung Pandang was hardly behind them when the sun sat up. Like a cable car on invisible wires, their small craft sailed through the air at a steady altitude of two hundred meters.

"This is an old model," she said.

"Not many flyers hereabouts. This would be considered modern by Asian standards. Look." Raul banked to the right and circled above a small village. On one side of the settlement several buildings stood on stilts.

"Is that to keep wild animals out?"

"No. They're rice barns. They build them high on smooth pillars and keep the pillars greased so the rats can't climb."

Haria's face was a half-mix of relief and horror. "Is there much twinning?" she asked.

"Very little, except among those in control. Bio likes to keep Geminizon for the northerners. Guess you don't have a twin in the bank, huh?"

"No. There was some kind of power failure. And you?"

"Me neither. Makes us ideal material for resisting the establishment, doesn't it?"

Haria didn't answer. After a pause, she said, "What happens if we get stopped?"

"We won't. The long arm of Bio doesn't stretch this far."

"Back home they tell us everywhere is under control."

"They would say that, wouldn't they? But not here. The size of the place protects us. If you combine the islands of Indonesia, and add in the seas between, you get an area as large as what used to be the U.S.A."

After several miles of looking down at lush foliage, Haria said, "I never imagined there could be so much vegetation. You'd almost think there'd never been a crisis."

"Hah," Raul snorted. "That *was* a crisis back in '015. American troops sent in to stop the felling, economic wars between the third world and the West, the second Japanese-American war, etc, etc. As far as freedom was concerned, it was pretty predictable what happened next."

"From what Mulroy told me on the 'hopper, you two guys don't exactly lead predictable lives."

Raul threw back his head and laughed as he set the controls for descent.

He landed the flyer in a grassy field no bigger than a basketball court. The hoverjets scared several grazing horses. Bucking and neighing, they galloped for cover as Raul maneuvered the flyer beneath overhanging trees. "They're about the nearest thing to wild animals." He pointed at the horses when they had touched down. "Practically all the large wild species have died out. Birds and insects, and most of the smaller mammals, survived okay. From here on we go at ground level to avoid radar."

From the midst of trees came Zenga, a Polynesian tall and handsome—a brown pearl of a man whose handshake promised much by way of strength, decisiveness and loyalty. He was in his early seventies, about ten years older than Raul, who introduced him as their guide.

"It's very easy to find a hiding place in Sulawesi," said Raul as they chugged upstream for forty kilometers in an old-fashioned *klotok*. "Impossible to search the place thoroughly—too many mountains, not enough rivers."

Vegetation soon clogged the river. Nipa palms sprouted from the water like forests of giant bulrushes. When they reached that part of the river where the water's surface was completely enveloped in a brown spiny sea, they steered to the riverbank where they hid the boat before venturing inland on foot. Zenga led the way—his trailmaker cut a swathe high and wide as a door through the undergrowth.

Haria felt her sweat shrivel up her clothes with rotten clamminess, melding them to her skin like a coat of hot molasses. But the jungle was new to her. There were enough distractions to keep her mind off the discomfort.

After what seemed an eternity—her watch had steamed up too much to reveal the time—they camped on the sandbank of a small river. When camp was made she propped the mosquito net up on sticks stuck in the sand and rested beneath it while Zenga and Raul went casting for dinner. Fish and sweetened milk made her feel better. The heat showed mercy, too. When darkness fell they sat on their sleeping bags around the fire. Zenga showed her his trailmaker, which looked just like an old-fashioned lightsaber.

"Before it was invented we had to hack our way through the jungle," he said. "The most ground we could cover in a day was ten, maybe twelve, kilometers. Now we go as far as our legs carry us."

"No wonder my feet ache," said Haria.

"The bad news," said Raul, "is that we've about thirty kilometers ahead of us tomorrow."

They set out early hoping to complete the remaining distance by nightfall. They stopped and rested frequently, mostly at Haria's request. Mosquitoes big as chestnuts picked on her, never on Raul or Zenga. Her arms turned to lead from swatting. Several times she jumped in fright, thinking things had moved in the bush alongside her. Raul read the signs of her terror and tried to convince her that in the jungle things were magnified, but that did little to relieve her anxiety. Complaining of tightness in her leg, she halted near a bamboo copse and reached down to massage her calf muscle. What she felt instead of muscle was all her worst nightmares rolled into a tube of slithering swollen slime. In blind panic she hitched up the leg of her jeans and saw that despite laced-up boots, tucked-in shirt and tight belt, a leech had got in and bloated itself on her blood.

The parasite clung like a limpet without a shell, soft and gooey as a piece of her own flesh turned inside out. Vomit rose in her throat at the thought of her blood being drawn, sucked, by that vilest of jungle creatures. Her face turned white as a jawbone in a jungle clearing. She would have fainted but for Raul taking her by the arms and easing her into a sitting position on a fallen tree-trunk. He held her steady as Zenga removed the leech and rubbed on calamine lotion to ease the irritation.

Hours limped by. Kilometers limped by. Haria looked about at vines and behind them saw vague shadows ready to swing. Undergrowth squelched beneath her feet—whatever filthy secrets it contained did not bear thinking about. Rivulets of sweat defied gravity's laws, invading her everywhere as if the rain from overhanging branches had drenched her to the skin. She wiped perspiration from her forehead and saw with revulsion that the back of her hand was black—the dye in her hair was liquefying, reverting her hair to the natural blonde color it had been when she had worked in Chicago Gemini Clinic. She thought of mosquitoes and all things creepy-crawly. Most of all she thought of the heat. It was in her mind like built-in radiators in her head. It lay on her now like a sodden blanket; sickening, overpowering, sucking her life like, oh Jesus, like a leech. She wanted to put on a brave face. She tried to convince herself the worst was over but the humidity sapped what little energy she had left and she had to sit and rest again.

Raul had a brief word with Zenga. Only ten kilometers to go, but they bivouacked on another riverbank. Food and

41

rest again had a medicinal effect on Haria. The rain stopped and night fell quickly like an umbrella of dark leaves spiraling down from the tallest tree.

They surrounded a small campfire. Raul and Zenga sat on their sleeping bags. Haria lay in hers beneath the mosquito net and joked that she should never have tried to rinse the dye out of her hair with her sweat.

Raul looked at her face veiled by the white net. Despite the mesh, he saw that her curls were branded with the golden sparkle of firelight, and realized that her hair was prettier blonde than dark. He said so, too, which made her smile in her fascinating way. She gazed abstractedly at the leaping flames. He studied her face even more and thought it pretty also, but this time kept his tongue in check. After a brief pause he said she was safe now. Bio would never find her or her baby here.

She lifted her gaze from the fire to look at him. What she saw and heard made her realize that here was a man whom, despite the age difference of more than thirty years, she could, maybe would, like to get to know better.

Raul went on to describe their destination in detail. He told her that though Camp Agrina and its school were primitive it was one of the safest Association sites on the planet. "Air-conditioned as well," he added with a smile.

"Leech-proof and mosquito-proof, too," chipped in Zenga with such a laugh his lips parted broad and high, and his teeth glistened in the camp light.

She told them how she had smuggled her cargo out of Chicago Gemini Clinic and brought it all the way to Sulawesi. "It's a bit like time travel," she said, "moving from the modern world up north to a place like this." She gazed abstractedly at the fire. Now, three weeks after switching capsules in the clinic, she was within ten kilome-

ters of Camp Agrina. Quite a journey, not to mention ordeal, but it was worth it, she said, glancing over her
shoulder at her basket. The campfire cast shadows that
danced across its intricately woven surface.

Raul was looking at the basket, too. "Do you know yet if
it's a boy or girl?" he asked.

"A boy."

"When is he due?"

"Early November."

"Have you got a name for him yet?"

"Bio designated him as Leonard MWC 970131," she
laughed. "I prefer to call him Lee."

Chapter Four
Carver

One week after Lee had been safely deposited in one of the three batteries at Camp Agrina's illegal womb-bank, and around the time that Raul Armitage and Haria Roberts realized that they were destined to live as man and wife, a hydrohopper skimmed over the waves of the Atlantic Ocean.

"Destination dead ahead!" The overseer shouted to make himself heard above the roar of the 'hopper's engines. The din and the headwind rendered his voice inaudible.

The 'hopper traveled at a full sixty knots, skimming over the waves like a cormorant. All nine passengers were out on deck. Like most fifteen-year-olds, they savored every minute of the ride. Hair flapping and fluttering astern, they braced themselves at the rails, gulping in great lungfuls of tangy air, joking and laughing, making themselves dizzy as they leaned over to stare at the waves rushing beneath the hull. The salt, sun and wind whipped up the ruddiest of complexions on their fresh young faces.

"We're stopping!" yelled a tall, fair-haired boy near the bows.

He was nearly right. Within seconds the 'hopper had slowed to twenty knots, dropping closer to the crests of the waves. The overseer pressed a button and the vessel belly-flopped onto the surface, creating a huge splash that thrilled the passengers. Now they were on a boat sailing through a veil of spray into the harbor. Two crewmembers stood fore and aft, keeping an eye on their cargo—a task made easier now that all nine were at the starboard rail, eager for their first glimpse of the leisure center on Flok Island.

Carver's island.

An old and gray-haired man stared down from a vantage point high on Station Hill. It had been quite a climb for his ageing limbs and gasping lungs, but it had been worth it— not just for the view of one of the prettiest harbors in all the Carolinas, but for a glimpse of the incoming 'hopper.

The man held his bino-lens steady and zoomed in on the approaching cargo. An overseer and a girl came into focus—he had no interest in them. There, up near the bows, was the blond teenager he sought. The hair, and of course the face, were unmistakable. The body looked in good shape beneath a light shirt and shorts. Soon, the 'hopper docked at the jetty. The old man could not help but chuckle as the boy sprang effortlessly ashore into a waiting courtesy cab.

He pocketed his bino-lens and turned to walk downhill past the hoverstation, the research center, the leisure complex and the womb-buildings. His steps were slow and measured with all the deliberation of old age, but his heart was light as he relished the stiff, painstaking rhythm of tired old limbs. He was still smiling as he arrived at the reception center. Tomorrow there would be no more aches, no more tiredness, no more old age.

"Pity about Sawyer," Quincy indicated an empty chair in the reception lounge.

"Sawyer?" For a moment Ronald Carver III was confused. Not surprising, given that he was more than a century old, but . . . unexpected.

"There were ten of us at the Activation Ceremony fifteen years ago, remember? I can still see him sitting in that seat watching as the womb machines birthed our twins."

"Oh yes," said Marge Philpott. "Whatever happened to him?"

"Homicide," said Quincy. "Mexico, I think."

"Such a pity." The old woman shook her blue-rinsed head. "I suppose the odds were against us all surviving for the fifteen years they've been growing."

"Yeah," said Quincy. "According to Doctor Ambrose, nine were brought over from the archipelago today. What I'd like to know is what they've done with Sawyer's twin."

"Termination, probably," said Carver.

"Oh my God, would they do that?" The old woman winced, drawing her hands together on her lap.

"That's right, Quincy," said Carver to the old man. "Nine on the 'hopper. Very healthy looking, too." He paused, waiting for it to sink in.

"You saw them?" said Marge Philpott, her mouth gaping.

"Yeah. Great view from Station Hill."

The old woman looked at Quincy, then at Carver. "How could you bear to look at the poor creatures—I certainly couldn't. Bad enough that they grow for fifteen years. You know, some people say they're conscious while they're being grown. Can you imagine that?"

Quincy stayed silent. Carver smiled.

"I don't know how you could ever think of looking at them," she repeated.

"It's reality," said Carver. "Why not face it?"

"I couldn't," said Quincy. "It's a matter of respect. I . . ."

"You should respect the living, not the dead."

Quincy looked shocked. Marge Philpott's hands were bound in an invisible knot that defied extrication.

Carver stood up—he had wasted enough time on these doddering old fools. "See you tomorrow," he said. Enjoying the perturbed look on their faces, he walked out of the lounge.

Doctor Ambrose's office was in the development lab on the other side of the island. Here work was carried out on the preservation and regeneration of brain cells. The research center back at the harbor dealt with the Geminizon drug and longevity of the human body. The lab was less than half a kilometer away on the northern shore. Reaching it meant another climb—though not as steep as Station Hill.

Carver could have taken a hover but he wanted to walk the last kilometer out of his weary limbs. There was a perverse satisfaction in the stiffness and soreness such a walk induced in legs and hips more than a century old. He took pleasure in every step, wallowing in his creaky joints. Today was his day to savor. Old age had been worth it for this. Everything he had worked for, longed for, lived for, was about to be realized.

The day's only blemish had been that shabby encounter with Philpott and Quincy in the reception lounge. Carver felt an approximation of guilt at the way he had shocked them with his comments. He continued on his walk, promising himself to be more tolerant of ordinary people in the next life, shaking his head at the crazy notion that people like Marge Philpott insisted on clinging to: that the twins somehow 'grew' in a comatose way, like fruit on a tree or herrings hanging upside down in a smoking kiln. It was obvious at Activation that they had been born into life as surely as if it had been a real mother, rather than a machine, that had birthed them. Carver looked out at the archipelago, knowing that the islands were full of children living, growing and playing in the normal healthy way—until it was time for Transposition. Down by the harbor, he saw the 'hopper glide gracefully over the waves—off to collect the next day's consignment, probably.

Something caught his eye. He looked up. A shuttle flew north from the Cape. He watched it, silver and silent, climb into the stratosphere. No doubt it was heading for station cluster *Atlantica* where it would transfer its payload to a long-haul freighter bound for Mars. Carver was tempted to wave, but chided himself inwardly for such sentimentality.

His own father, Carver Jr., had prided himself on saving Earth from disaster. One area where Carver's father could genuinely claim to have benefited mankind was in space exploration. The Bio Corporation had launched a series of service platforms, observational structures and docking facilities into orbit around the Earth. Stationed five hundred kilometers above the largest oceans, the cluster systems *Atlantica* and *Pacifica* were the new lynchpins of the space program.

Carver Junior's son watched the shuttle disappear behind a cloud. He kicked a stone off the rocky Flok Island path. Again, he scuffed his shoe in the dirt, harder this time. Memories of a childhood best forgotten bubbled up in his mind. The father, damn him, was the last thing the son wanted to think about. Half his life had been spent under his thumb, the other half under the shadow of his ghost. Now—tomorrow—a new beginning, a chance to lay low the past.

Lesser men might have wanted to destroy a brutal father's legacy, but Ronald Carver III would show them what real leadership was about. As for space, mere cluster systems were no longer enough. Now a red planet waited to be colonized, not by astronauts and scientists as it had been in the past, but by pioneers and their families. With a spring in his geriatric stride and muttering that old Bio slogan *bank your twin till you're old and gray, then live your life another day,* Carver turned and walked downhill to Doctor Ambrose's lab, knowing that his new life promised much by way of consolidating his position as head of Bio. Most of all, he hoped that the next hundred years would bring him more personal happiness—and less loneliness.

The doctor knew it would be unwise to keep the head of Bio Corporation waiting. He saw Carver into his office immediately. For minutes both men talked shop, each sitting either side of the doctor's real wood table.

"No success with triplets, I'm afraid," said Ambrose. "When the egg splits into three, the Geminizon effect is diluted. We get identical triplets, but they're identical only in the old-fashioned sense."

"So triple lifespan is still a long way off," said Carver. "What about brain research?"

"We're working on it all the time. Degeneration still sets in rapidly between one hundred and ten and one hundred and twenty years." Ambrose pushed his gold-rimmed spectacles up over the bridge of his nose. Purely ornamental, they served no useful purpose except to confirm and adorn his status as head boffin in Bio research. He fidgeted with some papers on his desk, knowing there had to be another reason for this visit. "The good news," he said, "is that Activation will shortly be at age ninety-two."

"That's official?"

"It will be next month, when average lifespan is announced as one hundred and seven years."

"A gain of two years in fifteen. Not bad." Carver felt gratified that he had postponed his own twin's Activation. It had been a gamble worth taking—but if anyone could afford to take the risk, it was he. After all, the world's richest and most powerful man was bound to have the best medical care and advice. He leaned forward. It was time to come to the point with Ambrose. "I want to see him," he said.

Doctor Daniel Ambrose tried not to look fazed. "Em, that's unusual, sir." One look at Carver told him refusal was out of the question. "Normally, it's not allowed—but for you . . ." The doctor was tempted to feign a laugh, but did not.

"Right now."

"Yes." Ambrose rose to his feet. "Of course."

"I want to see his file first."

Also unusual. This time the doctor made no comment. He picked up a sheet of paper containing nine rows of printout and repositioned his glasses on his nose—an affectation Carver was beginning to find tiresome. Ambrose turned and spoke to the console on his desk. "Quote, 'Display Yelric MWC 2586 A2116.' Unquote."

The doctor turned the screen toward Carver and noted with distaste that his visitor bore the look of a lion at feeding time. Ambrose had rarely seen such intensity, but knew enough about Carver's background not to be surprised. It was the face of a man tormented with ambition. How strange that one so idealistic, so charismatic, so widely admired and respected, could be so consumed by the desire to see his own twin. The doctor took off his glasses and stared down at his feet, not wanting to see that look again. He rubbed his nose once more, wondering how a man who owned the world could covet so much.

In the leisure center, all nine of them. At the back of the diving tower, behind a two-way mirror, Carver sat transfixed by the sight of the blond-haired boy climbing out of the pool. The last time he had set eyes on his twin brother had been fifteen years previously when the twin was a full-term baby emerging fresh out of one of Flok Island's many womb machines after ninety-two years in suspended animation. Following Activation, Carver's twin—known as Yelric, Male White Caucasian no. 2586, activated in the year 2116—had been farmed out to the archipelago to be raised.

What had Ambrose said—a new decree setting Activation at ninety-two? Medical science was advancing all the time, thanks to Bio-sponsored research. When his father pioneered Geminizon, Bio was the most influential political player in the world. Now, under Ronald Carver III, it was the only political player in the world. All because of this, thought Carver, grinning through the glass at the fifteen-year-old on the diving tower.

Carver watched those long athletic limbs sprint along the board. Legs pounding, calf muscles hard and firm, the boy drove his body on. He sprang off the end of the board, arching through the air, legs tucked against chest, held by arms that tumbled twice through three-hundred-sixty degrees before straightening out in a perfect vertical entry. A double somersault!

Such fitness, such finesse. Breathing hard, Carver watched the youth haul himself out of the water again. Someone else, a girl—probably the new Marge Philpott—stood at the ladder ready to climb to the boards. Through the mirror, he saw the boy mouth an obscenity as he pushed her aside. What words had the overseer put on Ambrose's file? Single-minded? Determined? Intense? Yes indeed, thought Carver, that's my boy.

The fifteen-year-old walked from the changing rooms into the sauna. Through the vapor he saw the dim figure of a man, an old-timer sitting on a bench.

"Someone said you wanted to see me, mister?"

"Yes. Sit down."

"Naw, I'll stand." Something about the old-timer made the boy nervous. He could not put his finger on it. Maybe it was the way the old man sat, clad only in a towel. He did not want a close-up of sagging skin, scrawny face, bony limbs.

"Think I'll stand, too. Mind if I call you Yelric?"

The boy shrugged, mystified as to why he had been sent for. Yet there was something vaguely familiar about the old man looming like a ghost out of the mist.

It amused Carver to see a shadow of perplexity flit across the boy's face. Looking at his twin was like gazing into a mirror at an image frozen in time. Ninety-two years was a long way back, but Carver remembered that handsome face—the smooth skin, jutting jaw, blue eyes—as if it was only yesterday.

It was hot in the sauna. Water droplets betrayed the opening of pores on the boy's skin. Carver was also aware of the temperature, but a different heat rose in him at the sight of long delicate lips and smooth wrinkle-free skin. He looked down at the hard hairless chest and flat stomach. He saw arms strong and smooth, rippled only by muscles. He could smell the boy's sweat and fear, and nothing ever felt so good. Not even Narcissus, in his wildest dreams, had looked into the waters and pined as much. This was what it was all about. The idealism that had turned Carver into a driven man was made manifest now in the presence of his twin. In that moment, Ronald Carver knew for certain that he was ruling the world the right way—even if his rule was unappreciated by certain people who were just too bigoted to know what was good for them.

The boy spoke in a dull mechanical voice, a side-effect of the drugs administered earlier—drugs designed to render a fit and strong fifteen-year-old incapable of fending off a feeble old man. "Is there something you want, mister?"

"As a matter of fact, there is." Carver liked the feature-less voice, and was amazed that his own twin could be so guileless.

He walked to the exit door and locked it. Turning around, he looked at the lean young figure standing before him and contemplated what Narcissus had never dreamed of.

At 2200 hours a team of surgical supervisors stood by as eighteen anaesthetized patients were wheeled into the Transposition unit. They were lined up in two rows; nine elderly patients head to head with nine younger ones. When all was ready, Doctor Ambrose gave the go-ahead and Transposition began.

Scanner-controlled instruments descended from the ceiling as the delicate task got underway. Biosensors embedded antibodies in the membranes between brain cells. Antigen molecules bonded with antibodies, distorting the membranes, releasing chemicals, causing them to flow, making the cerebra communicate easily. Millions of such effects over wide areas of the brain led to large-scale memory transfer. Inter-protein and antibody-antigen reactions, combined with dendril-neurone alterations, replaced the juvenile minds with those of their adult twins, erasing all traces of the originals.

Up in Control, Doctor Ambrose consoled himself with the thought that death for the fifteen-year-old minds would be quick, painless and—he hoped—unexpected.

Fifty minutes later, Transposition was complete; the minds of the centenarians transplanted, their bodies ready for disposal as feeding matter to the creatures of the deep. The fifteen-year-old shells of the children of the archipelago would rest in a deep sleep for twenty hours. Then they would awaken with minds ninety years older than the bodies that housed them.

Chapter Five

Several months later, the pulsing beat of Ender's music rocked the 'Dero Diner, a teenage club on the California coast. The 'Dero Diner was *the* Ender hangout, though the volume of the music was too loud for Ronald Carver III. Something would be done about it when he was in charge once again. A lot of things would be dealt with then. Carver lit his pseud-cheroot, raised his glass of cool beer, leaned his back against the wall, and surveyed the scene before him.

The amber seats and stools seemed to sway to the rhythm of the beat. It was hard to tell if strobing wall-screens or loud vibrations caused this. Not all the seats were occupied—they would fill up later. Those already here wore the regulation syntho-leather Ender outfit. Bleached hair radiated from the tonsures standard to all males; most of who, unlike Carver, seemed to enjoy the music.

It was mandatory for second teens to take leave of absence from careers and responsibilities. Carver was no exception. The world of Bio could look after itself while the most influential man on the planet re-sowed his wild oats. He caught himself bopping ever so slightly to the heavy beat, which made him realize how compulsive the second teenage years were. All the experiences real teens cram into that period could get packed in again—exponentially. This time nothing was illicit. Alcohol, tobacco, narcotics, sex—all the activities illegal in real teens were now condoned, except for serious crime. Most elder teens were all too aware of the negative effects of addictive narcotics on teenage physiology, and so were careful not to indulge too much in drugs. Sex, however, was a different matter . . .

Carver took another long draw on his cheroot. The music was getting to him. His feet surrendered to the rhythm and his mind drifted back four months to an island off South Carolina. Hard to believe that such a short time ago his feet had been an arthritic hundred-and-seven-years old. It brought a smile to his lips to realize how sweetly they were tapping now. Something else amused him: Tully came swaggering down the stairs, headbanging to the beat. He strutted purposefully toward Carver, radials of white hair flapping like the tentacles of a mad sea anemone.

"Chawke will see you now." Tully mouthed the words with all the subtlety of a grunting gorilla. Appropriate, thought Carver, considering his physique.

He followed Chawke's envoy to the upstairs dining area where the decor was not as garish as below. The tables were empty except for Chawke and a pair of goons. They were more than status symbols—protection was mandatory in the days and nights of gang warfare.

"We've considered your proposition." Chawke rose from his seat. "Deliver on this and the Enders are yours."

"Very civilized," snorted Carver. "How do I know I can trust you?"

"You have three witnesses." Chawke pointed at Tully and the goons.

Carver knew Tully was the key. Swing the second-in-command and the rest would follow. Tully was the foundation on which leadership rested.

56

"You know our rules," said Chawke. "Put a proposition to us—if it's daring enough. Bring it off and you're the man." Chawke smiled—no way could this scheme succeed.

"Delivery Thursday night," said Carver.

"Disposal?" Chawke still tried to look amused, though his eyes betrayed a trace of doubt.

"Memory erasers will take care of that." Carver smiled on the inside of his mouth, knowing he had the contacts and the nerve to make it work. "Immediate leadership guaranteed?"

Chawke looked first at Tully, then at his goons. "This guy has some neck," he said, expecting his right-hand man to echo his remark. To Chawke's dismay, Tully turned from him and uttered one word. "Guaranteed."

Carver turned around to walk out. This time the smile showed.

Matters more important than formal education preoccupied Reggie Brooks. She stared out the windows of San Andero High, past the schoolyard, the flyway, the hoverstation. Something white caught her eye. Thumbing her stringy brown hair over her eyes, she picked up a laser pencil and scribbled *surf* on the scratchpad at her fingertips. Five words were now on her list: *concert, Enders, Quickers, school* and *surf*. She was jacked into the State of California Learning Process and could easily have memorized the words using the school implant, but mental commands under SCLP might leave traces in the system. Reggie's word-list had little to do with North American history, the subject currently being expounded on by her tutor 'bot.

She had spent the whole of Thursday morning daydreaming. Between reveries, she had thought of those five topics to bring up should there be any silences. Nobody wanted uncomfortable pauses on their first date, and what a girl lacked in classic Californian beauty she could make up for with ebullience—Reggie had learned that in social development class, the only subject she ever paid any attention to.

She covered the list with her hand, closed her eyes and revised the words in her head. She knew them all and glanced at her best friend, Amanda Ullman. Reggie's looks were plain but her smile was lovely. Knowing the cause of her smile, Amanda returned it.

Reggie looked at the tutor 'bot. Her glance in Amanda's direction would have been noted, but not committed to file. When classmates exchanged more than three glances, the 'bot recorded a misdemeanor. They had already looked at each other twice. Reggie forced down a giggle and tried to look interested. The tutor droned on for ten minutes, then switched off. Reggie unplugged the learning jack from the socket behind her ear. The bell sounded and school was out.

The Brooks' household was never a place for talk. Even at the best of times it was usually of the shut-up-and-listen variety. Tonight it was more shut-up than usual.

"Is there any possibility you might get off that damn vid?" barked Mr. Brooks. "You've hogged it for an hour and a half."

"Daddy, it's Amanda."

"I don't care who it is. Who's going to pay the bill? Get off that vid or I'll unplug it right now."

"Okay, okay." Reggie upturned her already upturned nose, bringing her nostrils almost level with her eyes. Her friend thought this was hilarious and both girls broke into a fit of giggles.

Amanda recovered first. "Hey, I forgot to tell you about Hodder. Read the riot act to me after school for not having my homework done."

"He what?"

"Yeah. He said I wasn't being responsible."

"You didn't have your work done?"

"Are you slow or something?"

"REGGIE!" Her father was halfway up the stairs now.

"Gotta go."

"Call me when you get home. Tell me everything about your date, y'hear?"

More laughter. Reggie nodded furiously. She hit the off-button and the screen went dead.

"Think we're made of money? Think I can afford to have that thing on for hours?"

"No, Daddy, I—"

"Don't make excuses." Her father was not going to listen—he never did. "You have enough time at school to talk to that Ullman girl."

"Yes, Daddy." Reggie sighed and daubed a spoonful of salad cream over her lettuce. A fluttering of butterflies took flight in her stomach. Only an hour to go.

"And another thing—who exactly are you going out with tonight?"

"Amanda, Daddy." Reggie never could lie properly. "And two boys."

Richard Brooks stopped chewing, but only for a moment. He resumed eating his tomato and considered what a single father should say to his daughter on the occasion of her first date. His advice was brief; always was. Then the usual questions. Who? When? Where?

Reggie had her answers ready. She could not say that she was meeting Ronald Carver, elder teen, member of the

59

Ender's gang, alone, so she used her imagination. Satisfied that she would not allow herself to be separated from Amanda, Richard Brooks watched his daughter leave the kitchen and walk to the stairs. He felt nervous for her, but something else as well. Pride. He shook his head and raised his cup.

Reggie looked in the mirror. Nearly ready. *Concert, Enders, Quickers, school, surf.* The butterflies were in full flight. Occasionally, on looking in the mirror, she saw doubts. Ronald Carver. But why her? The Quickers had lots of prettier girls in their gang. It thrilled her to recall the way Ronald had singled her out in front of the others. Their astonishment was palpable, equal to their amazement that the Enders were making peace overtures at all.

Reggie squeezed a blackhead. Two weeks short of her sixteenth birthday and she still had puppy fat. No boy had asked her out before. That Ronald should do so was incredible. He was a warrior, drooled over by all the girls. She squeezed harder, forcing it out, hoping it would not leave a red blotch. He was an elder, one hundred and seven years of living crammed into a teenage body. *Think of the experience he has,* Amanda had said as they collapsed on each other, laughing. He was experienced, all right. No doubt about it. All the elders were, including girls. It was their second time around, after all. So why choose a Quicker? Why select her? Reggie felt uncomfortable when she thought about it. She had seen holos of the male organ in the sex program. No way was she ready for that. If he tried anything she would refuse, politely but firmly. Boys preferred girls who said no, she believed.

She forced herself to be five minutes late. As promised, Ronald was waiting outside the 'Dero Diner.

It was sundown. Litter devils swirled on the pavement.

Three Enders walked past, looking her up and down. Reggie was conscious of her figure, but this time the leering made no difference—she was already blushing in deference to Ronald.

"Hi," she said.

He said nothing, pushed open the swing door and cocked his head for her to enter first, patting her left buttock as she edged past.

"Hey, don't do that!" Not knowing how to react, she smiled.

Downstairs was busy. Wall-screens shimmered to the beat of iso-rhythms. Enders were everywhere. So many bodies milled about she expected to be jostled and shoved, yet they parted to make way for Ronald. He was such a dish, obviously very popular and important.

Reggie never liked being ogled at. She avoided eye contact with them all, except her date. He nodded, indicating the stairs.

She went first again. This time he did not touch but she felt his gaze burning holes in her clothes. A sign at the first floor dining area read *this section closed*.

"Never mind that," said Carver, pushing the door open.

Reggie asked for a regular diet fry, diet veggie-burger and diet mineral water. Ronald ordered the same, diet-free. Instead of mineral water, he called for a beer. For a moment there was uncomfortable silence between them. Reggie searched frantically for something to say. The jukebox play list on the wall reminded her of her five-word agenda.

She was in the middle of describing the concert light-show when the servobot returned with their orders. Ronald tapped a credit number on the dial in the palm of the servo's hand. When the 'bot had glided away, he turned to

Reggie and said, "Go ahead. Eat."

Apart from that, and telling her to ignore the sign at the head of the stairs, and choosing his order, he did not speak again. The silent treatment fazed Reggie, but it was the macho thing to do and Ronald was very macho. He was also extremely handsome; curly blond hair, hard jaw, eyes that sparkled like diamonds. They also displayed other carbonaceous qualities—coldness and hardness, for instance. Reggie wondered were these the same eyes that had twinkled at her the night he asked her for a date. They were, but for an instant she wondered if their sparkle had been for his friends rather than her. Dismissing the thought, she tried to look cool. At least there was something to do now besides talk. Between munches, she chatted about the concert but did not really say much. She did not want to talk with food in her mouth or, heaven forbid, chew with her mouth open.

Ronald's lips occasionally tightened into a smile. Gazing at the street below, he often seemed not to be listening to her at all.

"Gosh," said Reggie. "The glass in this window is very thick."

"Five centimeters," he said. "It keeps people from jumping out."

Sometimes she saw him glance at her tray and her hands, maybe her breasts, in a way that made her anxious. This was not what a first date was supposed to be like. Glad to finish the food, she pushed the tray away and folded her arms on the tabletop.

"Want some dessert?"

She was ready for this. "No thanks. I have to watch what I eat." It made her nervous to say it, but why not admit what was obvious?

62

"Really," said Ronald Carver. "I thought you'd enjoy getting stuffed."

Reggie unfolded her arms and fidgeted with her hands beneath the table. The urge to get up and walk out crossed her mind. She stifled it and put on a brave face. Her pale blue eyes darted from tabletop to play list to Carver. Following the line of his gaze, she saw a pair of Enders staring up from the opposite side of the street below. Of course! Enders—the second word on her list.

"Tell me about the gang, Ronald," she said, hoping he might open up.

Carver looked at her momentarily; a hangdog expression—a half-moon leer of contempt—drooping from his lips. He glanced at the sidewalk and beckoned the two gang members to come upstairs. Reggie looked down and saw them cross the street. She glanced again at her date. He was staring blatantly at her now, sizing her up and down.

A nervous half laugh, more like a gasp, escaped her lips. "Got to go powder my face," she said. As she got to her feet, a change—subtle at first—came over the dining area. The quality of light was altering. One glance at Carver told her why. He was staring at the window. The streetlights faded fast as the glass grew increasingly opaque. Within seconds, the pane was black.

"Did you do that?" Reggie's mouth hung open.

"I sure did." Carver took his finger off the button beneath the tabletop, stood up, turned his back to her, and walked toward the counter at the far end of the dining area. No sign of the servobot now.

Reggie stood by the darkened window, not knowing what to do. Halfway to the counter, opposite the exit, Carver turned around. "Want to see some Enders, honey? Here they come!" Like a magician introducing his assistant, he indicated the door.

Reggie took two steps forward. The door opened. A dozen Enders pushed into the room. One look at their faces told her what was on their minds. Panic rose in her like a geyser, foundering her to the spot.

She could feel the iso-rhythms throbbing in the floor beneath her feet. Someone had pumped up the volume, but that did not drown out the blood pounding in her ears as her breath quickened and her heart raced. She could smell the sweat erupting all over her shaking skin. The taste of a regular fry jumped up her throat. She could smell the air too, as it pushed through the door with the Enders. For some reason, her last rational thought was that the air reeked of stale vinegar. Then she saw the first Ender in the queue. He was fat and greasy; the gum he chewed stuck to the floor when he spat it out. He stepped forward, undid his belt, and opened his trousers.

Though her eyes opened spasmodically during the next six hours, they may as well have been closed for all the sense she could make of what surrounded her. Her vision was as blurred as the rest of her senses, except for touch— which remained painfully tactile throughout. After the first seven or eight rapes, her screams died down. They served no purpose anyway, the relentless music saw to that. As the will to live ebbed away, her screams became pathetic whimpers lost amid the grunts and whoops of those around her.

Fifty minutes after the first violation of Reggie Brooks, Jim Chawke was let up the stairs of the 'Dero Diner. Her screams had died down. There was no need for excessive volume. Carver ordered the beat toned down to less than its normal loudness.

"Want some o' this?" The greasily overweight Ender made it sound like a piece of his chewing gum was on offer.

Chawke looked at the table. One was on her face. Another, priming himself, was ready to mount. "No thanks," he muttered, the need for a strong beer uppermost in his mind. He turned to the counter hoping to satisfy his thirst. What he saw was Carver, sitting on a high stool. "So," said Chawke. "The goods have been delivered."

"On time, as promised."

One look at Carver's smug face and Chawke knew that what had once been his gang had kept their end of the bargain, too.

"I thought you liked real teens," said Carver.

Before Chawke could reply, he heard a high-pitched shriek from the other end of the room.

"The bitch is wailing again," said Tully, who was standing at Carver's shoulder.

Carver snapped his fingers. "Deal with it!"

If Chawke remained in any doubt as to the identity of the new leader of the Enders, his doubts were dispelled by the speed with which Tully obeyed the order.

Chapter Six

Fifteen years after a young girl's naked body was dumped in a gully off the West Coast Highway, a man called Elie Sacchard walked toward Bio's headquarters, the State Militia Building. As he made his way through the security gate, Sacchard saw that SMB was large and squat, its shape and location dictated as much by seismology as by security. It was essentially an enormous bunker—if it appeared to be growing out of the soil, that was because its architects had employed the iceberg principle: they buried most of it below the surface. They also stole another glacial idea: color. The entire edifice was a dirty off-white, like a monstrous concrete slab dropped from the sky.

As far as Elie Sacchard could make out, SMB had no windows. On the few occasions he had been in it he had seen no evidence of natural light—but he had visited only a small portion of it. The building was so large the recommended way around its interior was not by foot, but monorail. That and elevators—there were an awful lot of those. He rode in one now, descending deeper into the bowels of California than he had ever gone before; his queasy stomach caused not so much by G-forces as by the prospect of meeting Ronald Carver III.

Within minutes of disembarking from the elevator, Sacchard stood at one end of a long dark room, light-stick ready to point at the projections that would illuminate the wall behind him. He was grateful to have something in his hands, even if the smooth surface of the light-stick served only to accentuate the clamminess of his palms. Waiting never came easy to Sacchard. Once started, he was determined to impress the thirteen members of Bio's Central Council. A good performance guaranteed promotion. Most of all, he wanted to impress the man at the far end of the table.

Carver and Sacchard were physically the same age, just turned thirty, though for the head of Bio it was second time around. They had in common fair hair, blue eyes, slim build. There, comparisons ended. Ronald Carver III had *power*—the sort other men dream of when they're on mind-expanding drugs—and large doses, at that. From what the files had told him, Sacchard knew that Carver exercised power mercilessly. One wrong look and he could be out of a job. Or worse. But his nerves were driven as much by adrenalin as by fear. If only the Council would let him start.

One minute later he had his wish. Lights dimmed and the wall glowed with a high-definition image.

"This was taken some time ago. Location: Sulawesi, South East Asia. The subjects are male Caucasians, mid-teens. Hold it right there. Note the figure on the river-bank—his fetus was reportedly lost in the Idaho womb-bank fire of July '130. His five-year-old twin was subsequently executed in accordance with the Resolution of '143. The other boy—move it on a fraction—that's it, stop right there—his image is also quite clear. These pictures were taken by drogue bird—he was turning as it flew past. His face did not match up with *in vitro* losses—until recently."

Sacchard paused and noted with satisfaction that Carver was leaning forward, eyes on the screen. He continued,

"We sent the drogue up the Ludese River because we had suspected for some time that a clandestine womb-station existed somewhere in the region. We had combed Sumatra, Java, Kalimantan and the Moluccas without success. The drogue-shot indicated that Sulawesi might be it.

"Renegade twins have been spotted in many areas. Their presence does not necessarily confirm the existence of an enemy stronghold. However, our suspicions regarding Sulawesi were confirmed last week . . ." Sacchard stepped aside, leaving the image on the wall-screen to speak for itself.

The riverbank dissolved to a scene that was anything but pastoral. A man sat strapped to a chair in the center of a darkened room, chair and man illuminated by a spotlight shining down. The camera provided a back view, a full figure shot of its seated subject.

The man was black, naked, and babbling in an almost incoherent manner. Slowly, the camera roved, altering the shot from back to side, long to medium. The lens zoomed in, eliminating the man's feet, shins, knees. As the image of his head grew large, the back of his skull was lost to view as the camera continued its slow-motion pan in quest of a full facial.

He was jabbering about womb batteries, three of them. An underground complex . . . The lens was turning through ninety degrees. His thighs dropped out of shot, then his hips. His head filled one third of the frame . . . A school, the Association . . . In profile now, his face sweat-soaked, the blue pigment of his skin turning his sweat to purple, to red. Blood . . . Adults, seven. Raul . . . The overhead spot lit up his forehead, his cheekbones, his nose. It threw the hollows of his face into shadow. The head was turning—no, it was the camera's motion. Three-quarters frontal now; his eyelids flapping listlessly. Red rivers, deep as the Ludese, on his cheeks . . . Sixty-three children . . . The image froze. The man looked straight at the camera but did not see it. He did not see it because—when he raised those listless lids—he had no eyes.

Sacchard held his breath at the frozen image of the eyeless man. Audible disgust from some members of the Council brought a smile to his lips. The screen faded to white. He turned to the Council and said, "Subject's name: Leroy Wethers. Supposedly lost in a womb-bank accident in '122. Raised in Sulawesi. He was picked up in Fiji one week ago. As to the details he, uh, volunteered . . ." No trace of nerves now, Sacchard was in full flight, reiterating all the information confessed by Wethers, this time with articulation and a mass of details added. A nod to the audio-visual operator elicited the appearance of a map on the screen behind him. "The island of Sulawesi," he said, "is shaped like the capital letter K. As the map shows, it has an incredibly long coastline. When the Portuguese discovered it, they refused to believe it could be one island, so confusing is its shape . . ."

"We're not here for a history lesson," Carver's voice cut through the air like an ice pick. "Get to the point. Show us exactly where the clandestitutes are."

Sacchard fumbled with his light-stick, focusing its arrow on the Ludese River. "Here," he said, "in the interior, a hundred kilometers upriver."

Again Carver spoke: "How can—how many? . . . seventy people?—live in such a place without being detected?"

"The canopy, the topography . . ." Fumbling for words, Sacchard felt the perspiration ooze from under the collar of his shirt.

Reynolds, second-in-command, California State Militia,

rescued him: "It's the third world situation, Mr. Carver. So long as we let them survive, as long as they muddle along in that primitive way of theirs, the clandestitutes will find plenty of havens for their activities." A man of few words and fewer principles, Art Reynolds had made colonel on the backs of third world peoples. For years he had pushed for a takeover of the entire southern hemisphere, an idea Bio was gradually coming around to. He hoped such a campaign would make him general, so he advocated it whenever Central Council was in session.

If Carver had heard the colonel's argument, he chose to ignore it. "Tell me," he addressed the man standing in front of the screen, "how do they survive? How do they feed themselves?"

"They rig up artificial sunlight in clearings under the canopy. They grow maize, sugarcane, onions, chili, garlic, coffee. They fish. They have supplies of sweet milk, rice and dried vegetables. The clandestitutes—or the Association, as they call themselves—are extremely well organized."

"When did you extract this confession?"

"Five days ago."

"And the drogue-shot of the two boys—you said it was taken some time back?"

"Yes."

"Precisely how long?"

"August thirteen. Last year."

"What!" Carver strained forward, eyes fixed firmly on Sacchard. "Five months ago!"

"Yes." More than ready for this, the Surveillance man said, "I only identified the second boy a week ago. His twin is still alive."

The six men to Carver's left wore military uniforms, including Reynolds, the colonel who had urged a military assault on the third world. They all gasped, astonished by Sacchard's revelation. Those opposite—the half a dozen members of Bio's Inner Chamber—showed no reaction.

Carver waved his hand dismissively at the military and said, "There were some exceptions to the Resolution of '136."

Colonel Reynolds was about to ask for elaboration. The sound of "Wha . . . ?" had barely left his lips when Carver cut across him, leaving the militiaman gaping like a kissing gourami.

"Where's the twin?" Carver demanded to know.

Sacchard nodded and the AV operator screened the drogue-shot of the Ludese River boy again. "You may recall the event. His fetus was smuggled out of Chicago Gemini Clinic, June 131. The clandestitutes exploded a device in the hoverpark to distract security. The fetus was never actually womb-banked. The womb-cot capsule was switched—it was empty by the time it got to the womb-bank—so it did not appear in the usual files. When the drogue-shot was scanned for match-up, the result was negative." Sacchard gripped the light-stick tighter, hoping the next part of his speech would have an upwardly mobile effect on his future. "There was a foul-up. The matching process was not carried out as thoroughly as it ought to have been. Nobody checked that boy against twins allowed to survive the Resolution of '136."

"Whose responsibility was it to ensure that matching was thorough?" said Carver.

"Well," Sacchard paused and swallowed, deliberately. "It's a whole section of . . ."

"Specifically?"

"Eh, my boss. John Saunders delegated the task to various personnel."

"Who discovered the error?"

"When we picked up Wethers last week, I decided to check all surveillance records."

"You decided this? Not at your boss's instigation?"

"No, sir." Sacchard could not believe it was falling into place so easily. "It was in my own time."

"Your name?"

"Sacchard, sir. Elie Sacchard."

Carver leaned back in his chair, looking past Sacchard to the boy on the screen.

Colonel Reynolds jumped in. "May one ask exactly who, and how many, were allowed to survive the Resolution of '136?"

A member of Carver's Inner Chamber, a behaviorologist in her second twenties, smiled sweetly and said, "Of course you may ask, Colonel. The Resolution of '136, the 'Purge' as the clandestitutes call it, was introduced that year and made retrospective so that no singletons would remain alive. Even if a twin died accidentally, the surviving twin was to be terminated no matter what their age or status. The reasoning was simple: by eliminating all singletons we were guaranteed to thereby eliminate those working clandestinely. However, as an experiment, certain exceptions were made, mainly to see if any of these singletons might eventually, in the fullness of time, lead us to secret clandestitute womb machines and hideaways. There have been sixteen known cases of fetus smuggling similar to that outlined by Sacchard. The first, in '125, was around the time the clandestitutes began to organize into the Association—or whatever it is they insist on calling themselves. The last—prior to the Resolution, that is—was in '135. All these cases were allowed to survive beyond '136."

"But why let them live?" asked Reynolds.

The colonel's open-palmed plea for understanding was met by knowing glances from the Inner Chamber members sitting opposite him.

Carver blinked as if coming out of a reverie. "Call it . . . human interest, Colonel. As the lady said, we let them survive as guinea pigs in a long-term experiment. We decided to be patient to see what might happen. We've been waiting a long time for this. It's the first time one of those sixteen twins has shown." Carver's lips curled into a smile. "I remember now," he leaned forward to examine more closely the image on the screen. "The Chicago incident—it was around the time of my own Transposition. Who's his twin?" he snapped at Sacchard.

The Sulawesi image dissolved to a high-school portrait of a fresh-faced, sandy-haired boy. "His name is Grant Maxwell. Turned fifteen in November last year. Brilliant student. Hopes to go to med school. As you see from the uniform, he attends Golden Gate High."

"Clandestitute tie-in?" asked Carver.

"None whatsoever. His family's been under surveillance since '131 when his twin fetus disappeared. They think his twin is safely womb-banked, of course. No subversive connections at all."

"Has there been an attempt at surgery?" asked Helga Wren, the behaviorologist.

"I'm glad you asked that. Computer enhancement lets images speak for themselves."

Sacchard stepped aside. The portrait of the high school student shifted slowly to one side, leaving room for the boy in the Ludese River to fade in, his face gradually enlarging until it matched that of his Californian twin. Both faces came together until they gelled flawlessly, one overlapping the other.

"Incredible," said Carver. "Absolutely identical."

"Damn fools, those clandestitutes," quipped Colonel Reynolds. "You'd think they'd have the sense to change his face."

"The jungle obviously suits their primitive ways," said Wren with a sneer.

"Even so," said Reynolds. "We ought to tox those places right away. The sooner Bio's writ runs everywhere, and the whole world's twinned, the better. Do you agree, sir?"

Carver looked contemplative for a moment. There was substance to Reynolds' argument. Existing policy was to turn a blind eye to many parts of Asia and the southern hemisphere. Control their resources and their economies; otherwise let them fend for themselves—that was the current philosophy. It was cheaper than building the necessary womb-banks and colonies for activated fetuses. How many times during his first life had Carver heard that policy defended? Too many times. Father-thinking, he called it. Now he was convinced there was a cheaper way. Wipe them out—they're only the dregs of humanity, polluting the planet. Wipe them out and give their land back to nature. Use their resources and the long-term saving to finance the space pro . . .

"Sir?"

"Perhaps you're right, Colonel," said Carver, returning from his reverie. "Maybe the policies I inherited were those of a weak man." Ignoring the stunned looks of those around him, he went on, "How soon can you take out the womb-station?"

If someone had put a mirror in front of Reynolds at that moment, he would have seen a general's epaulettes appearing as if by magic on his shoulders. "We can have a task force ready in a matter of days . . ." Unsure if Carver's frown was caused by concentration or by his loose initial estimate, the colonel backtracked quickly. "Say thirty-six hours."

"That's better."

"How about the boy in the jungle?" Reynolds nodded at the screen. "Do you want him dead or alive?"

The head of Bio thought for a moment. "Kill them all. We already have the boy's twin right here in California."

Early the next day, Elie Sacchard walked into the Surveillance Bureau in downtown Longevity City. His former boss was nowhere to be seen. Sacchard had never liked Saunders, though he admired his taste in secretaries. It pleased him no end to see the smile on Esther Varnia's face that morning. It was a broader smile than usual—the sort normally reserved for bosses. Her firm thighs and silky lips promised much in the days and nights ahead. When it came to promises, Esther was known to deliver.

When she told him there was someone to see him in the office, and a sweep of her hand indicated Saunders' office, he knew. And the kick he got out of seeing his own name emblazoned where Saunders used to be was nearly as good as the hard-on he got at the thought of what he would put between Esther's long slender legs.

Helga Wren sat waiting to see him, member of the Inner Chamber of Central Council, behaviorologist with responsibility, among other things, for selecting Ronald Carver's top personnel. Her message to Elie Sacchard was simple:

"Officially, you are the new Surveillance Bureau Chief. In reality, your sole task is to keep the boy Maxwell and his family under the closest scrutiny. The smooth running of the SB will look after itself—you don't have to worry about that. Other than this Maxwell business, you will spend your time with Mr. Carver."

Wren wore a white skirt to just above the knee. As she spoke, she noticed that Sacchard could not keep his eyes off the silky cloth that peeped below the hem. She leaned forward until her blouse revealed a hint of cleavage. "My boss doesn't suffer fools, Mr. Sacchard. He's a busy man. Bio and the Mars project take up most of his time. What leisure he has revolves around the conservation of endangered species. He was impressed by your performance in the State Militia Building yesterday. We researched you. You're the sort of person he can get along with. My boss doesn't have many close associates to share his hopes and visions with. We think you could fill that gap. You might understand and appreciate what he's trying to achieve for our world. He needs men who share his vision. Unofficially, you will be a personal assistant, an advisor to Mr. Carver."

As he listened to the round-headed, dimple-faced emissary from Bio, Sacchard realized that here was promotion beyond what he had ever dreamed of. Now one of Bio's top executives, he hardened again at the prospect of power that promised much more than anything his nubile secretary might deliver.

Chapter Seven

Raul Armitage switched off the lights in a room deep in the underbelly of the Camp Agrina complex. He picked his way between the children and young adults squatting on the floor and those fortunate enough to be sitting on stools. By the time he reached his seat at the back of the room, the film show had begun and all eyes were on the screen which was datelined *Washington, September 12th 2024.*

A black stretch limo turned off the freeway into Cypress Avenue. It swung through a pair of electronically controlled gates set in the rim of a high-walled estate and rolled slowly along a driveway lined with slender evergreens that cast long shadows across billiard-table lawns. The sun slanted through the Lincoln's plate glass windows. It illuminated the graying hair and pale face of the passenger in the rear seat, bleaching out wrinkles around eyes that grew narrow in the early morning light. Tree trunks swished past every other second, strobing the sun's rays in a way the passenger found unsettling. He closed his eyes to the intermittent light and turned his head the other way.

The cypresses ended and the driveway fanned out into a large concourse in front of what the caption called the Eastern Security Building. The limousine rolled to a halt before two security guards manning either side of the main entrance. A voiceover said that neither of the guards would be aware of the identity of the VIP now stepping toward them from a chauffeur-held door. The voice added that security men at ground floor level would also fail to recognize him because, 'the heads of multinationals are not always household names—not even the chairman of the largest pharmaceutical company in the world'.

The viewpoint then switched to the security man guarding a conference chamber somewhere within the building. The voice said that he was a hot property on the Washington quiz scene, though this morning his head was not the best. Too many beers had made it difficult for him to recall the trivia normally at his fingertips. He rubbed his pot-bellied stomach—which the narrator said was also a result of too much alcohol. Drink-induced upset stomachs were an experience that some of the older viewers in Camp Agrina, such as Lee and his friend Hugo, could identify with—particularly as Lee and Hugo had, only weeks previously, tapped illicitly and abundantly into the Association's precious supply of alcohol. With some amusement they heard the quiz buff mutter to himself that the great thing about waking up with a hangover was that from then on the day gets better. They saw him scratch his head and ask himself who said that first. It took a fraction of a second for him to remember. Then a cartoon light bulb lit up over his head. The old black and white image delighted the audience—early twentieth century comedy films, though two centuries old, were a staple part of the entertainment facilities in Camp Agrina.

The security man sat at his desk and opened a sporting almanac. The narrator said there was a sports quiz in the Grove tonight and he needed to read up for it. The audience watched attentively as the security man leaned back in his swivel chair, eyes glued in concentration, trying to remember who won the Super Bowl in 2009. The screen showed some old football footage. Organized sports in huge stadiums were something beyond the experience of the Camp Agrina children, so they found this segment fascinating.

Raul Armitage sat with his back to the wall, watching them watching the screen, thinking to himself how well made this historical docu-drama was. The Association's filmmakers knew all the tricks, but would it hold their attention all the way?

The buzzer on the security man's desk jolted him upright. He slid his almanac under a console and straightened his cap. The voiceover said he had already let five people through to the chamber, now who could this last one be? When the elevator door opened, it revealed the VIP from the black stretch limo. The voice said the security man recognized his face from somewhere, but could not put his finger on the name. He confirmed clearance from ground level and let the visitor through. The narrator said the security man could not make up his mind if the VIP was a politician or a media mogul. Such uncertainty irked him because he had only recently seen a photo of the man in a magazine article—trouble was he could not recall the name beneath the photo. It just would not come. Was it something like Cutter? Cotter, maybe? No, not that. Cleveland? That was a nineteenth century American president. Cleaver? Close, but still not right. As the door to the conference chamber closed, the quiz buff returned to his almanac, his inner voice telling the audience that he would be unable to concentrate fully on Super Bowl history until it dawned on him who exactly the man was.

The rest of the film revealed what occurred in the conference chamber of the Eastern Security Building that fateful day so many years before. Seated around a polished, circular table were: Hal Beecham, Chief of Security; Lawrence Petty, presidential candidate and chairman of the Senate House Committee on Internal Affairs; Sam Seaver, United States Attorney General; Professor Timothy Armstrong, head of Behavioral Studies, Harvard; and General Hugh Whitney, a four star soldier with responsibility for the National Guard. All four were captioned, name and position, whenever they spoke. The fifth person, the VIP from the black stretch limo, was not name-checked, though he was captioned throughout as head of the Bio pharmaceutical company.

"Gentlemen," Hal Beecham tapped his mineral glass with a pencil. "I think we're about ready to . . ."

"Hold on just one minute," interrupted Petty, the presidential hopeful. "As Chief of Security, have you taken every precaution to ensure that this location is absolutely solid?"

"Mr. Petty," said Beecham. "We're in a bunker forty meters beneath the safest building in North America. I think you can relax."

"Maybe the candidate is worried in case some reporter's tunneled his way up from *The Lone Star Chronicle*," said Seaver, the Attorney General. "It might cost a few votes in Abilene." Seaver knew votes were a sore point, particularly in Texas.

"Now you listen here, boy." Petty pointed his snub-nosed cigar at the Attorney General. "The man who appointed you is leaving town 'cos his second term is up and the way things are going in the primaries I might just end up replacing him. One more smart-ass comment outta you and come the new year we might see a high-class, blood-suckin' lawyer like you kickin' ass in some hick town back in Wyoming."

Raul chuckled. Such an exchange probably never happened in reality, but it held the attention of the young audience.

On screen, Attorney General Sam Seaver was about to retort with the latest opinion poll, but the Chief of Security got in first: "Gentlemen," said Beecham, "I think we ought to . . ."

". . . put an end to this bickering." The head of Bio spoke. "I think we can dispense with preliminaries—has everyone read my report?"

Security Chief Beecham put his pencil on the desk and waited for someone to respond to the man who had interrupted him. No one did.

"Any questions?" Again, the voice was that of the Bio boss.

Beecham sighed and looked at his sheaf of papers. No point in trying to chair this meeting, let the man at the other end of the table do it—it was his baby, literally.

"One question, sir." Candidate Petty again. "This drug—uh, Geminiozone?"

"Geminizon—though the name isn't definite yet."

"Right. This, uh, Geminizon, it splits the human embryo in two, right?"

"Correct. The fertilized egg implants itself in the womb in the normal way, then divides into two parts. Both fetuses develop with a single placenta. But Geminizon ensures the birth of twins who are identical not just in the traditional way. It carries the process further than nature intended. Even fingerprints and voice patterns become identical. Personality and character develop to be essentially the same also. What it guarantees is two copies of one individual."

It was an explanation plainly spoken not just for Petty's benefit, but for the Association's young audience. They sat glued to the screen in front of Raul. Anything to do with childbirth and related matters would hold their interest anyway, he knew.

"We're not just talking common-or-garden-variety fertility drug, huh?" Candidate Petty nodded sagely as he spoke.

The Attorney General cast his eyes to the ceiling, then looked scathingly at Petty. "What we have here is a breakthrough unparalleled in human history."

Petty sneered at him as if he was a fly on a dinner plate. "Tell me, sir," he turned his attention to the head of Bio. "Is this drug safe?"

"All manufacturing companies like to think in terms of a hundred per cent success rate. Mistakes sometimes occur, but Geminizon-related failure is so small it's insignificant."

"Are we to understand that it's been tested on a large scale?" he asked.

"That's a very interesting question. A forerunner of Geminizon was tested in the nineteen nineties. All side effects have been eliminated over the last few years."

"You mean that this has been going on for thirty years? Without the press sniffing it out? So much for your damn reporters, Seaver." Petty took the cigar from his mouth to make room for an even broader grin.

"It may come as news to you," said Attorney General Seaver, "but people have acted as guinea pigs in the interests of medical science since time immemorial."

"Sure. People do anything for money." Petty exhaled a stream of smoke at Seaver. "In the interests of science, of course."

Security Chief Beecham sought to break the build-up of tension. "I think we're digressing. It's not so much the gynecological effect of the drug—what's at issue here is how it can be used to increase human lifespan. Can it work?"

"Of course," said the head of Bio.

"Will people want it?" asked the Presidential candidate.

"Would you say no to the chance of living a second time? To do everything over, only better? To be twenty, again? Would you turn down *a second term*, Mr. Petty?"

"Very droll, sir. But you're forgetting one thing. The people we're selling this to will not benefit directly from it."

"Their children will."

"Is that enough of a carrot?"

"Professor Armstrong is best qualified to answer that."

The Harvard man cleared his throat. "By and large, people will do anything for their offspring. Human instinct, human nature, is to want the best for your children. The need to propagate the species, to pass on genes, is what brings this about. Research shows . . ."

"What that means," said the Attorney General, "is that if you promise someone that their children will have the gift of an extra eighty or ninety years, you are making them an offer they will find hard to turn down. Our trump card is that Geminizon counteracts the infertility that is so widespread nowadays. Cures it, in fact. Childless couples, and they are in the majority in our society, will not refuse a drug that promises fertility."

Petty's cigar was almost out. He pulled hard to get it going and said, "But it's a drug, isn't it? What about the side effects you mentioned earlier?"

For a moment there was silence. The man responsible for the development of the drug said, "Mr. Petty, everyone at this table is in favor of the introduction of Geminizon— except you. I called this meeting and arranged to have these men attend to convince you of the need to legislate. Our future is Geminizon. The world's future is Geminizon. Every

83

person around this table agrees—except you. Nobody is putting forward any arguments—except you. And Mr. Petty, for what it's worth, my wife is four months pregnant with twin boys."

Lawrence Petty carefully balanced his cigar on an ashtray and looked at those around him. He joined his hands under his chin and said, "Well, if it's good enough for the head of Bio, it sure as hell ought to be good enough for Joe Public. When can I—we—announce it?"

"A few weeks," said the Attorney General. "End of next month, at the latest."

"Do I have your word on that?"

"On announcing it before Super Tuesday?"

"No, no . . . not necessarily. I mean can we tie up the legal end of things by then?"

"Sure." There was nothing the Attorney General liked more than seeing a politician squirm. "We'll get the legislation through on schedule. Geminizon will be mandatory a matter of days after the announcement."

"Won't there be a problem with the second fetus? Won't people object to its removal and long-term storage?"

"No problem there. Abortion has been legal for half a century."

"We're not just talking abortion here, Seaver," said Petty. "We're talking about a second child. We're talking abortion *after* the birth."

"Gentlemen," Security Chief Beecham raised both palms. "Let's hear the professor's views on that."

Armstrong placed his hands on the table before him. "Our conviction is that people will accept the, eh, sacrifice of one child for another, especially as both children will be essentially the same. We will present it as abortion after the event. The spare twin will not become conscious, at least not as far as the public is concerned."

"Can you guarantee that?" asked Petty.

"There may be a problem in some cases. There are always non-conformists."

"And how do we deal with them?" said Petty.

For the first time, General Hugh Whitney made his presence felt. "The anti-abortion movement was very strong at the turn of the millennium, but the wars with Japan and the third world, and the subsequent economic downturn, as well as the population nosedive and widespread infertility, have seen to it that people no longer have the luxury of pre-occupying themselves with ethical issues. The moral compass points with no certainties these days. Our citizens are easily led by television, and the media is firmly under our control now. With the mood of the nation in our grasp, plus the logical argument that what we are proposing is *not* abortion—after all, we're not in the business of killing fetuses, but of storing them and bringing them to term at a later stage—then I think those who disagree with us will be in a small minority. As for those who might act subversively, rest assured you may have no qualms on that score, gentlemen. State militia will deal with all dissenters."

"You're not a man to mince words, General," said Petty. "I guess that covers everything."

"Any further questions?" asked Security Chief Beecham.

Presidential candidate Lawrence Petty chewed on his Havana Special, preoccupied by matters electoral.

"Very well," said Beecham. "That wraps it up."

Raul knew that this important development in human history had not been rubber-stamped in such a simplistic manner. The imposition of Geminizon required a regime hell-bent on denying freedom and choice—there were other Association docu-dramas to outline just how authoritarian

America had become in the wake of the terrorist wars, the second war with Japan and the resource conflicts with other countries. In the meantime, the closing scenes showed Professor Armstrong leaving the chamber first, but not before being buttonholed by Petty who was eager to know if the Behavioral Studies Unit at Harvard had ever investigated voting habits. "Look here, professor," Petty followed the Harvard man out the door. "We could be talking extra finance here. You college boys are always looking for extra cash, right?"

Attorney General Seaver waited until the general and the security chief had also left the conference chamber. When he was alone with the chairman of Bio, he said, "Our incoming president is some dumb ass, huh?"

"Can we control him?"

"Yes," said Seaver.

"Strikes me he could stir up trouble."

"Only when he's drinking water—and he's not too used to that." Seaver nodded at Petty's untouched glass of pure New England Spring. "Matter of fact he prefers something that looks like water, only stronger. If Petty gets out of line all we have to do is announce that he's a dipso."

"What about the incoming Attorney General?"

"Already in the bag."

"Good. Has this been lucrative enough for you?"

"Yep, and I sure appreciate it." Sam Seaver shook the other man's hand as they headed for the door.

The last man in was last out. As the quiz buff security man ushered him to the elevator, the voiceover returned to confirm that he was still mystified as to who exactly the man was. He had spent ages trying to put a fix on that name, but the knowledge he sought bubbled infuriatingly out of reach in his subconscious. It was something like

Cutter or Cleveland or Cleaver. It started with C—he was certain of that, but the rest of the name just would not come.

He watched as the elevator numbers counted up to ground level. He stood with cap slightly askew, rubbing his forehead, concentrating. When 'G' lit up, it hit him like a locomotive. He snapped his fingers in triumph as another cartoon light bulb appeared overhead. Of course! The head of the world's largest pharmaceutical company; one of the richest, most influential men in the whole world. He remembered a magazine article he had read. It contained a thumbnail sketch portraying the head of Bio as a conservationist with an interest in saving the rain forests. It also outlined Bio's sponsorship of the space program, in particular its plan to establish station clusters around the planet. To dispel any lingering doubts, he sounded the name out loud—the name he had seen in the caption beneath the magazine photo, the name he had confused with Cutter and Cleaver and a former American president—the name of Ronald Carver, Jr.

Raul Armitage spoke briefly at the conclusion of the AV presentation. He knew there was no need to emphasize the Bio leader's name—the Association's filmmakers had been adept enough at their job to ensure that the young Camp Agrina audience would not forget it in a hurry. Raul watched them file from the room, the younger ones first, followed by older ones like Lee and Hugo—and Tamara and Sharon, the two girls who seemed inseparable from them these days.

Chapter Eight

The footfalls were light, but Lee heard them coming and guessed to whom they belonged. It was Zenga, tall and straight as ever, though now—in his eighty-sixth year—the shoulders were beginning to droop. The Polynesian did not speak—there was no need. Lee was on his feet, apologizing for forgetting the time.

"Two minutes," said Zenga. "At the garlic patch. Then we go."

"Right." Lee shook the grass from his legs.

The jungle around Camp Agrina was crisscrossed with pathways, some so well trodden they resembled leafy avenues through which people could walk two, even three, abreast. Other paths were rarely used. Rapid growth soon reclaimed them. Trailmakers were useful tools for venturing far afield. In Lee and Zenga's case a trailmaker was essential. Their destination—a salt spring twelve kilometers distant—was well off the beaten track. A return journey, counting a couple of hours for salt gathering, would take the whole day. With the aid of a trailmaker they hoped to be back by sundown.

One of Zenga's few concessions to the approach of old age was the surrender of the trailmaker to the younger generation. Lee wielded it expertly, slicing a precise swathe through the underbrush. Zenga followed close behind, twenty-five kilometers still within the compass of his long gangly legs.

Halfway to the spring, they rested. Time for refreshment and a chat. Zenga made it a rule not to talk while trekking— a waste of energy, he said. When they were seated on a tree trunk he asked about Tamara—the Wild Woman of Agrina, he called her. "She's Hugo's girlfriend, isn't she?"

Lee nodded, quaffing a mouthful of cool water.

"It surprises me she's so friendly with Sharon. They're so different."

Lee nodded again. Mention of that name and his face brightened. One look at Zenga and he knew the old Polynesian had noticed.

"Is Sharon your girlfriend?"

Lee's heart stepped up a gear. No adult had called her that before. They had been sweethearts for weeks but had tried to keep it a secret—except from Hugo and Tamara. Yet the grand old man of Agrina had it all sussed. Zenga had this way of looking straight ahead while simultaneously peering at you out of the corner of his eye. It was his way of keeping tabs. Recognizing the look, Lee laughed more from pleasure than embarrassment.

Slapping his knees with both hands, the old man stood up stiffly. "Come, young man," he said. "We can't wait around forever for you to get your breath back."

The mind-numbing chore of salt gathering was tolerable when accompanied by thoughts of Sharon. Lee spent quite some time thinking about what they had been doing after the film show of the night before. It dawned on him that he was finding it difficult to keep her out of his mind. Not that he wanted to, but when three bags were packed, he found something that banished her from his thoughts.

"What's this?" He picked up a small round stone—a

vague human outline engraved on one side.

"A talisman," said Zenga, examining it closely. "Keeps evil spirits at bay. Probably belonged to the cannibals who lived here for thousands of years." Zenga settled himself on a rock. "You can still find traces of their village." He held the stone in the palm of his hand.

"We might find a pot for lunch," quipped Lee.

"I'm serious," said Zenga. "They didn't cook them in pots, either. No, not like that. The tribe that lived here was cultured. Literate, too. They were feared as powerful magicians and well known as cannibals. They ate captives and criminals. First, they tied them to a stake. Then they lit fires and played music. The chief addressed his people, explaining to them that the victim was not a person but an evil spirit. The only way of keeping the evil one at bay was by putting a piece of him in your stomach."

Zenga paused and stared off into space for a moment. He went on, "The chief would cut the first piece—usually a cheek or a slice off the arm. He would hold it up and drink the dripping blood. Then he would go to the fire and roast the meat a little before eating it. That was the signal for the other men to help themselves. It was considered a sign of bravery to eat the flesh raw. It usually took maybe ten minutes before the victim lost consciousness, fifteen to . . ." Zenga never finished the sentence. He stared upward, preoccupied.

Lee thought his sudden preoccupation might have something to do with his Polynesian origins. "They never told us that at school," he said, giving a weak little smile.

"Listen," said Zenga. "Do you hear that?"

Lee heard nothing beyond the usual noises of the wild, but Zenga's expression grew darker. Lines of fear and concern etched themselves on the old man's face. A strange foreboding rushed through him as though icy fingers were hovering at the gap between his shoulder blades. Something was happening, but Lee could not fathom what it was.

The old man stared upward, his Adam's apple vaulting once, twice, as he craned his neck and rolled his eyeballs in a bid to discern whatever vibrations were passing through the air. After a moment he hurried to his feet and said, "Let's go back."

"What's wrong?" asked Lee.

"I don't know yet. Trouble at the camp, maybe. Best travel, not talk. Here," he tossed over the stone. "Put that in your pocket, for luck."

No need for a trailmaker now that the outward journey had been made, but that did not stop the return leg from seeming twice as long. The way Zenga moved—he insisted on taking the lead—told Lee that something cataclysmic had happened. The old man had sensed it, and as they marched closer to Agrina, Lee felt it, too.

The nearer they came to the camp, the quicker Zenga's strides became. Lee shouted at him to take it easy but Zenga ran the last kilometer. Lee feared for the old man now. Such exertion was bound to take its toll. He sensed a different fear as well—a sickening realization that the worst had happened. *Some sort of ray, wave, vibration, oscillating into their heads. Sharon, Hugo, Tamara . . .* Where that foreboding came from he could not tell. Perhaps it arose from his subconscious mind. Most likely it emanated from the anxiety-ridden old man loping between the trees in front of him . . . *Haria, Raul, all fall down . . .* Wherever the foreboding originated, it formed a knot in the base of his stomach—a knot that grew larger, tauter, with each stride until finally they turned the corner down by the garlic patch.

The trees bent over, bowing under the weight of immeasurable sadness. Zenga leaned over, too, holding onto the railing at the edge of the herb garden. Breathing hard, he tried to say something but the words would not come. Lee ran past him, eyes only for what littered the surface around the camp.

The detritus of crushed bodies squelched under Lee's nervous feet—a carpet of dead birds and insects. Snakes too, and small primates, lifeless as everything else that had fallen out of the canopy. Here and there lay human bodies, corpses with no wounds. One look at the wildlife and the bodies was enough for Lee to know it had been a condenser attack. The trees bowed not out of sympathy, but because they too were dead. Every living organism within the target area had been killed by an assault designed to take out only living cells. Amid the debris and the grass—drooping blades had already begun to curl at the tip—were boot prints: the unmistakable calling cards of Bio troopers.

Heart thumping and breathless, Lee searched for those that mattered most. Raul Armitage, his foster father, had keeled over at the entrance to the underground complex. He was stone dead. Haria was on her knees in the passageway behind Raul. She had toppled forward and listed to one side; her corpse against the wall, face on the ground, body in the air like a Moslem at prayer. Lee knelt too, cradling his mother in his arms before laying her in a prone position alongside her husband whose beard he stroked in one last, loving gesture of farewell. Then he noticed the acrid stench of melted womb-batteries and burnt-out support systems. The smell permeated the labyrinthine tunnels, stinging his already misty eyes. He sprinted from passageway to passageway, stooping over corpses, searching for Sharon, Hugo and Tamara.

He found them in the recreation chamber. Hugo on the floor, head down. Tamara on a couch, hunched over. Sharon had collapsed sideways onto Tamara's lap. Her strawberry hair was streakier now, and certainly more crimson. Rivulets of blood streamed onto it from Tamara's ears. On the floor a coffee cup, untouched until Lee knocked it over, spilling its contents in his haste to escape an underground complex that had become a tumulus, the brains of the interred frizzled by the vibrations of a Bio wave condenser.

Outside, in the beautiful jungle light, he fell to the ground, vomiting. Whether it was the gut-wrenching smell or the sight of so much death or the shock of it all that brought on the nausea, he cared not. When nothing remained but bile, he looked frantically around for Zenga.

The old man lay on his side in the herb garden, clutching his chest, head against the railing. Lee dropped to his knees, grabbed him by the collar and almost shook what little life was left out of him. "You shouldn't have run!" he screamed. "You shouldn't have run!"

"Are they . . . all . . . ?" gasped the old man.

"Yes," sobbed Lee.

Zenga grabbed him by the arm and held on tight. Between gasps, he told him of a place to go and a name to contact. Then the old man grimaced. His heart was racked by one last spasm. He stared at Lee, eyes bulging as he tried to say something. It was too late. His last breath came raggedly, like a whimper.

Lee laid Zenga's head against the railing, sobbing and cursing him for running that last fatal kilometer. Then he saw a tear roll slowly down the old man's cheek. He stared in horror, and wondered who could be so cruel as to make the dead weep. He stood and cursed the sky, screaming at

Bio for what it had done. Most of all, he cursed himself. Raul had said no other drogue bird had been spotted near Agrina. If only he and Hugo hadn't sneaked down to the river that fateful August day . . .

He ran about like a lunatic, stomping on the footprints of Bio troopers, as if by erasing them he might erase their massacre. He fell to his knees. From his lips came a shriek so piercing in its crescendo that the trees seemed to bow even more, and whatever dead creatures were left on the branches rained down on him in a final death shower.

He dragged the bodies of those who had made it outside into the main passageway. In the storerooms he gathered supplies, including foodstuffs undamaged by condenser rays, and explosives for use in stunning fish. He set off devices at both entrances, sealing off Camp Agrina.

The underground complex was now a burial mound, a mausoleum before which a young man stood, head hung low like the setting sun. Darkness came and silence, except for the sobbing of his tears and the beating of his heart.

Chapter Nine

The wallvid glowed as soon as Colonel Art Reynolds arrived home from his raid on Sulawesi. The head and shoulders of Esther Varnia, Surveillance Bureau secretary, filled the screen with a look so Californian it could have been patented. Surgical compukit, probably. How many operations, Reynolds wondered, had it taken to sculpt a designer face so flawless even the dimensions of her teeth seemed set by spirit level. He was so busy admiring her cosmetic beauty that, at first, her words did not register with him. Her boss's office? Right now? But he was just back from . . . Mr. Carver? Oh.

Colonel Reynolds' wife, Dolly, had a perpetually furrowed brow. Now there's a case for surgery, he thought, as he watched it furrow even more at the realization that her husband, barely home, was going out again.

"It's Carver," he said. "The top dog wants to see me."

"But you're hardly in the door . . ."

"Duty calls, Dolly." He knew that no matter how cheerful he sounded, little could be done to lift the cloud of depression she seemed to be permanently under these days. "Cheer up," he said. "Looks like your man, Art, might make general after all."

He left her with a peck on her cheek and was gone before she could ask when to expect him home. He knew it was not easy—being a career officer's wife—as he watched her feeling sorry for herself on the doorstep. He wondered too, for the millionth time, what a gung-ho soldier like him was doing married to a woman like her.

He put his flyer into alto-mode, chiding himself for his smart-alec cynicism. More time with her—that's what the doctors advised. She needed company, but he—well, Art Reynolds pointed his flyer in the direction of downtown Longevity City knowing that his needs, his career needs, were a major part of Dolly's problem. Dammit, you can't blame a soldier for being a soldier. He locked on to a vacant homing slot to city center and tried to forget about his wife. He concentrated instead on the promotion that was surely his. He would have more time for Dolly then, he told himself as he eased her yet again into the future tense.

Reynolds hitched a homing beam from fifteen kilometers out. Relaxing in his seat, he let comm-control do the flying. Rush hour was over. He looked forward to a gentle glide and a view unhindered by too many passing flyers.

His route took him low over the western suburbs of Longevity City, past villas with verandas, patios and pools. Residents lay in the sun, confident that PseudOzone levels would never dwindle above their houses and gardens. One of the great breakthroughs of the mid twenty-first century, PseudOzone's presence in the stratosphere had made a tremendous difference worldwide, diminishing global warming and the cancerous epidemics that had ravaged the planet in the 2000s.

People could sunbathe again. A lot did, especially in the western suburbs where there was so much leisure time. The flyer was only a couple of hundred meters above the rooftops. Reynolds wished he had a bino-lens to peer down on the rich and idle. So much time to soak up the sun, so many states of dress and undress.

The flyer descended to level two. Comm-control slotted it into a stream of traffic that flew by high-rise amusement arenas and multi-functional recreation parks. Two blocks past the concrete slab of the State Militia Building, Reynolds descended to level one and was pulled along Gemini Boulevard at a steady 80 K. A second homing beam took over, drawing the flyer to an opening fifty meters above ground level in a multi-story hoverpark across the street from the Surveillance Bureau.

Esther Varnia looked even more stunning in reality than she did on vid. Reynolds could see more than her shoulders now. Yes, the surgeons had been there, too. He followed her through reception to John Saunders' office—at least, it used to be Saunders' office. Now the sign on the door read, *Elie Sacchard, Surveillance Bureau Chief.*

Elie who? A millisecond later, the penny dropped. Of course, the whiz kid with the light-stick who had stolen the show at the State Militia Building. That had been only three days ago. He had not been SB chief then—promotion is in the air these days, Reynolds thought as Sacchard introduced himself. He did not need to be introduced to the other man in the room. Reynolds had met Ronald Carver several times—usually on official business and always with the Central Council in attendance. Never in such intimate circumstances. The newly promoted surveillance chief, the head of Bio—why else would such exalted company want to see him so soon after the Sulawesi raid except to congratulate him and to confirm that, yes, those extra bars would soon adorn his uniform. Art Reynolds felt his chest expand with pride. How thoughtful, how efficient, how . . .

"Sit down, Reynolds." Carver indicated a seat by the window.

When he heard that tone of voice, Colonel Reynolds had the uncomfortable feeling that all was not well. As soon as he was seated, the head of Bio also sat on a chair, legs crossed, facing him. Sacchard stood some distance away at the other end of the office.

"Tell me, Colonel," said Carver. "Do you recall the face on the wall-screen in SMB three days ago—the face of a young boy on the banks of the Ludese River?"

"Of course I do." Reynolds wondered what on earth this could be about.

"Do you recall seeing his body in the aftermath of your assault on the Sulawesi womb-station yesterday?"

Oh shit. Visions of a generalship took a back seat in Reynolds' mind. "We took out the site as directed. No one could have . . ."

"Did you body-count?"

"Y-yes. Sixty-eight."

"Wethers, the clandestitute we arrested some time back in Fiji, admitted to sixty-three children and seven adults. That makes seventy."

"He must have been wrong. No one got away. Condenser range for human cells was ten K."

"Colonel, the riverbank boy was not in the bag. How do you explain that?"

Reynolds shifted in his chair. It was not easy for him to concentrate, not with the way Carver kept swinging his right leg to and fro as if in time to an inaudible tune. For some reason Reynolds wondered if those slow-motion knee jerks were some kind of nervous reaction. Then he said, "Mr. Carver, my orders were to take no prisoners. We wiped out every human cell within . . ."

"Your orders came directly from me. My precise words were, 'kill them *all*'. That, Colonel, you failed to do."

Reynolds was suddenly aware of his shirt collar. It had shrunk a size or two in the last few seconds. It was time to insist that he was right. "The fact is, sir, we went in and took 'em out. Every last one."

The colonel knew he had lost the battle when Carver said, "Do you want to go through each scanshot, Colonel? Your troopers did go in for vids after the condenser wave. You at least got that bit right."

Reynolds found himself counting to ten. He knew that if the boy was not dead, it must have been because he had been outside condenser range. If an adult had gone missing also, that made two who had escaped. He said, "We got our information from that Wethers nigger a week before we went in. They must have moved the boy. You can't blame me for that."

For the first time, Sacchard spoke. "If you had reconnoitered the womb-station properly, Colonel—you know, staked it out before going in, you would have noted that a boy and an adult left the site early yesterday morning, five hours before you attacked. They returned less than an hour after you pulled out your troopers."

The temperature inside Reynolds' collar soared hotter than Old Faithful on the boil. He felt like calling Sacchard an arrogant little shit, but stopped himself. He was tempted to yell that he had been chasing clandestitutes since before Sacchard knew his ass from his mother's tit. What came out was: "Don't you tell me how to stake out an ambush. Besides, how d'you know all this about 'em leavin' and comin' back?"

"Simple, Colonel." It was Carver who responded, not Sacchard, and in the instant that he spoke, Reynolds knew that not only the battle, but the war, had been fought and lost.

Carver explained that the scanshots taken by the Bio vidmen had been checked out as soon as the troopers had returned to base. When it emerged that the riverbank boy was missing, a sortie was organized to revisit the site. A reconnaissance team had gone in that morning and found a trail in the underbrush. Imprint analysis revealed it to be newly made—no more than twenty-four hours old. It led to a salt spring where bags of freshly packed salt were discovered. The site was twelve and a half kilometers distant, beyond condenser range. Two distinct trails were found: one large—an adult, the other smaller—judging from the footwear, a youth. Another set of prints, similar to the youth's, led away from the camp. Analysis showed them to be a matter of hours old. They led to the Ludese River and disappeared.

"Clever little bastard probably left at first light," said Sacchard, "using the river to cover his tracks."

"Not before he buried his minders," continued Carver. "Sealed off their underground lair, too. Spectrographic read-outs of the womb-station showed that the seventh adult, the one you missed, had been dragged inside. His boot prints matched those found on the salt spring trail. Son of a bitch died of a heart attack, not condenser damage. Of course, you would have known all this, if you hadn't been in such a damn fool hurry to get in and out."

"Probably anxious to get home to your wife, huh, Colonel?" grinned Sacchard.

Once again the anger rose in Reynolds with geyser-like intensity. He felt the urge to smack Sacchard right in the middle of his sarcastic sneer, but smothered it, knowing it would be a useless show of frustration. Biting his lip, he ordered himself to maintain dignity—and make one last play.

"You just show me where he is, sir." He made his plea

directly to Carver. "Give me one chance. I've never let you down before." He almost said please, but stopped just in time.

"Mr. Sacchard is right, Colonel." Carver stood and walked to the door. "According to medical opinion, your wife needs someone to look after her." He paused, enjoying the bewildered look on Reynolds' face. "We've arranged your transfer to Camp Waverly. She can live right there with you in the marriage quarters. Waverly's a calm place. Nothing much ever happens there. You'll be able to devote plenty of time to Dolly—and," Carver indicated the door with his hand, "you'll still wear an officer's uniform."

The emphasis on 'wear' was enough to convince Reynolds that Camp Waverly was the only career option open to him right now—other than a downward plunge to corporal rank. He mustered enough pride to salute Carver on the way out. It gave him a minor sense of victory to ignore Sacchard entirely.

On the way home he tried to persuade himself to devote more time to Dolly. Yes, he thought, he would now have little to do but take care of his wife. He knew that because of her mental state her twin might not be activated. Rumor had it that Bio was shutting down the womb-banked fetuses of those with mental problems. Mentalers in the lower classes were already being targeted. Even the vulnerable members of military families were under threat. Supposing Dolly's twin was shut down, what would be the point in activating his own twin, in living all over again, with such a blemish on his record? Everything he had hoped for, worked for, fought for, was gone. It was the end of all his dreams. There was nothing left to live for—no more army, except in disgrace. And Dolly. Yes, now that the future tense was gone, he would have nothing to do at Camp

Waverly but devote himself to Dolly. And when Art Reynolds dwelled on that, he swung his flyer out of the homing slot and set the controls for the nearest convenient wall.

Sacchard and Carver missed the commotion caused by Reynolds' fatal impact with a wall down Gemini Boulevard. They were too busy flying toward the coast.

"You've got to be more subtle, Elie."

Carver banked the flyer onto flyway three.

"Sir?"

"You're thirty-one, right?"

"Yessir."

"So am I—only I've been around before. In my experience, one thing I've learned is that subtlety works better than going for the jugular. If you had been in charge today, you probably would have had Reynolds executed or at least stripped of his bars. There was a time when I would have done the same. Now I prefer to treat people more . . . psychologically. Understand?"

"Yes," Sacchard nodded.

"Good. You learn fast." Carver adjusted the controls. "Let's descend on autopilot. It takes longer but gives a better view of the sort of place you might live in one day."

Sacchard leaned to his left to look out the side, the smile on his face proportionate to the beach beneath them. The color of the sand could have been put there to remind him that he was Bio's new golden boy, favored by Carver as his new right-hand man, constantly under his tutelage, being trained—trained for what? He tried to figure out what Carver meant by 'the sort of place he might one day live in'. Did he mean just anywhere down there? Or did he mean . . . ? No, he couldn't, could he? Things had changed so fast over the last few days. All Sacchard's birthdays, all his Christmases, all his lottery numbers, had come at once. As far as 'living down there' was concerned, he did not know what Carver's place looked like, but he saw nothing in the neighborhood that was less than status-class quality, at least.

The flyer descended in a wide arc, curving over surf and sand toward the houses of the super rich. Sacchard looked down with envious eyes at seafront villas; resplendently white, each with its own wave pool, games arena and multiple hoverbay.

They leveled off over a greenbelt area protected by century-old legislation, then climbed above a headland and descended into a small cove. One glance at the head of the cove left Sacchard speechless.

Behind a small beach was a sandy area on which stood the strangest structure he had ever seen. It was circular, a hundred meters wide, enclosed in a semi-flattened, tinted dome. Glistening in the sun, it reminded him of a washed up jellyfish; the bell sectioned off by tentacles and ring-like structures beneath a gelatinous umbrella. Carver's building also had its sections, though it was difficult to see what they were made of through the opaqueness of the dome. As the flyer descended, an opening appeared near the apex into which Carver maneuvered.

When they stepped from the flyer he took his guest on a guided tour, pointing out how the building was made. If the structure had rendered Sacchard speechless from without, it left him breathless from within. It was sectioned off by walls of coral encased in panels of water. A designer-reef habitat; living, breathing, *growing* on all sides. Sacchard's eyes were drawn every which way as vivid colors grappled for his attention.

Rainbow parrotfish gnawed at coral with beak-like mouths; four-eyed butterflies flitted among neon-colored angels; clownfish darted between the tentacles of sea anemones flapping about in hidden currents. Here and there were sandy ledges decked with worms and mollusks, cones and cowries, great clams and burrowing crabs.

"Fantastic," said Sacchard.

"The building is made of animal organisms. We grow them artificially now. The many endangered species that live here would otherwise be lost to mankind."

"I knew of your interest in conservation," Sacchard turned around slowly, admiring the coral walls. "But this is just incredible."

"I thought everyone already knew how keen I am on protecting the environment. That's partly why I got so angry with Reynolds. Damn fool used a condenser to kill seventy people. A condenser with a human range of ten K! At its core, a half-kilometer radius, it would also have taken out a whole area of forest." Carver clucked his tongue and said, "Imagine the satisfaction there is in helping one of these creatures survive. Think how good it feels to breed an endangered species." His finger trailed slowly along the glass, attracting a small sea trout.

"Your father was a great conservationist, too, wasn't he?"

Carver's finger jumped off the glass, scaring the small fish.

Sacchard inwardly kicked himself for being so tactless. Three days previously he had attended a meeting at which Carver had openly criticized his own father—what had he called him, a weak man? And here was Elie Sacchard heaping praise when he should have kept his mouth shut.

Carver kept staring at the reef, at where the fish had

been, which did Sacchard's nerves no good. His scalp tightened, he prayed his *faux pas* would be looked on kindly, that it would not provoke the reaction he had heard about so often.

Carver turned around—for a moment a cold look in his eyes. Then he said, "Enough of this. What do you suggest we do about the boy?"

"The riverbank boy?" His mind a blend of relief and uncertainty, Sacchard glanced at a passing triggerfish.

"No, his twin—the Maxwell kid living here in California. Would you bring him in for termination?"

The head of what looked like a moray eel peered at Sacchard through a cleft in the coral. Remembering Carver's advice as they had flown here in the flyer—about being subtle and not giving in to knee jerk reactions—he said, "I suggest we leave him as he is. Sooner or later—it may take years—he's bound to attract the renegade from the riverbank."

"You mean . . . use him as bait?"

"Why not?" Sacchard wondered if he had said the right thing.

"Yes, indeed. Excellent idea. Come, Elie. I've something to show you."

He led him to a coral wall that was particularly sheer, taking up the entire side of a small room.

"Quote, 'lights down. Map.' Unquote," said Carver. The coral shimmered in the dimming lights. "The planet," he said. "Present day. You can see the areas under Bio control."

Sacchard was astonished to see that the coral was shaped like a world map. The northern hemisphere was exclusively red, plus much of Africa, Asia, South America and Oceania.

"You know, Elie, that idiot Reynolds was correct when

he advocated at the Council meeting that we spread our wings in the south. That's exactly what we're going to do. We've let them muddle along in their stupid ways for too long. He looked at the map and whispered, "Quote, 'one year plan'. Unquote."

Sacchard watched mesmerized by a crimson tide rolling down until all the world was wrapped in the arms of Bio. Then something distracted him—a glow flaring and fading, and moving, in the region of Patagonia. "What's that?" he asked.

"A passing fish."

"But it glowed."

"Many species glow in the dark. A coral reef has its own innate lighting system."

A pair of headlamps showed briefly in a crevice to the north of the Great Lakes.

"Wow," said Sacchard. "Did you see that?"

"That's nothing. It takes time for the reef to really light up. Remember, this is artificial darkness—their circadian rhythms are still attuned to daylight."

"I'd love to see this place at night."

"I believe you will, Elie." Carver placed a hand on Sacchard's shoulder. "When darkness falls you can look up from my bedroom and admire the stars and planets, all perfectly visible through the dome."

Aware of the hand on his shoulder, Sacchard looked at his boss and smiled.

Part Two

Chapter Ten

Fifteen Years Later

Late Thursday: the best time. Most of the regular shift gone on the weekend by four o'clock. Surveillance Bureau staff were thin on the ground—skeleton crew, they called themselves. An appropriate title, considering that the files they made available to the public were mere bones—a framework from which the flesh had been deliberately and carefully picked.

Mandy Ullman was not a member of the general public. She was an enforcement officer whose secondment to surveillance duties gave her access to the meatier parts of the State Record Department's files. But her access was limited—seconded officers were allowed view only those items appropriate to their studies.

She showed her credentials at the check-in. The desk-sergeant was impressed by her dedication. "Studying at the weekend again?" he said. "They sure push you guys hard."

"Yeah," Mandy smiled. "Worst thing is to let the work pile up."

"That's right. Who is it you want access to?"

"These three." She showed her authorization. The names Moorehouse, Mason and Rully all had a bearing on the assignment she was doing as part of her HEO (Higher

109

Enforcement Officer) course.

"Those three shouldn't take long. Aural?" The desk sergeant's fingers hovered over a button.

"No—manual," said Mandy, opting to key in her requests rather than use the more up to date 'quote-unquote' aural system.

A trace of surprise registered on the desk sergeant's face, as she knew it would. "You know how it is," she said, pretending to strike invisible keys with her fingers. "Got to keep in touch, otherwise typing gets rusty."

A window on the far side gave her a good view of a busy streetscape below. The terminal she wanted was nearby, the window her excuse for being there, but it was not the cityscape outside the window that attracted her. It was the fact that the console seat she now sat on afforded a wide view of the open-plan room. She could see the desk sergeant sitting at the check-in, his back turned. No other staff members were visible. Of the five people scattered here and there around the department, none were students on her course. Which was just as well—the last thing Mandy needed was someone coming over for a chat. She was not used to subterfuge, least of all in the Surveillance Bureau. This was her second—and, she vowed, her last—time doing this. She keyed in the first name.

Moorehouse.

Number?

213.

Alan Moorehouse's file appeared onscreen. It consisted of sixteen pages (thirty lines per page). This was four times above the legal limit. Details were exhaustive, including the fact that the secret eye in his cell had recorded him masturbating six times in one day during his spell in solitary (crime: rape, LA area). Mandy's HEO project concerned violence against women, specifically gang rape. She fed the details into the 'corder on her lapel. Done with Moorehouse, she whispered 'integrate'. Her lapel unit merged his file with her project database.

Mason.

Number?

465.

His file was as expansive as Moorehouse's. Mandy recorded the relevant information and wondered, not for the first time, what her own file might look like. Probably not as long, certainly not as villainous, but every bit as personal. If people knew how much information the state possessed . . . But people didn't know—and did not want to know. In a society where knowledge was dangerous, ignorance meant security.

Keyboards come and keyboards go. Different styles flirt briefly with popularity, but way back when people used typewriters—Mandy never could figure out how anyone could work with a machine so primitive it lacked memory— even then the most popular top row was *qwerty*. Materials may change, the cosmetic look of a keyboard may change, but *qwerty* goes on forever. So when Mandy typed 'T' instead of 'R' and the name Tully appeared, she pretended not to notice. She glanced furtively around to see if anyone was looking over her shoulder. No one was.

Number?

The world's foremost keyboard wizard might accidentally type Tully for Rully, but 218 for 38? That's pushing it a bit, Mandy told herself. Illicit access would take some explaining—she hoped it would never come to that. All the motivation she needed for what she was now doing had occurred thirty years previously when her best friend Reggie

Brooks had been viciously gang-raped and left for dead in a gully near San Andero. Thirty years is a long time—long enough for most things to be forgotten, if not forgiven. Finally, after all these years, Amanda Ullman was able to use her position as an enforcement officer to track down the perpetrators of that horrible crime—a crime she knew had been covered up by the authorities at the time. Scrolling quickly to the relevant reference—Tully's current whereabouts—she committed the information to the memory in her head, not the one in her lapel 'corder. Then she exited from the forbidden file and keyed in Rully.

The desk sergeant expected people to pause on the way in, not out. "Yeah?" he said to Mandy.

"I want to report a misread. Typo on console twenty-two." She struck another row of invisible keys with her fingertips.

"Oh?" Her fingers were long, like her limbs. She was late thirties, he reckoned. "How so?"

"I accidentally typed 'T' instead of 'R'. Out of practice, I guess. Databank coughed up Tully instead of Rully. I didn't notice until I'd scrolled halfway through."

He looked at *qwerty* on his keyboard, then stroked his chin. "Understandable, I suppose. Do you want me to report it?"

"Whichever you think." Mandy shrugged.

"Which Tully did you get?" he asked.

"Dunno—don't think I used Rully's number, either. Guess I knew subliminally that something was wrong. I wasn't thinking about numbers. You know how it is—it's been a tough week." She raised a laugh, knowing she had to get him to report it. That way it goes straight to storage and doesn't lie waiting in the memory for someone to examine it and make the connection between Tully and . . .

"Quote," the desk sergeant addressed his console mike. " 'Misreading on Rully 38. Typological.' Unquote." The file showed Mandy's date of birth. He did a quick calculation. She was well preserved for forty-four. "Have a nice weekend," he said. The wiliness was gone from his expression. He was just a tired old man—old enough to be her father.

"You too, Sarge," she said, turning from his desk and making her way out of the Surveillance Bureau.

Out on the street, Mandy Ullman tried not to walk too quickly to her enforcement hovercar. She opened it and locked herself in beneath its dull blue dome. She sat alone for long moments, realizing that if the authorities ever cottoned on to her illicit accessing of files, she would be arrested and probably accused of Association membership. Mandy had several times entertained the idea of contacting the clandestitutes with a view to joining them, but had never actually done anything about it. She was a lone operator, a maverick with a single-purpose mission. From now on she would have to be careful. Whatever additional information she needed would have to be acquired tonight. There could be no more illicit access. What she had done just now was crazy. *Never again,* she whispered to herself as she turned the ignition. *Never again.*

Darkness falls along with the rain. All good citizens leave the greasy streets to those who thrive on the night. The East Side belongs to them: hookers and hoodlums, racketeers and pushers, pimps and crooks. This is their town. This is their time. Night brings out a sleaze that hangs pall-like on the sidewalk. Men and women stand like desperadoes in doorways, hustling for customers. Everything is for sale or rent: power, death, sex, dreams. All available upstairs or on the ground floor or in the basement. Everywhere. Everything is available except twins. Twins are at a premium down East Side. Most of the desperadoes don't have them. They are onetimers. East Side is a onetime town set up at the turn of the century by the last generation, the lost generation, with no twins in the bank. No ticket for a return visit, no second time around the roller coaster and they *feel* it. They feel it so much it kills them to see teenagers walk around with a double lifespan they can never have. Drives them crazy. Mostly they sit back and let it eat them up, but some cannot take it. They cut loose: gray crime, dementia crime.

The last of the genuine onetimers died off in the 2120s, but that did not solve the problem. Bio's Inner Chamber, in a special protocol to the Resolution of '136, decreed that all citizens convicted of a felony automatically forfeited the right to a twin. They thought that would weed out the criminal element. Instead, it created a new generation of onetimers, more hardened than the last. Now there was a new crime: onetime crime.

Charlie Tully was a pusher, not a onetimer. His second life began as a gang member in the 'Dero Diner, San Andero, back in the summer of '131. In those early days he traded in robbery and rape—now he specialized in drugs. Narcotics were rampant down East Side, fed by pushers like Tully supplying a never-ending stream of psychosis drugs. The latest craze was korsing, called after Korsakoff's Psychosis—a syndrome once confined to alcos who drank so much they suffered selective amnesia. The brain suppressed recent events: far-off memories of youth dominated the mind. Now, a lifetime's drinking was not necessary. Just pop a pill. Onetimers loved korsing—it made them forget about old age, made them think they were living the second youth available to all but them.

A hooker stood in a doorway. She was pushing seventy, at least. Tully knew her from way back. Probably kills her to see a young guy like him—in his forties, but nearly fifty years older. She looked like she could do with a fix. She was rotten and reeking of clammy tuna. How anyone could mount her—even look at her—man, there should be cobwebs between her legs, but a score's a score.

Tully sold her the stuff and was about to ask if she'd had her downstairs replaced yet when the look on her scrawny face killed the sarcasm in his throat. She was standing on the sidewalk, back to the door. Tully's back was to the street. What she glimpsed over his shoulder brought a look to her face that meant one thing. Enforcement officers. Even before Tully had swiveled around she had stepped back into the shadow land behind the doorframe.

Tully had often disregarded the golden rule: never turn your back on the street. One look and he knew that this time he had disregarded it once too often. A pincer came fast at him from out of the dark grille beneath the dull blue semi-spherical cab of the hovercar. Tully jumped instinctively to one side but he was too late. The three triple-jointed claws of the hover's mobile arm grabbed him before he could think of running. The outer claws clasped his hips; the third poked between his legs, pushed beneath his testicles, raised them up, squashing them painfully against his thighs. Then it wrapped itself between the cheeks of his ass—catching him by the balls, and more.

As soon as the arm had him in its vice-like grip, it retracted violently, pulling him off the sidewalk, groin-first. Head, trunk and limbs followed: shooting forward, ramming him against the hovercar's metallic body. Tully's head was above the rim of the dome-like cab. His eyes were open but rolling from the jolt of the retracted arm.

Gradually, his vision sharpened up.

A face glared at him from beneath the cab's dim light. By the time Tully had focused his watery eyes, the face had turned through profile and beyond. Now he saw the back of a head—but not because the enforcement officer had turned around. The entire cab of the hovercar had swiveled on its chassis through one-eighty degrees. The front was now the rear, with Tully sitting like an indignant stunt rider on a particularly sharp ball-hitch. He held on for all he was worth to the outside of the cab as the hover sped through seedy streets up to level one, out into Manulands—an industrial area otherwise deserted on a weekend night.

A dead-end between two factory walls. No light except the dull pulse of the dark blue enforcement car dome. Silence save for Tully's breathing—ragged now after the rough ride. Another sound: the dull whirr of the rotating cab. That face again. This time Tully made sense of it. Short hair cropped in regulation style. The face beneath the hair was grim, determined, set with the sternest of purposes. In another light, another setting, it might even have been a pretty face. Jesus, thought Tully, a rampaging female cop—the worst kind.

A hand beneath the face touched a button. The mobile arm shot forward, ramming Tully's back hard against the factory wall. His head cracked off a brick, making him fuzzy-eyed again. As soon as he got his breath back, and his eyes re-focused, he yelled, "What the fuck d'you want? You can't do this!"

"Want to bet?" The voice came through a speaker—the harshness of the tannoy matched its tones perfectly. That button again. Once more Tully's back became a battering ram.

"Had enough?"

116

Hanging like a rag doll, head bowed, limp-limbed, dazed; Tully's iron-clawed diaper had him pinned to the wall.

"Let's talk about the Enders gang."

Tully hadn't heard that word in years. "Enders?" he gasped.

Another button. The claw tightened between his legs. He screamed in pain.

"Don't play games. Enders. San Andero, 2132. Remember?"

Memories flooded back, encouraged by the playful pincer. "Stop! Stop!" he yelled as she squashed his scrotum further up, further in.

The claw relented.

"Okay, okay," he gasped. "What d'ya want?"

"Information. Remember the gangbang in the 'Dero Diner?"

"Y-yeah."

"Tell me about the guy who organized it."

Oh Jesus, not that. No way could he mention *him*. Panic. "There was different leaders . . ."

A sudden dart of pain somewhere near the pit of his stomach. His testicles were riding high now, higher than they had ever ridden before.

"Stop!" he screamed. "You're gonna bust me!"

"I won't book you for korsing—not if you tell me what I want to know."

"I mean you're gonna—I'm gonna bust! Jesus, stop! I'll tell ya whatever—"

Once again the claw eased off.

"It was Carver, wasn't it?"

"How do you know that?"

"I had a little chat with a former associate of yours. Very

117

co-operative he was, too. Didn't need much encouragement, either. Seems he was booted out the night of the
rape."

The years peeled back and Tully saw Jim Chawke
standing at the counter of the 'Dero Diner, stunned by the
realization that Carver had replaced him as leader. A picture of Chawke's face flashed before Tully's eyes. So did an
avenue of escape. "Will you let me go if I tell?"

"It'll be like we never met."

"No drugs charge?"

"That's right."

"Then for chrissake don't squeeze me any more!"

"You ugly bastard. You know what Reggie Brooks went
through and all you're worried about is what's between
your legs."

"No! NO! PLEASE!"

"Then tell—everything."

"Okay, okay."

"You were Carver's second-in-command after he de-
posed Chawke, right?"

"Right."

"Okay, so squeal—and if you don't answer every question I'm going to put my finger on this button and keep it
there until your privates come poppin' up your throat. Got
it?"

Tully nodded furiously. He told her about more than the
rape. He knew better than to admit that Carver had instructed him to take Reggie away after the gangbang and let
her live by fixing her up with memory erasers. He lied that
he was merely obeying Carver's orders in dumping her body
in a gully off the West Coast Highway. The lie saved his
skin that damp and dreary painful night in Manulands.
Mandy Ullman asked endless questions about Carver's

leadership, his dealings in matters relating to the gang, his policies, his background, his personality.

When Tully had finished coughing up, the three claws eased their grip. The mobile arm retracted, dropping him to the ground. He fell in a heap and lay against the factory wall. He watched the blue light disappear, hoping he was not too badly ruptured and praying that no one would find out it was Charlie Tully who spilled the beans on Ronald Carver.

Chapter Eleven

Camouflaged by coral, an anglerfish dangled its bait optimistically in the passing current. It stayed perfectly still, waiting for lunch to swim up close. Ronald Carver had watched it for minutes, but his attention was wandering. Years had passed since Elie Sacchard had left him for Bio's top behaviorologist, Helga Wren. Since then Carver's sense of personal well being had been in the balance. Now it was perched as precariously as a codling peering into a conger's lair. The certainty and conviction of his previous years had been replaced by ambiguity and paranoia. How strange it was that he—Ronald Carver, the most powerful man in the world—could be stricken by a malady as profound in its lonesomeness as this.

As he stood in front of the anglerfish in his coral-walled home, Carver knew that some things could neither be bought nor controlled by money or power—genuine affection, for instance. It can be faked, as it was initially by Sacchard in his upwardly mobile rush to a position of importance in the Bio hierarchy, as it was by Carver in his hunger for sex and companionship. Both men had used each other. In the wake of their mutual manipulation, Carver was left with an authentic love for Sacchard that prevented him from having his Surveillance Chief fired as soon as he realized that his affection was beginning to wander.

An unspoken understanding had sprung up between them both. Sacchard realized that for the sake of his own hide he would have to carry on the pretense of loving his boss. Carver knew that life would have its burdens, even for the richest man. So they lived a lie: a life of pretense like a loveless marriage of convenience. Finally realizing that Carver was losing his drive and quick-wittedness—and that, no matter what he did he would never be fired—Sacchard announced that he was moving out of the coral-walled home, back to downtown Longevity City—back to Wren.

Carver took it with the morose indecisiveness of a manic-depressive at the wrong end of the scale. In the three years since, he had lost interest in what went on around him, becoming more and more reclusive and preoccupied with inner thoughts. In a strange kind of way his condition might have been diagnosed as lovesickness. But there was more to it. As leader of the world he felt incomplete, dissatisfied, unfulfilled. The supernova brashness of his ideals and ambitions had long been thwarted and betrayed by the hands and minds of mundane men. No wonder a drawn languid look masked the eyes that stared unseeing at the patient anglerfish. Failing to notice the glass cloud over in front of him, he sighed and shook his head once more.

"Quote," he whispered. " 'Lights down. Text.' "

The sheer coral wall darkened in the dimming light. He wiped away the condensation caused by his breath and studied Helga Wren's report. At least she had remained loyal on a professional level, if not personally. Her words glimmered on the coral wall-screen that had once shown Elie Sacchard a map of a Bio-dominated world. Now it displayed text, not maps. Carver watched Wren's words—words that seemed to glow with an indignation all their own. The report had been compiled from her Surveillance

121

Bureau records of a secret discussion held by five members of Bio's Central Council. The sixth, and as far as Carver was concerned, now the only loyal Council member—a man called Wallace—had been wise enough to decline the invitation to attend this secret meeting. He had chosen to contact the Bureau and so the meeting was scanned. Wren's report outlined in detail who said what. Then she added her own list of recommendations.

"Scroll," he ordered. As the text obeyed his command, he studied their treachery yet again.

According to these traitors, there had been four crucial errors on Bio's part. The first two, the Resolution of '136 and its protocol decreeing that criminals forfeit their twins, could easily be reversed. In their treacherous eyes, the purge of singletons under Resolution '136 had led to a hardening of Bio's image. The felony decree was equally detrimental. There was a finality about it that upset people. Its blanket imposition made them distrustful of authority.

Other blunders were more critical. If only the colonies of growing children had remained classified, if only speculation about them had remained a treasonable offence, then public disquiet might have stayed under wraps. Now, in the year 2162, the existence of the colonies was a major reason why so many people nurtured sympathies for the clandestitutes.

Another error, the attempt at a third world take-over and the laying waste of its people to create vast nature reserves, was roundly condemned by all five men. They felt it unnecessary, an irresponsible power play that overstretched Bio's resources and sowed seeds of dissent in the public mind. All these blunders combined to create a climate that spawned the growth of the Association. Clandestitute cells were now widespread and gaining in support.

In conclusion, the five Council members felt it was no coincidence that these events had occurred since the death of Carver Junior, who had favored a policy of *convincing* the population that everywhere was under Bio rule. *Influence their thoughts, control their actions,* had been a catchphrase of his. He had also urged the construction of womb-bank facilities where fetuses could be brought to term and nurtured through fifteen years without gaining consciousness. *Farm them like a crop,* he had said. Logistics of storage, as well as exercise and physiological problems, were stumbling blocks to this, but the scientists at Flok Island had been working at it all the time—until Carver Junior's son shoved it way down the priority list. Finally, the five traitors had sneered at the fact that more money was being spent on the Mars project than on population control . . .

Seething now, Carver read Helga Wren's recommendations. They perked him up considerably—he saw the writing on the wall, in more ways than one.

" 'Delete text. Lights.' Unquote," he said, storming out of the display room.

As instructed by Carver, Sacchard had flown in from downtown and was sitting behind a desk in the study of the coral-constructed home. He was scanning the latest reports on Grant Maxwell, the twin of the Sulawesi boy who had disappeared fifteen years previously. Carver had long since warned Sacchard to keep a close eye on Maxwell. In fact, that had been his sole responsibility in his early days as Surveillance Chief. In the intervening years Maxwell had qualified as a gynecologist and Sacchard had assumed other responsibilities—but he had never forgotten his initial duty to monitor Grant Maxwell.

Politically and socially, the gynecologist was as clean as a whistle. Always had been, though lately he was having a relationship with an enforcement officer called Mandy Ullman. Sacchard felt that there was something incongruous about a gyno having an affair with a cop. It just did not make sense. They were from different social classes. According to the latest reports, they were now living together. Sacchard decided that the cop clearly warranted further investigation. He was about to order enhanced surveillance when Carver walked in briskly.

"I want a Central Council meeting today, Elie. State Militia Building at four o'clock. Full attendance, no excuses. All members of the Council and the Inner Chamber to attend. Organize it."

"Sure thing." Sacchard, too, was aware of Wren's report. He was also surprised at how suddenly Carver had snapped out of his lethargy. The old authority, the old decisiveness, had returned.

"Put the flyer on standby," said Carver. "I want to be there early. You can help me with my speech."

"Yes, sir." Sacchard was genuinely delighted that the boss seemed to be back to his old self. It was not natural that a man in his mid-forties should be so morose and dispirited.

Deep in the State Militia Building, a small room. A U-shaped table, Carver at the head. To his right, Sacchard took one glance at the wall-screen at the far end of the room and congratulated himself on coming such a long way since first impressing Carver with a slide show of two boys fishing in the Ludese river. Next to Sacchard, Wren. Further down from her, four others made up the seven members of the Inner Chamber. Along the left side of the table sat six members of the Central Council. Military men one and all, they represented the strong arm of Bio control.

"Fellow members," Carver began. "For years I've been charged with governing this great organization. It's not easy, living with the responsibility of leading the human race. Oftentimes I've asked for your assistance and your advice. It has never . . ." With a flourish of his hand he indicated the Inner Chamber members, ". . . been less than forthcoming.

"I have a vision," he turned to face the Central Council members. "For years it's sustained me through the burdens of my responsibilities. That vision I have shared with you. I have nurtured and cared for it with policies that have sometimes been incomprehensible to the common man. This is not unusual—men of vision have been misunderstood and maligned throughout history. It is history that is the cause of the world's problems. For millennia, we have killed off wonderful creatures of nature—whole species wiped out by our selfishness and our carelessness. Sometimes I can't sleep nights because of this. My blood runs cold when I think of what our greed has done. But I wake up feeling good because I know that every day I help redress the balance. Each day I set things right. How I wish we could start over with a new beginning on a new planet. We've betrayed this one with our treachery. Most of you Central Council members are, in fact, traitors."

He paused. Five Council members looked up at him with more than a glint of concern in their eyes. Their fretful scrutiny reminded Carver of the petrified look of rabbits caught in the glare of headlights. The sixth member— Wallace, who had betrayed the others to Helga Wren— avoided eye contact as he sat at the far end of the table. He stared down at his memory pad, no doubt wishing at this moment to be somewhere else, anywhere else.

"We have polluted this planet with our products, with

125

our waste, most of all with ourselves. Population growth was so out of control that nature had to find a way to fight back. War and disease were not enough. Nature found another way—through Bio, through Bio policy. That's why I ordered the extermination of those masses of indolent peoples who clung like parasites to the face of the Earth."

Carver rose from his chair and made his way to the far end of the room. He took his time, walking slowly behind the Council members, pausing to look down on each of them. His eyes bored holes into their heads, his gaze filled their starched collars with sweaty dread. He did not gaze for long at the last in line, though he saw with satisfaction that geysers of sweat were erupting on the back of Wallace's neck, too. The Council members did not turn to meet Carver's stare, though each felt its presence as icily as if the scythe of death was at their shoulders. At the head of the room, Carver turned and said, "Now that we have controlled quantity, it's time we turned our attention to quality. That's what nature wants us to do; that's what nature wants me to do.

"When my father developed Geminizon he bestowed on the human race a great gift—the gift of two centuries of life. Such a treasure should not be allocated lightly. If nature had intended us all to have a double lifespan she would have been far more selective in her breeding. That, gentlemen, is the key—breeding. Unfortunately, my father was not a man of vision. He saw the signposts but misread the signs. Making Geminizon available to the unworthy was a grievous error. I have tried in small ways to divert the gift of a double lifespan away from those who don't deserve it— criminals, for instance—but I have been handicapped by Council members so blinkered they can't see the past correctly, let alone the future."

126

Carver stood near the door. Though he had a perfect view of the twelve before him, he only had eyes for the Council. Slowly he spoke, staring at each of the five, examining their faces in turn, searching for signs of uncertainty and fear.

One look at their ringleader and Carver knew his message was getting through. The man in the middle of the five twirled his laser pencil around and around, nervously bouncing each end off the tabletop. He could read between the lines of Carver's speech—and could guess what was coming.

"We need to extend our restrictions beyond the criminal element. Nature does not protect those who are mentally or physically scarred, so why should we? Enemies of the state are another category that we ought to have eliminated by now. Yet elements that contaminate our society are still with us. Why? Because I've been too reticent, too circumspect, too tolerant of those unable—and unwilling—to share my aspirations. They say I have made errors—purging singletons and criminals, for instance. My detractors have accused me of major blunders, such as ridding the planet of its parasitic third world citizens and allowing the truth to filter out about how we farm our activated fetuses. To them I say: why should we hide our achievements? Those who misunderstand us do not deserve the benefits they derive from sharing our world. To those who criticize me I say, yes, I ought to be criticized—for being too lenient with those who would betray me. More discipline is needed. Nature understands discipline. People understand it. They also understand example. Where better to start than at the top? Right here in this room?"

Carver watched mounting alarm spread across the faces of the five. He could smell their rising fear. He could see their rabbit-eyes bulging with the realization of what was about to happen. Their hearts pounded so hard in their chests he could hear their frantic beat. Edging closer to the door, he said, "More than two millennia ago, there lived another man of vision. He also shared his dreams with twelve whom he trusted with his life. He, too, was betrayed—though in his case there was but one traitor." He paused. Silence reverberated around the room. Then he said, "Council member Wallace, stand up!"

Uncertainty oozed from the man's small unctuous eyes as he rose to his feet. Not sure if praise or damnation was coming his way, he awaited Carver's next pronouncement with trepidation.

Recognizing the confusion in Wallace's eyes, pausing to wallow in it, Carver drew breath before saying, "Take your chair in your hands and step forward."

The room-lights glistened off Wallace's bald head as he took two hesitant steps, holding his chair before him.

"There," Carver indicated a space at the other side of the table—the wing normally reserved for Inner Chamber members.

Wallace slithered around the head of the table as if the space on the other side might disappear if he did not get to it quickly enough.

"I've decided to implement several directives immediately. Some are for public consumption. Some are classified." Carver put his hand on the door. The steel handle felt cool and solid in his grip. He looked at the five, particularly at the man in the middle whom he knew to be the ringleader of this ragbag of traitors. He saw that the man's knuckles were white—his fingers were working that laser pencil so hard it might break—and his face was welded with fear and outrage as he glared across the table at Wallace.

"As of now," Carver went on, "Wallace is promoted to the Inner Chamber which, from this moment, will consist of eight members. Central Council is abolished forthwith."

Carver opened the door.

The pencil snapped.

"You groveling bastard, Wallace!" On his feet now, the color of the ringleader's face matched his knuckles. He was about to launch himself across the table at the man who had betrayed them when he heard militia jackboots storm into the room. He saw then that the troopers had their pulse guns ready and were aiming right at him. He froze, knowing it was too late. Nothing he might do mattered any more.

"Count your blessings," Carver said as the militia pointed their guns at each of the Central Council five, cornering them at the far side of the table. "Death will be merciful. The cerebral incapacitator is instantaneous and humane—perhaps a fate too lenient for traitors."

As the militia escorted the grim-faced gang of five out of the room, Carver instructed the sergeant-in-charge: "Leave their leader until last. Make sure he sees what happens to the others."

When the doomed men had been led into the corridor, Carver closed the door and turned to face the Inner Chamber members. Once again Wallace stared at the table-top, the corners of his mouth twitching almost out of control. The four members seated alongside him had turned pale. Even Sacchard and Wren, seated together as usual these days, looked chastened.

"Quote. 'Recline eighty-five. Turn three-sixty.' "

Carver's chair responded at once. So did the rotating floor. He looked up. Stars were on parade tonight. The Milky Way was flung high and wide like a starry net cast across the heavens. This was Carver's nest, an astronomer's dream perched at the apex of his dome-covered home. Below him walls of coral, above him a ceiling of sky.

Not far above the horizon, Mars winked its reddish eye invitingly. Another light, a brighter red, rose vertically from below. The flyer returning to Longevity City. Carver did not need a telescope to know who was on board. Elie Sacchard and Helga Wren disappeared into the arms of Orion, leaving their boss to contemplate the emptiness overhead.

" 'Halt,' " he whispered. The floor stopped moving. The chair was reclining almost horizontally now. There was a time when Elie Sacchard shared that chair, and more, but ultimately Elie was attracted more to women than to men. When Helga Wren made her move, three years ago, the result was never in doubt. Carver pretended not to mind, at first. There were other lovers, always would be, but they could never give him what he craved for most. They too would pretend, but pretense is like a shooting star; all show, very little substance.

He looked straight up. The sky was hazier now—not just because of the Milky Way, but from the tears he so copiously shed. It was not stars he saw, but the dark spaces in between. In the vastness he saw a desolation and despair so immeasurable it matched the emptiness and loneliness he felt inside. He felt truly tortured. Nine-tenths of him told himself to lash out, to have Wren and Sacchard shot, to deal with them in the way he dealt with the Council traitors. But deep down that little one-tenth ruled his heart the way Sacchard once did. Here he was, the most powerful man in history, trying to balance his own sanity with the vengeful urge to strike, to maim, to kill . . .

He looked with misty eyes at the constellations overhead

and not for the first time wondered why the warmth and affection he had always longed for was destined to stay forever out of reach. As he lay in his chair, Ronald Carver realized that true happiness was about as far from him as Cassiopeia's five bright starry jewels—and just as unattainable. With that realization, the old uncertainties, the self-doubt, the lonesome paranoia of previous years, returned to haunt him once again.

Chapter Twelve

Mandy Ullman stepped from her enforcement car. Out of the corner of her eye she noticed something move. By the time she turned, she was nearly flattened by an officer twice her size hurrying past, oblivious to her opening door.

"Hey! Watch where you're going!" she yelled, but the man who had collided with her kept running as a stream of officers poured out of the Enforcement Building and hurried down the steps. She moved aside to let them pass.

Mandy's duty officer was not her favorite person. She regarded him as cynical at the best of times and rarely spoke to him, except when she had to. This time her curiosity won out. "What's the flap?" she asked. "Everyone's running around like jackrabbits."

"Some kind of riot down the Bay area. But don't let it worry that pretty little face of yours—you're off-duty now."

"Oh yeah?" Mandy handed her stunset over his desk, checking it in. One more sexist comment and she might show him how it worked. "Do we have enough officers available to handle the riot?"

"Plenty. You volunteering?" he asked.

"No. I've had a hard day."

"You hardly need the overtime, not with that rich doctor friend, huh?"

Pity that stunset was out of reach now. Her tongue was

not. "Aw gee, Sarge. Riots down the Bay but you're nice and snug behind your desk. Got to keep ourselves safe from the big bad world, haven't we?" she said, sidling out the door.

Mandy was in and out of the locker room in five minutes. She could not wait to strip off her uniform and get out from under the same roof as that duty officer. His sarcasm made her workplace an unhappy one, not that it would have been much better without it. She had spent years carrying an enforcement officer's badge, working her way to Higher Enforcement Officer status partly so that she could find out what had really happened to her classmate of long ago, Reggie Brooks. But it was beginning to dawn on her with great clarity that in the end the truth would not matter. So what if she discovered what had really happened—what use answers when the closer she got the more corrupt she realized the system was? Justice? Forget it; that was not what enforcement was about. Sometimes, in the empty nights before she met Max, she wondered if she was going insane investigating a thirty-year old crime like that—but she had to find out.

Reggie had not been the only victim. Mandy's parents had reacted to the rape with an overprotective regime. They rarely let her outside the door. The few times she did get out she was introverted and uneasy in the company of others, especially boys. Reggie had been her best and only close friend. Lonely and friendless, inadequate and insecure, sometimes suicidal, it became an obsession with her that one day she would track down those responsible for Reggie's death. She suffered a breakdown of sorts in her twenties and remained emotionally aloof until the age of forty-three. Then along came Grant Maxwell and out the door went her emptiness and her frustrations.

She stepped onto the sidewalk outside the Enforcement Building and thanked her lucky stars for the night she had met him. She looked at the trees in the park and from the far side of the road she could see the buds. Her lungs expanded with a breath that felt crisp yet mild. Spring was in the air . . .

Sirens were in the air. People in motion walked quickly to the hoverstations and hoverparks. Mandy looked up. Homing beams were busy. It was mid-afternoon but levels were filling up. Trouble down the Bay could easily spread. Unlike most of those around her, she knew the riots were localized, otherwise off-duty officers would have been called in. But she was in a hurry too, walking quickly to a bar down Petty Street.

"Mandy," said Max, "this is Violet. Careful what you say, Vi—she's an enforcement officer."

Violet laughed. "Pleased to meet you," she said, offering her hand.

"What'll it be?" Max was on his feet, turning to the bar.

"A large bourbon."

"Tough day?"

"Don't ask." She watched him walk to the counter, then said to Violet, "I've been looking forward to this. Max has told me a lot about you."

"I hope it wasn't all bad. He talks about you all the time."

Mandy smiled. "He says his medical practice would be in bits if it wasn't for you. How long have you been with him now—two years?"

"Yeah. Ever since he set up. He needed an experienced receptionist. I was looking for a new job. I must say he's great to work for. The man knows how to treat people—not like other people I know, believe me."

Mandy glanced at the bar. Drinks were being poured.

"How long have you been an enforcement officer?"

"Too long—about five years. Before that I drifted around. Different jobs, travel—that sort of thing." Mandy looked across the table. Violet was fifty-ish and pretty. Her round ebony face was as black as darkest Africa—those large sharp eyes did not miss much. Mandy continued, "I'm not like Max. He went straight from med school into practice. An organized guy."

"Change the subject. Here he comes."

"Have you two been talking behind my back already?" he said.

"Of course," said Mandy. "Say, Violet, has this guy ever thanked you for that ticket for the New Year's concert?"

"He's never mentioned it—not even once. That's how you two met, right?"

"Yeah. Three months ago today."

Max leaned over and kissed Mandy. Then he looked around at the fake oak panels, brass fittings, mirrors, and other twentieth century decor. "Know what?" he said. "This is a great place. Genuine bartenders, none of this servo stuff." Pulling up his stool, he leaned in close and whispered, "Pity about that holo though. I wish they'd turn it down."

Behind them, on a circular stage in the center of the bar, two cartoon characters acted out a cat-and-mouse drama.

"That's all they show these days," said Violet. "It's vacuous stuff. Still, what better way to start the weekend than with a drink? Cheers."

"Cheers," said Max. "Hey, the bartender was talking about the protest down the Bay."

"Protest?" Mandy raised an eyebrow. "I thought it was a riot."

"It probably is, by now." Max drained two centimeters of long cool beer.

"Didn't you hear the news?" said Violet to Mandy. "Channel Eight announced this morning that Bio intends destroying all womb-banked fetuses, and activated twins, of what they called 'mental defectives'. So, people are protesting."

"That'll be the end of Channel Eight," said Max.

Violet leaned in close. "First, they destroyed the twins of criminals. Now it's mentals."

"Hold on," said Mandy. "Anyone with a low IQ is now a onetimer, right?"

"Not just that," said Max. "It applies to mental illness as well as IQ. Goes right across the board, regardless of concordance."

"Regardless of what?"

"In ninety-five per cent of cases where Geminizon-induced twins develop schizophrenia, the other twin does likewise when he or she reaches the same age after Activation. That's concordance. It's more or less the same with other illnesses, though studies yield variable rates."

"You're talking shop, Max." Mandy put her glass on the table. "What's the bottom line, in English?"

"They're killing off one in twenty fetuses that would otherwise grow up to have no mental deficiencies or illnesses."

"The bottom line," said Violet, "is who's next after mentals?"

"Channel Eight reporters," snorted Max.

Mandy felt suddenly afraid for her own womb-banked twin. Who was to say that the twins of those who had nervous breakdowns might not be next for termination? Such a cold thought made her shiver. She was brought back to the conversation by Violet, who leaned over and asked, "What do you think of the Association, Mandy?"

"You mean clandestitutes?" Mandy shrugged. Violet's use of the word 'Association' might be interpreted by some as a sign that she was sympathetic to their cause. It was unusual, not to mention risky, for a civilian to call them by their own name in front of a law officer. "Don't know much about them," she lied, and sipped her bourbon.

"What did you say?" said Max. "I can't hear a thing. I wish they'd tone down those damn holos."

Five minutes later his prayers were answered. The cartoon faded. A uniformed holo took center stage. It turned slowly through three-sixty degrees, its cam-eyes recording all it saw. Then its mouth broadcast a militia newsflash, instructing all citizens to leave the downtown area at once.

"You were right, Mandy," said Violet. "The protest must have turned into a full scale riot."

"And it's spreading," said Max. "Let's go. Fancy going somewhere else?"

"Not me." Violet was on her feet. "I have a date tonight. See you bright 'n' early on Tuesday. Bye, Mandy. Nice to meet you."

Max stood up, helping Mandy with her coat. "She's some character, isn't she?" he said as Violet went out through the door. "I'm glad you met her."

"So am I." Mandy struggled with a sleeve. "But I got this funny impression that she was sizing me up."

"Sizing you up for what?"

"It's just a feeling. I thought she was fishing—trying to sound me out on Bio and the clandestitutes and . . ."

"Keep your voice down. She was only doing that because they're hot news. Violet was just making conversation—you know, being friendly, interested in your opinions. She's the salt of the earth, believe me."

"Perhaps you're right, but . . ." The bleeper on Mandy's watch cut off her reply. "Oh no," she said. "Those riots must be bad. I have to report back. There goes our anniversary. See you whenever."

One kiss and the bartender intervened between them. "Sorry folks, you heard the announcement. We're closing. Looks like trouble is coming our way."

Grant Maxwell avoided downtown by taking his flyer up over the hills to a grassy headland overlooking the Bay. He sat on a bench and looked out over the city, trying to make sense of it all.

Smoke hung low over Gemini Boulevard, at least four buildings were burning. Fires also blazed down East Side. Who could blame the unfortunates down there? The new directive would hurt Eastsiders harder than most—more mentals lived there than anywhere else. Max looked out over the western suburbs. No fires breached the boundaries of the rich. He tried to reconcile himself to what was going on. If the world order was rotten, and he was becoming more and more convinced that it was, then how could he justify his lofty status as a gynecologist? Eminence did not always equate with collusion, he knew, but maybe that was just an excuse.

Somewhere in the distance he saw the roof of Golden Gate High, the exclusive school his parents had sent him to. They died in a hover crash when he was in first year med. An only child, that left him with plenty of cash to pay for the completion of his medical training. Midway through his studies, he had opted for the most lucrative, most coveted branch of medicine. Gynecology. Now, at the age of thirty, he was beginning to earn real money. And now there was Mandy—he hoped she would be safe on the streets tonight.

Max got up off the bench. He had always been a part of the system, always would be. He was just a drop in a vast tide of people. A drop can't change the ocean. He stepped into his hover and took one last look at the riot-torn city. There was enough paranoia in the world without doctors like him getting infected. It was bad enough that he thought he was being followed all the time, without blaming himself for the world situation as well. Hell, his whole life was ahead of him—twice. He switched on the speakers and listened to music as he hovered back home to wait for Mandy.

Chapter Thirteen

Bald-headed girl on a couch, blood flowing from her ears. A drop rolls down her cheek, gathers itself into a globe at her chin, falls onto the head of another girl. The other girl has hair, blonde hair, though now it's blood-entangled, messy. They sit on a couch, one collapsed on the other's lap. Both dead. Yes, dead. Who are they? Don't know. Friends? Sisters? Cousins? Maybe. Maybe not.

Don't hang around. On the floor a boy about sixteen years old. Dead? Probably. Want a closer look? No. Go quickly. Be careful passing the dead boy's head. There's this coffee cup. Now you've spilled it. Jesus, it's not coffee—it's blood. Got to get out of here.

Endless corridors, getting smaller, narrower. Corpses everywhere. Rotten, stinking, maggot-ridden corpses. A light in the distance. Freedom, but the corridor is shrinking. Run!

A dead woman up ahead, kneeling forward, face on the floor, backside in the air like a Moslem praying, blocking the way. Who is she? Don't wait. Jump! There's not enough room. Go for it!

The roof is closing in. Unable to run now, unless hunched over. Stoop, but keep running. The roof is falling in . . . Bend! Keep going for the light. Can't stand now, must crawl. Earth everywhere, bits of corpses. Have to tunnel out with bare hands. Walls are caving in. The light is small, shrinking, out of reach.

Fading, getting dark, can't breathe . . .

"Max? Are you okay, Max?" Mandy grabbed him by the shoulder.

A pair of sleepy eyelids blinked open.

"You were having a nightmare."

He hauled himself up on the pillow, his startled mind hovering in that crazy half-space between lucid dreams and cock-eyed reality. For moments the dream clung to him until he shed it like dead skin. Realizing where he was, he asked, "What time is it? It's bright."

"Time you were up in two minutes."

He forced himself to look at the bedside clock. 7:28. "Shit. Did I wake you?"

"No. I was awake already. It's early shift today. No riots this week, so I'm back on earlies. Do you want to talk about the nightmare?"

"It's just a bad dream I get from time to time."

"Tell me about it."

"It's nothing much. I usually end up suffocating."

"That's not much, huh! Is it just you—there's no one else?"

"There are others. I don't know who they are but they're always the same."

"How often do you get this dream?"

"I got it first when I was fifteen. Since then it's come on and off, maybe three or four times a year. How come you're so interested? I'm supposed to be the doctor around here." He turned on his side and took her in his arms. It was hard to believe she was almost fourteen years older than him. She looked almost as young as he did.

"Dreams fascinate me," Mandy said. "Besides, I'm an investigating officer—that entitles me to investigate."

The bedside clock squawked its alarm. Max quenched it

and turned back to Mandy. He pulled her close and said, "Okay, officer. Let's conduct an investigation."

Violet's blonde head peered into Grant Maxwell's office. "Mrs. Chapman is here to see you, Doctor," she said.

Max's eyes never left his console. They didn't need to—he could see Violet's head reflected on the screen. "Fine," he said. "I'll be with her in a minute."

The monitor also reflected his own face. Right now it showed a smile. Good receptionists were hard to come by. Violet was a model of discretion, never calling him by his first name while at work, even though they were friends. It was always 'Doctor' when patients were on the premises. He called up Mrs. Chapman's file. It appeared onscreen, wiping his smile away. Before he could study it fully, Violet said, "Did you enjoy your walk down by the pier last night, Doctor?"

"Yes. You were down there, too?"

"There was a nature-music concert on the pier. I'm a fan, remember. I saw you and Mandy passing by."

"You should have called us over for a chat."

"We were inside the pier gates. I only saw you in the distance. Anyway, I was on a first date. You know how it is." She smiled briefly and leaned in close, resting her hand on the console table. "Mrs. Chapman appears a little apprehensive today, Doctor. I think she knows."

"Well, that's good. The bad news won't come as a shock."

Violet walked toward the door. "If there's nothing else I'll tell her you'll see her shortly." On her way out she nodded in the direction of the console.

The note was at the edge of his keyboard. It read: *'You had a tail down by the pier last night. I had a good view so I'm sure I'm not mistaken. Two men—militia in mufti, by the looks of them.'*

Max was not surprised. Watchers were widespread, easily spotted. Totalitarianism breeds inefficiency: whoever had installed the vid-cams in his office had failed to do the job properly. Max had the angles figured out. There was a blind spot near the console. If he seated himself in a certain way, like he was sitting now, the keyboard became invisible to the cameras. He had told Violet about it.

He turned sideways to the cams, pocketed the note, stood up and looked out the window. To the south, a distant boardwalk jutted into the sea. The concert pier. The Bureau of State Enforcement loomed large in the foreground. Somewhere in the distance, around the corner, was the concrete slab known as the State Militia Building. In a society where a certain type of pregnancy was encouraged, the gynecologist was king. But what's the point in being a king if they keep you under surveillance, access your files, follow you around and bug your office? Max turned and walked pensively to the door connecting his office to the opulent room in which his clients came to consult.

Violet was right. Mrs. Chapman knew. He had barely set foot over the saddle of the door when she stepped forward. "Doctor," she said. "Have you analyzed my scan?"

"Please take a seat, Mrs. Chapman." He placed a comforting hand beneath her elbow, guiding her to the high-backed chair in front of his desk. She was a capable woman, well able to read body language and draw her own conclusions. He hoped his delaying tactics would make it easier for her to assimilate what she was about to hear.

He leaned forward on his swivel chair, his hands joined on the broad expanse of desk before him. Mrs. Chapman sat rigid, features sculpted in apprehension. Her dark protruding eyes bore the look of an alarmed cat.

"Mrs. Chapman," he began. "I'm afraid the results are not good."

She shuddered just a little. Her jaw dropped. She was about to speak but he knew it was best for him to keep talking.

"The initial hyperscan showed nothing unusual. The fertilized egg implanted in the womb in the normal way, but the second scan revealed that it did not divide as it should have." He drew breath and went on, "I'm afraid that soon after implant the egg separated into more than two parts."

"You can't possibly mean that they're not twins?" Mrs. Chapman's large round eyes were like headlamps.

"I'm sorry. The egg split into three. It happens once every eighty pregnancies. There's nothing anybody can do."

"But I took the right amount of Geminizon. That guarantees identical twins, doesn't it? It has a one hundred per cent success rate, hasn't it?"

"The manufacturers of these chemicals like us to think that there is no failure rate, Mrs. Chapman, though it happens." Max knew he was sailing close to the wind by indirectly criticizing Bio, but the woman at least deserved the truth.

"My egg split into how many parts?"

"Three."

"But aren't triplets . . . ?" Her fourth word was uttered so forlornly it was inaudible.

"Triplets are not allowed," he said, anticipating what her question might have been had she completed it.

"Couldn't two of them be identical? Couldn't we terminate just one?"

He shook his head. "If it had been two eggs and one of them had split into two and the other had not, then you would have triplets consisting of two identical twins and one non-identical individual. In that case, yes, we could abort the odd one at the embryo stage. But it was a single fertilized egg."

"Then aren't they three identical twins?" Marsha Chapman bit the corner of her lower lip, embarrassed by her tied tongue and tangled thoughts. "I'm confused, Doctor. If Geminizon works with two, why can't it work with three?"

"The drug works best with twins. With triplets, Geminizon becomes diluted. Correspondence rates would not be high enough to satisfy society's demands. Your triplets would be identical only in the historical sense. And . . ."

"And that is not permitted."

Max was surprised that she should take the words from his mouth. Had he uttered them, they would not have been loaded with such bitterness.

"I'm truly sorry," he said. "There is no choice."

"I knew I shouldn't have picked a young doctor like you." She was on her feet, heading for the door. "I'm going to get a second opinion from an experienced gynecologist."

"It's not me, Mrs. Chapman. It's the scan. Not a doctor in the world would say different."

"That's the trouble with doctors!" She swiveled around to glare at him. "You've turned the world upside down, changed all the natural laws for this stupid double-life. A woman can't get pregnant unless it's twins. Then you take one child and raise it for, what, fifteen years? And what do you do then? Kill it, that's what. No wonder there's so much trouble. What about all that warfare in the southern hemisphere a few years ago? And the riots in the city last week? Is there a point in living twice? Tell me that!"

"Please, Mrs. Chapman . . ." She was saying too much,

but he could not tell her that the room was bugged.

"I'm asking questions, Doctor, but you're not an-
swering. What's the point? Life's not worth living when
there's so many laws you can't breathe; when children are
getting killed. It wasn't like that in my mother's time. It
wasn't like that when I was younger. And where's all the
perks, all the leisure, all the freedom we were promised?
Down the tubes like—oh Lord!"

Her choice of words brought a spasm of grief to her
mouth. She put her hand to her face and looked at the
young man standing patiently before her. "Oh God, I'm
sorry, Doctor. I shouldn't get so . . ."

"That's all right, Mrs. Chapman." He wanted to tell her
to be more discreet in condemning Bio, but such comments
might compromise him. All he could think of saying was,
"It's best to let your feelings show, but be careful. Share
your emotions with your friends—with people you know
you can trust. Do you understand?"

She sighed. "Well, looks like I'll have to try again. It's
not your fault, Doctor. I realize there was nothing anybody
could do." She was wearing too much foundation. The light
caught her cheek and her make-up glistened.

Grant Maxwell momentarily felt his throat go dry. She
was sixty-eight, too old for further implantation.

"Have you mainlined my file to the databank?" She
asked as he reached for the door handle. It was a remarkably clear-headed question considering her emotional state.
It threw Max slightly.

"No," he said. "Not yet. When will you terminate?"

"Tonight. Will you prescribe me?"

"Yes. Violet will look after that for you. I'm sorry, Mrs.
Chapman." Feeling totally inadequate, he opened the door
to reception.

When his patient had stepped out into the reception area, Max closed the door behind her and walked across the carpet to his desk. As he passed the high-backed chair in which Mrs. Chapman had sat, his right hand caressed the headrest.

Despite the spring sunshine, his office felt cold and uninviting. He sat at his desk, glaring at the console. Its blank screen reflected his surroundings. He saw reflections of the sunlit window, the door to reception, the walls of his office. He saw a wall adorned with certificates. He could not read their mirrored commendations—there was no need to. He had seen them too often. Phrases like *eminent gynecologist, pillar of society, member of the noblest profession.* Beyond the words, he saw his own face staring out: bleak, moody, accusing.

Something to the left of his reflection caught his eye. The door opened. Violet's head appeared, tilted at an angle. This time he turned around.

"I've prescribed Mrs. Chapman for tonight, Doctor. Do you want her file mainlined today or shall I wait until after the weekend?"

"I'll take care of it."

"Will there be anything else?" Violet's face exuded its usual Thursday afternoon cheeriness.

"No, that's it." Max looked at the time. It was three o'clock. "I'll lock up. See you Tuesday."

The door closed. He keyed up Mrs. Chapman's file. For five minutes he stared at it, or rather at his reflection on the screen, but did not mainline it. There were too many things on his mind, like trying to justify once again his own position in the Bio scheme of things.

The directionless nature of his life had but one calming constant: Mandy. She, too, was unhappy in her work. It was a factor that they had in common but it was something they would have to talk about more. How could Max explain things to her without him seeming to be off the rails? He was in love; he held down a lucrative, respected and sought-after job; he and Mandy lived in a nice apartment out West Side—yet these strange dreams were coming more often. Jungle dreams, entombed visions of being buried alive and robotic birds that leave a cold stare as they fly past . . . He had told her about some of them. What he had not yet told her was that sometimes, when he lay awake, his thoughts were disturbed by the weirdest visions that seemed to come out of nowhere. Like now, for instance, his mind was full of spaceships long and sleek, and a blue-white planet looming up close, and a stub-nosed shuttlecraft edging ever closer to the planet's surface . . .

Chapter Fourteen

A rookie air traffic controller thought he saw a speck of dust on the control tower window. He stepped sideways to see if the speck moved. It did not.

"There she is!" he cried, pointing to the sky over Walker Lake.

Most of the tower personnel ignored him, preferring the dot on their plasma screens to the dot on the windowpane. Multi-colored graphics displayed the incoming shuttle's parameters much more reliably than naked-eye observation.

The shuttle left the lake behind. Dipping its tail, it came in low from the northwest, hitting the runway with a screech that was audible inside the distant tower. Its turbulence tossed up a golden cloud as it careered along the sand-strewn track, eventually rolling to a halt half a kilometer on the far side of the terminal building.

Three flight crew and ten passengers alighted from the shuttle and hovered the short distance to the ground complex. Nine of the passengers were regulars who had come down on the shuttle from the wombship *Catalina*. After scanning, they went to the canteen for lunch. The tenth passenger was a supply crewman provided as last minute cover for an ill colleague on the *Catalina*. As soon as his scan showed the necessary clearance, he left the complex.

Once outside, he looked up, holding an engraved stone

in the palm of his hand. It was small and round. There was a vague outline of a human figure etched on one side. He looked at the stone, flicked it once in the air and returned it to his pocket. The spring sun played on his face, illuminating hair once fair, now dark. For a moment he savored the warm rays—something he had not experienced in more than a year. Then he stepped back into the shade. Not much PseudOzone over this neck of Nevada, but there was a militia bus going east to Tonopah. From there a waiting hovercab took him several hundred kilometers south.

Xiao Qi Ching opened the door and poked his head out. His was a great globe of a skull, a freak of nature that posed a serious dilemma for those who jump to conclusions and base their opinions on first impressions. Was the man a simpleton or a genius? Stepping out of the hovercab, Leandro Vialli knew the answer. He also knew that the cranium's size had killed its twin fetus. The cerebra of both brothers had developed as one—in one skull. Two brains do not necessarily mean twice the brainpower, though in Ching's case the evidence seemed irrefutably positive. The death of his brainless twin had made him a singleton. Clever enough to play the fool, he had masterminded the growth of the Association and avoided the singleton purge of '136. Now in his eighties, he lived in a secure location near the foothills of Mount Whitney.

Ching thanked the cabbie and held the door of his house open for his guest to enter. The equally ancient cabbie saluted the clandestitute leader and returned to his hovercab.

As soon as the door was closed, Ching said, "Sit down, Lee. Relax. I'm sure you're glad to be back on Earth after a year wombshipping up there." The old man pointed to the ceiling and added, "They no speak Italiano on Mars, no?"

"Not yet," said Lee. "But if you wanna, I go maka them an offer."

"Good, good," laughed Ching. "The vastness of space has not affected your sense of humor, nor old age mine. I'm glad to see ethnic surgery has worked well for you. A credit to our doctors. How long is it now? Fifteen years?"

"Fourteen."

"When has it to be renewed?"

"Every seven years—otherwise it starts to peel. Also, the ethnic aspect of the implant—the accent and family tree memory—starts to wear off. Physically, the molded bones crumble and the skin flakes. It literally falls off," said Lee, "unless it's renewed. Renewal's due now."

"Make sure you get it done, in case Bio grabs you. Our latest information is that they have technology to revert a face to its natural state if the implant is waning."

Lee looked surprised. "What about the ethnology—can they revert that?"

"We're not sure," said Ching. "Whatever features the implant gave you—the dark hair and brown eyes, plus the ethnic knowledge of family and Mediterranean history and culture—all that is irrelevant. They only need your face. Wine?"

"Please."

"Do you still get those headaches?"

"Haven't had one in years."

"Good," said Ching. "Leandro Vialli—quite a mouthful. Hungry?"

"Starving."

"Excellent. This Martian business can wait. Never report on an empty stomach. Any problems getting here?"

"No. The cabbie was very professional."

"You met him once before." Ching paused for a moment, enjoying the perplexed look on Lee's face. "He worked in Chicago back in '131."

"*That* cabbie. You mean . . ."

"Yes. He was the one who ferried you and Haria from the Chicago Gemini Clinic to Oregon. Remember the incubator in his dashboard?"

"Very funny, but why . . . why didn't you tell me before he left? He took care of my mother."

"It's better for him that he doesn't know who you are. As you say, he's a professional. So are you."

"Of course," said Lee. "Now that you mention it, I couldn't keep my eyes off that dash the whole damn trip. Thing is, back in '131 it was a different color."

"Why you . . ."

He ducked past Ching's flailing arm. "Haven't moved the dining room, have you?" he joked, pretending to run from the old man, laughing not just at Ching's reaction, but at the joy of being reunited with his old friend.

The dining area was small—mock granite walls gave the impression that it was carved out of rock. It reminded Lee of his childhood on Sulawesi and the inside of Camp Agrina, though everything there had been on a larger scale. Ching's present home was more modest—a hunter's lodge in what used to be Sequoia National Park.

Though the surroundings were modest, the food was not. Ching had prepared a delicious Char Siu and chicken with bean sprouts. Lee's eyes followed every bowl as the Chinaman took them from the preserver and laid them on the table. When the main courses were eaten, Ching pushed his bowls out of the way, put his chopsticks to one side and asked about the Mars project.

"It's completed now. It's just a matter of waiting a couple of years for the first harvest, as they call them."

"Once Bio build Transposition facilities up there," said Ching, "they'll really have gone native. Then our friend Mr. Carver will have his perfect little world on Mars. From what we know already, his colony is well underway. What's the population of doomed children?"

"Five hundred have already been activated—plus a thousand womb-banked fetuses."

"What about the colonists themselves? Is the settlement at an advanced state?"

"Completely self-sufficient. Their closed-loop environment works well. The life support systems require only solar radiation. Everything else is produced beneath the domes. They get oxygen from carbon dioxide and drinking water from body wastes. Basic foodstuffs are grown. They even have a lake and a small forest. Waste products of fish fertilizes the plants—makes them grow better."

"Sounds almost idyllic."

"The twin towns are linked by shuttleway. Simulated gravity makes it feel like home. Sitting by the lake, you'd think it was paradise—except for the children behind the forest. Know what?" said Lee. "They reckon there's enough water locked up in the Martian ice and enough vapor in the clouds to terraform the desert."

"No wonder they want their own Transposition facilities to enable them to transfer their minds into the fifteen-year-olds."

"This is good stuff." Lee gulped down more wine.

"You saw doomed children before going to Mars, didn't you?"

"Will I ever forget?" Lee drained his glass and tried not to dwell on his six months working undercover for the Association on the island of Hokkaido. More specifically he tried not to think about Melinda FWC 3892 A2143. Mel, as everyone called her, was due for Transposition within the year. She did not know that, of course. She thought she was getting out of school. But Mel was bright—near the end she realized Hokkaido was not an educational center but a death camp. It broke Lee's heart to think of the questions she had asked him and it broke again when he thought of the answers he had to give and what they did to her. Sometimes, in the darkest nights, he saw Mel's face again—and other faces. Young, beautiful, hopeful, vibrant—dead. All dead.

"More wine, please," he said. "They don't allow it on Mars yet."

"And the wombship?" asked Ching.

"It's capable of carrying five hundred fetuses. Quite a sight, the *Catalina*. It's a new design based on the old supershuttles, makes her almost as big as a long-haul freighter."

"Quite a name too, *wombship*."

"Yes," said Lee. "She has this ethereal quality. When you look out from the shuttle and see her hanging from the station cluster she looks almost preternatural. Once aboard, you realize she's just a cargo vessel—a hateful one at that."

"It would certainly have an ethereal quality if we could blow it up," said Ching.

"The *Catalina*? Surely we don't have . . ." Lee paused. "Things obviously went well while I was away."

"You could say that. We're doing well in the battle for hearts and minds. You see: Bio's gone too far. While you were up there, they introduced new directives that have cost them public support. Carver just recently had five members of Central Council executed—he said they were plotting some kind of coup against him. They were all military leaders. As a result, we hope to swing some of the armed forces behind us. If we succeed, the Association may soon be in a position to strike hard at Bio—even an attack on their space program might not be beyond our capabilities. A lot depends on the information you collected on your trip— which should be very detailed, considering you worked up there for more than a year."

"All safely locked up inside here." Lee tapped the side of his head.

"Good." Ching rose to his feet. "Do real astronauts eat dessert?"

"Do fish swim?"

Lee sat back on his cushion, preoccupied by the military matters his host had hinted at. Halfway through a delicate toffee-banana, he said, "So they're losing the propaganda war?"

"Exactly. Double lifespan is only of value if life is worth living over, otherwise it's no good. As Bio becomes more totalitarian, and society becomes more paranoid, so the quality of life goes down. Know what the newest craze is?"

Lee shook his head and poured himself another glass.

"If a citizen dies before Transposition, they sell the activated twin as a sex slave. People know about that because, try as they might, Bio can't control all the media. This business of making Mars so self-sufficient its population won't have to return to Earth for Transposition, that's totally unnecessary. It's a grave mistake, and people are beginning to see it as such. A strike against the Martian program would drive Carver wild—it might just provoke the reaction we want from Bio."

Lee knocked back his wine as if it were beer. "You're trying to turn me into an alco," he said, "talking so much, making me do all the drinking."

"Think of a more important soapbox and you might

even get a fourth glass. It's good wine, you know, from Fukien. Though you better report officially before you drink any more. Care to do it while I wash the dishes?"

"Sure." Lee put his glass on the table. "By the way," he asked, "any news of my twin?"

Xiao Qi Ching nearly choked on his lychees. "Your what?" he blurted.

"You heard me. One night in Sulawesi, the night the drogue bird came, I asked Raul. He wouldn't say yes. He wouldn't say no. He gave an evasive answer, just as you did six months later when you took me into your household in Zhiantung. Just like everyone's done since—but I know he's alive."

"How do you know?"

"I feel . . . vibrations from time to time. It happens between twins."

"I see." Ching molded the last of his lychees into a neat pyramid in the middle of his bowl. "We're researching him," he said. "His attitudes can be interpreted in particular ways. You can read certain signs, if you look for them. Signs that say he is unhappy with the world as it is today." Ching looked at the broad smile on Lee's face and continued, "No approach is to be made, especially by you, until we know more about him. All I will say is that he is in good health and living in California. Bio tails him night and day, naturally. Now go make your report. That's an order."

In a corner of Ching's bedroom, Lee took a little plug from the wall and inserted it into the tiny socket in the skin behind his ear. Once jacked in, everything was downloaded. All he did was concentrate as the transcanner converted memory blips into coherent information. Mental images were transformed into graphic outlines, drawing up plans and particulars of the wombship *Catalina*, right down to the smallest specification. He was back with his host before the wine had warmed.

As soon as he had finished his fourth glass, Lee asked, "When do we attack the *Catalina*?"

"That is long-term. You won't be involved, so don't let it concern you."

"What? Why not? Why send me up there for a year if you're not going to use me?"

"But we are," said Ching. "We're using your information. As for you personally, the Association has great plans, Lee. There's the small matter of a pharmaceutical plant on the Gulf Coast. It's the biggest manufacturer of Geminizon in the northern hemisphere. We want you to pay a visit. Interested?"

"Sure. Anytime."

The dregs of Ching's bottle caromed around in Lee's glass. He felt disappointed at being left out of the plans to attack the *Catalina*. As always with drink, he saw visions of Sulawesi . . . *Raul, Haria, Zenga* . . . The condenser attack . . . *Sharon, Hugo, Tamara* . . . Hokkaido . . . *Mel* . . . So much bitterness left a residue that festered in his heart. It was always there, swirling around consciously and subconsciously, like the wine at the bottom of his glass. He had just been through twelve months deep cover on Mars, where there had been nowhere to relax and no chance to unwind. Now he was at last with a friend, someone he could trust with his life—a chance to forget it all, to ease his twisted mind. That's it: get twisted. Raising his voice, he began to sing.

"Italian folk song, Leandro?" asked Ching.

"Naw. Twentieth century American, written by some guy—what was his name? Say, you got any more of this Fuk—what d'ya call it?"

157

"Fukien." Ching laughed and got up off his cushion. "You are obviously out of practice with alcohol," he said.

"Thasright. Never was able to hold liquor anyway. 'Cept like this." Lee held the bottle upside down over his empty glass.

Chapter Fifteen

Mandy Ullman never could stomach false values. Not for her a designer apartment, thank you very much. Her down-to-earth tastes were reflected in the geraniums and bonsai that embellished the small apartment she shared with Max in the western suburbs. He was making plenty of money so they could afford to eat out often. Tonight, for instance.

"How about the Dolphin?" he suggested.

"Sounds great. Let's go."

He changed his mind in the flyer, suggesting instead a small restaurant down by the pier. They took quite a few turns on the way, and it seemed to her that Max took the long way around. Whenever Mandy looked at him, she thought he was preoccupied with the rear view mirror, but she said nothing.

The meal was pleasant—tortellini with mozzarella cheese washed down by a carafe and a half of medium dry. When Max had paid the servobot, he said, "Why don't we go for a walk along the bank?"

Below the restaurant there was a large inlet surrounded by trees—a greenbelt lung protected by laws centuries old. A bank walk undulated above the waterline. Half a kilometer out, the walk dropped into the high-tide mark and petered out into a small cove. It was a moonlit night, a night for lovers holding hands under trees.

"You really like this place, don't you?" she said.

"Yeah, it's great. No people, just water and trees. And it's far enough away from over there," he pointed to the far side of the inlet, where the amber glow of Longevity City was reflected on the underbelly of gathering clouds.

"Know why I changed my mind about where to eat?" Max did not wait for an answer. "Because we were being followed, that's why. And our apartment's probably bugged. That's why I mentioned the Dolphin, to confuse them, though I don't think they tailed us in the flyer."

"How much wine did you drink tonight?"

"Mandy, it's not that . . ."

"Four or five glasses, right? You're going to get one of your headaches."

"Listen, Mandy. Two men tailed us down by the pier last night. Violet saw them—she told me about them today. My office is bugged. My files are accessed. If you don't believe me, ask Violet. You've met her, go ask her."

She looked across the water, then back at Max. "You've had this fixation about being followed ever since you were a kid, right?"

He sighed. "I don't like the way you use the word 'fixation'—like I said, ask Violet."

"I will. There's enough paranoia in the world without you wandering around the apartment pretending to talk to me but in reality trying to fool a bug that isn't there."

"It mightn't actually be in the apartment. It could be a scanner across the street."

"Max!"

"You know what things are like. There's surveillance everywhere."

Mandy drew him close, rested her head on his shoulder and looked up at the stars. Overhanging branches and burgeoning clouds obscured her view. Through a gap in the cover, a red planet hung low over the inlet.

"Did I ever tell you about my research?"

"Your Higher Enforcement Officership—the multiple-rape thesis?"

"Not that exactly. I've done some private digging about Reggie."

"That was years ago."

"Thirty years last month. It's taken me that long to get my hands on the records."

"And I'm the one with the fixation?"

"Max," she lifted her head off his shoulder. "A long time ago I promised myself I'd do something about what happened to Reggie. That's why I joined Enforcement, to dedicate myself to nailing the animals that do that sort of thing. Call it militancy or vengeance or whatever, I don't care what it's called. I never dreamed I'd really get close to those responsible, but lately I've been in a position to do my own research. The fact is that I've found out more than I bargained for. I've broken through the cover-up and the deceit and the disinformation. Now I know exactly who raped her and why—and how."

Max studied her face. For a moment, a fifteen-year-old girl looked up at him; lost, confused and bewildered. He pulled her closer again.

"Do you know who organized the gangbang?" she said.

"Who?"

"Ronald Carver III."

Max let out a long low whistle. "He raped your friend?"

"Not him exactly. Our great and glorious leader just orchestrated the whole thing. Actually, he prefers men."

"I never knew that. But why organize a rape?"

"I think it must have been a power thing. He couldn't

161

just be in a gang—he had to be number one." Mandy stared into space for a moment, then looked at Max. "All I can do is speculate, but from what I know, and I've done a lot of research, I think I know why he did it. It was a mixture of ego and, this is where I'm not so sure, I think he's very insecure."

"Ronald Carver—insecure? Give me a break, Mandy. The guy owns the world. He's untouchable."

"Not according to the clandestitutes. Have you noticed how active they've gotten lately?"

"Yeah, but they'll never get rid of Bio."

"Can't you see, the reason the clandestitutes are so active is because of Carver's insecurity. You have to go right back to his father, Ronald Jr. That guy established Bio as the world's major controlling power by the mid twenty-first century. He was a wizard when it came to public relations. The man convinced everyone he was saving the planet from military and ecological disaster. He promised a double lifespan—two hundred years of bliss—for every citizen. He delivered too, at a price. Know what kind of man he was, deep down?"

"From what I recall . . ." Max shrugged, ". . . they told us at school that he was into conservation and the space program . . ."

"No, no. I mean do you know what he was like as a person?"

"How would I know? You tell me."

"He was a selfish bastard. Let me give you one fact. He had an only child, Carver III, but he couldn't stand children and didn't trust maids. Know what he did when his little son got on his nerves, you know, the way kids do? He locked him up in a room, that's what. And I don't mean for a little while. I mean for a whole day, or more. His wife, before she met with an accident, disclosed that as divorce evidence to a lawyer. Imagine! Locking up a two year old—it went on until the child was five or six—in a room for most of the day. Then the son was carted off to a posh private school."

"How do you know all this?"

"Digging. Ronald Carver III had an awful childhood. That's partly why I think he's insecure, but he's also arrogant. Psychology is part of my HEO and one thing I've learned is that insecurity and arrogance make a deadly mix. Carver's trying to be just like daddy, only more so. He's trying to *outdo* daddy. He's interested in the same things, conservation and space travel, only he tries to do them better. His father was content to control the developed world, so the son takes over the whole planet and how many people die? Millions. His father sets up experimental space stations, cluster systems like *Atlantica* and *Pacifica*, and what does the son do? Colonizes Mars, for God's sake.

"I'm telling you, Max, it's a classic syndrome. His father rejected him when he was young so now he's trying to prove that he's better than his old man. He can't have any real relationships because of his terrible childhood. He has no loyalty to anyone so he tries to find happiness in fish and mammals and . . ." Mandy looked at the planet hanging low over the inlet. ". . . Mars. All the loyalty that should be directed at others is directed within. He uses people, period. So he used Reggie, just like he used the gang who raped her."

"How did you find out about his involvement in the rape? You said there was a cover-up."

"I accessed certain files and . . . interviewed some of those involved."

"That's risky. If . . ."

"I know, but if people knew what I know about the man who runs the world, their skin would crawl. Are you listening?"

"Sure." He transferred his weight from one foot to the other, then back again.

"The funny thing is," said Mandy, "some kind of change came over Carver a few weeks back."

"What kind of change?"

"Rumor has it that for a couple of months he'd been withdrawn into himself, like a recluse. His long-time lover—the Surveillance Chief, Sacchard—left him for a woman. Carver apparently lost all his appetite for Bio and became very introverted as a result of being jilted. Imagine—the most powerful man in the world being dropped like that. His moodiness went on for ages, though if recent events are anything to go by, he appears to be re-kindling his interest in world affairs."

"How do you know all this?"

Mandy knowingly tapped the side of her nose. "Private research," she said.

"Like I said, it's risky."

"I've been very careful." She rested her head on his shoulder again. "Nobody knows what I've been up to. You're the only person I've told."

"If they find out, they'll accident you."

She had never heard it as a verb before. She looked up at him and smiled.

"I'm serious, Mandy. They might start following you now. Maybe that's why the apartment is bugged—so they can listen to you, not me."

"Very funny. Have you told anyone except Violet and me that you think you're being kept under observation?"

"No."

"I like the way you regard Violet as a friend. I imagine a lot of doctors treat their receptionists as dogs' bodies. You're different. She respects you for that and so do I." She kissed him gently on the lips. He seemed preoccupied. "Penny for your thoughts?" she said.

"It's just that you reminded me of my job and I'm not too happy about that at the moment."

"Why?"

"The usual thing. I'd prefer not to talk about it."

"Who was it this time?"

Max rested his forehead on hers and moved it about as if he was burrowing into her head. He chuckled at how easily she could read his mind. He raised his head then and told her about Marsha Chapman's visit that afternoon, including her emotional outburst against doctors. "She blamed me for everything as if I was single-handedly and personally responsible for Bio policy."

"Of course she blamed you. To her, you represent the world gone wrong. She took it out on you because to her you *are* the system. You are the establishment. Mind you, she had a point. If the system is rotten, so are you because you're part of it. You uphold it."

"So I earn a living. Big deal."

"Yeah, but you're saying it's got nothing to do with you. Well, it has. Don't pretend you're whiter than white. You work in a rotten business."

"Don't talk like that."

"Why?"

"It makes me feel guilty. Sometimes it bothers me, sometimes it doesn't. It's as if there are two of me. One wants to be a gynecologist, the other rails against it." Max leaned back against the tree. Misjudging the distance by a fraction, he stumbled slightly and fell against the bark.

"There goes that wine again," said Mandy. "God, you talk nonsense when you're drunk. You're not happy in your job, Max—that's your trouble. Women come crying to you and you can't take it because you know they're right. So what do you do? Cry on my shoulder, that's what."

"Not true."

"It is true. Look at you—your practice is expanding. Pretty soon you'll be a fat cat living off Geminizon and Bio. At the same time you whinge about society and the way it's structured."

"So I'm a hypocrite, is that it?"

"You said it. If you don't like what you're doing, get out of it. Otherwise you are a hypocrite."

"Oh yeah? Well, look at you. I've had to listen to you complaining about Carver. You feel the same way about things as I do and what are you? An enforcement officer, for chrissake. Now who's the hypocrite? What's the matter with you today anyway? Is whatsisname, that duty officer in the Enforcement Building, is he getting at you again?"

"Shut up! I had my reasons for joining . . ."

"Let me interrupt you for a change. If I'm such a hypocrite, how come you're down here with this fat cat tonight?"

"Because I love you, you bastard," she said, burying her head in his shoulder once more.

Chapter Sixteen

Lee lay on the ground with his chin on the hard metallic surface of the ventilator shaft. Like a boy with a catapult, he lined up his handheld Y-shaped deflector with the sides of the grille that closed off the ventilation duct from the floor of the pharmaceutical plant. He adjusted his angles until the deflector's electronic eyes were aimed directly at the point where the security beam fed into the grille. He pressed the yellow button in the middle of his Y-shaped instrument. Like a crossbow drawn taut, the ray jumped back four meters. Instead of taking the short route across the metal fretwork of the grille, it was diverted between the tips of Lee's deflector.

"Go!" he hissed, admiring the trigonometry of two thin red beams splaying out from his hand-held instrument.

Harkes was one meter thirty, but she had to stoop to keep her head from hitting the roof of the duct. Carefully negotiating the deflected beams, she knelt before the grille. Lee applied a quick-working adhesive to his deflector. Then he looked up. Harkes cut a diminutive figure in her skintight assault suit. Aiming first at the top right corner, she carved her way slowly down the grille, across the bottom and up the other side. She switched off her electro and attached it to the magnetic strip on her belt. She lay on her back and brought her feet to bear on the grille. A little pressure opened it wide enough for her to slide forward and drop to the storeroom floor. When the other two members of the assault team had gone through the opening, Lee checked that his deflector was securely attached to the duct before he too negotiated beam and grille. Then he forced the metal fretwork back into position while Harkes put her electro into reverse mode and applied it to the cuts. One minute later the metal had melded and the grille looked as if it had never been touched.

The four-member assault outfit stepped out of the store-room into a passageway that was off-limits to the control booth's surveillance cameras. "Check pulse guns," said Lee. Harkes and the other two gave their weapons a once over while he stole one last glance at a floor plan of the plant. A quick check of his own gun, a muted "Let's go," and they were in a corridor leading to the processing chamber.

Geminizon production was fully automated. On Saturday nights there was little danger of bumping into maintenance workers. With ancillary staff off-duty for the weekend, Lee reckoned there would be no problem getting as far as the chamber.

He was right. The corridors were bare except for one-meter-high drones that trundled by every now and then. Harkes found it unnerving to have to jump out of the way whenever a cone-shaped drone approached, but Lee assured her that they were harmless. "So long as you don't interfere with their progress," he whispered, "they carry out whatever task they're doing regardless of what's going on around them."

Never one for wasting words, Harkes turned her attention back to the long corridors. They resembled passageways on station cluster *Pacifica* where she had worked undercover for the past three years. Earthbound for a month now, she still had her space legs—the flatfooted way she stomped down the corridor vouched for that. She wished for zero gravity so her legs could float above the hard energy-sapping surface, away from meandering drones. Not much further now, she told herself. Around the next bend, the corridor ended.

Lee inched forward, craning his neck to peer into the chamber. Similar in size and shape to a fifty-meter swimming pool, it was guarded by twin vidcams, one at either end. Assembly lines carried rows of vials through the central processing unit. Line after line disappeared into one end of the unit only to reappear, ionized and impregnated with Geminizon, at the other end. Then they were marched on conveyor belts through a cooling system at the far end of the chamber. The parading vials were concealed beneath metal casing three meters wide, battleship gray in color. Though the vials were hidden, the noise of their progress through the chamber was betrayed by a rhythmic clickety-clack on the conveyors.

Lee looked up. Along one wall, a window—the control center. As anticipated, the shutters were down. Behind them a semi-darkened room with one, maybe two, security men gazing at banks of screens and warning lights.

"Okay," Lee whispered. "Take 'em out."

The taller of the two clandestitute troopers inched forward, praying his head and shoulders would go unnoticed in the view from the vidcam at the far end of the chamber. Taking careful aim with what looked like a sawn-off shotgun, he pulled the trigger and rolled back into the corridor as quickly as he could.

The gelatinous mass that hit the cam-eye coated the entire lens with a transparent film that literally was a film. On impact, the photographic plasma took an image of the chamber, promptly showing it through the cam-eye lens.

A security officer glanced at screen eight. Somewhere in his periphery, it had blacked out. By the time he focused his eyes on it, normal service had been resumed. He examined the other screens in his security array. At the end of row two, another flicker caught his eye. Screen nine had also hiccuped, but vision had restored itself almost immediately.

He stood back, hands on hips. Cameras eight and nine seemed to be functioning fine despite momentary lapses. Just in case, he reached for his memory pad and scribbled a note below the one he had written five minutes previously about the glitch in the ancillary light. But a note was not enough—weekend nights were lonesome and boring, always were. No one to talk to; nothing to do except wait while time limped by. Flickers like these were unusual—an excuse for talking to someone. He spoke into his lapel mike. "Hello, maintenance," he said. "Better get someone up here right away. We seem to have gremlins in the system."

Both cameras safely veiled, the clandestitute swung his videogun over his shoulder and gestured for the others to enter the chamber.

Harkes provided cover from the corridor as Lee and the other two infiltrated the processing unit. Running low and hard, they ducked their heads below conveyor belt level and made for the processor in the center of the chamber. They huddled down using the bulky geminizing unit as cover in case a security guard opened the shuttered window up in Control.

Lee knelt down. The troopers on either side of him

caught their breaths as he opened the straps on his backpack. He was unsure if his palms were sweaty from exertion or from the thought of handling the highly volatile explosives he was taking out of his pack. Preferring not to think about it, he said, "Okay, guys. Here's the stuff." The troopers exchanged nervous glances before taking a limpet in each hand. "Right," said Lee. "Go to it."

The door to Control opened with a soft swish.

"What's the problem?" A maintenance engineer stood before the array of security screens, examining each in turn.

"A couple of glitches—perimeter light flickered fifteen minutes ago, then an ancillary. Processing cams blinked just now."

"The two of them?"

"Yep."

"It's probably nothing." The engineer examined both screens. "They're perfectly steady now. Still, they shouldn't . . . Say, what's that?"

"What?"

The maintenance man pointed to a dark patch at the entrance to the corridor. "A shadow?"

The trooper had been quick but not quick enough. His blurred image had appeared in the cam-shot as he had rolled out of the chamber.

"Unusual all right," said the security man. "It could be the shadow of a drone up the corridor."

"But there's no movement. A 'bot ought to be moving."

"Right. You know, I'm damned if that shadow wasn't there earlier. It could be something on the vidcam lens."

"There's one easy way to find out." The maintenance man reached for the window shutter toggle.

The trooper was on his knees, back to the window, attaching his second limpet to the processing unit. The dull whirr of moving shutters prompted him to look over his shoulder. All the training, all the muscle-building he brought suddenly to bear as he sprang back, sprinted five meters, and rolled himself tightly against the chamber wall. Almost directly beneath the window, he was invisible now unless someone up there put a nose against the glass and looked down.

Lee and the other trooper did not have to react so strenuously. Out of view on the far side, they crouched beneath the conveyor belt casing. Harkes stood with her back to the corridor wall, heart pumping, fingers tensed, pulse gun ready.

The trooper lying by the wall eased his weapon off his shoulder and held it firmly against his chest. Looking up, he could see a horizontal slit where moments earlier there had been gray shutters. He glanced across at the processor. His second limpet was plain as daylight, hanging from the side of the unit. "Jesus," he muttered, knowing it was bound to be noticed by whoever was looking down from above. With flashing eyes and nodding head he indicated to Lee that they were about to be discovered.

The security officer stared at the corridor entrance. "No shadow now," he said. The maintenance engineer glanced back at screen eight. The blur was still visible. He looked out the window. It was on screen but not there in reality. He looked at the cam-eye responsible for the blurred image. Something was veiling the lens. He swiveled to examine the camera at the other end of the chamber.

Down on the floor, Lee knew there was no time to lose.

The man above might take less than a second to reach a certain conclusion, three seconds maximum to reach the alarm. Lee leaned back—a flick of his head indicated the Control window.

Harkes sprang into the middle of the corridor. Feet wide apart, she steadied herself and sprayed Control with a stream of pulse rays.

The engineer was reaching for the security button when the glass shattered. A pulse caught his shoulder, spinning him to the ground.

The security man saw a figure at the corridor entrance. Instead of ducking out of her way, he looked at her face. She was staring up. From somewhere beneath her gaze, a pulse ray seared. It smashed the window into a million shards, catching him full in the chest, ripping him apart. The last thing he saw was the room going into parallax as the pulse blasted him off his feet across the floor.

The rest of the troopers were on their feet now, spraying Control with more deadly rays.

"Go!" roared Lee.

On their feet and running, they arrived at the corridor simultaneously. Harkes jumped out of the way to let them pass. Lee grabbed her arm, pushing her in front. "Get the electro ready!" he shouted as they sprinted down the corridor.

Up in Control, the maintenance engineer lifted himself up on his one good arm. He tried to raise his other hand to reach the console alarm button but his arm refused to respond. One look at where his shoulder used to be told him why. With supreme effort he raised himself on his feet only to collapse on top of the console masterboard. His good hand reached over to push the alarm. Then he slipped slowly down off the console unit. Falling back, his head hit the floor with a sickening thud. As he blacked out, the fanfare of trumpets that welcomed him to the next world sounded remarkably like wailing sirens.

No time for being kind to drones now. "Zap 'em out of the way!" roared Lee. According to clandestitute information, drones went into search-and-report modes during security flaps. If screaming alarms were anything to go by, there certainly was a flap now. No point in taking chances—not that Lee's troopers needed encouragement. They blasted every drone as soon as it appeared in their sights.

Around the last corner, the storeroom door. Still no sign of security guards—they could only be moments away. One trooper smashed the door in with his shoulder, then crouched to cover the right-hand side of the corridor while the other covered the left. Harkes and Lee jumped in between, the electro ready to undo the earlier repair work. Lee put his hand on her arm, stopping her as she prepared to carve a way out. The idea of covering their tracks by repairing the damaged grille had only been of value because there was a slight possibility of maintenance men entering the storeroom while the raiding party was still in the chamber. On Saturday nights the chances of that were so slim they should have risked it anyway. Now they were faced with a thirty second delay—a delay they could no longer afford now that their presence had been detected.

"To hell with electros." Lee pushed Harkes out of the way. Taking aim with his pulse gun, he blasted the grille to bits. The Y-shaped alarm deflector he had so carefully positioned four meters back from the fretwork went flying down the duct. So much for the adhesive, and so much for the ancillary alarm that would now pinpoint precisely where they were.

Harkes climbed into the duct. Her colleagues threw delayed action blasters down each arm of the corridor. As soon as Harkes disappeared into the opening, the other Association troopers followed. Lee placed a small limpet where his catapult-shaped deflector had been. No sooner had he positioned it than the blasters went off in the passageway, taking out the first wave of security guards.

The clandestitutes crouched as they ran; legs vertical, torsos horizontal, like stooping giants. Harkes led the way. She was the shortest and the fastest. She also possessed radar-like direction when it came to negotiating the maze of shafts and ducts. The further they ran into the maze the harder it would be for Bio to pinpoint their precise location, and more importantly, where they might exit. The ear-splitting scream of rending metal told them that Lee's bomb had demolished the storeroom duct, hopefully hindering pursuit from behind.

Control was a lonesome place no more. It was full of troopers under the command of the plant security chief who took one look at the dead body of a maintenance engineer, minus a shoulder, and the mutilated corpse of an overweight security guard. Filled with distaste, the chief glanced at the security man's memory pad. It contained ten words. The last five were *Screens 8 and 9—blinked.* One glance at the plasma-coated chamber vidcams confirmed what that meant, but the top half of the note was more interesting. It read *Perimeter 20, Peripheral 9—flickers.*

"Attention, troopers." The security chief addressed his lapel mike. "Raiders are making for Perimeter Twenty. Repeat, Twenty." Confident that the clandestitutes would now be cornered, the chief walked on shards of broken window glass and looked down into the processing chamber. For the first time in half a century he found himself praying—hoping that Bio's defusers would dismantle the limpet bombs in time. What happened next, had he lived long enough to think about it, might have made him doubt the power of prayer. All six limpets exploded simultaneously, demolishing the geminizing unit and creasing the security chief to the back wall of the control center, which promptly collapsed from the blast.

Shockwaves reverberated through the warren of ventilation ducts and maintenance shafts. The raiding party was almost out. Legs pumping, head bent low like an ostrich in a headwind, Harkes led the way unerringly to the appointed exit. She halted five meters from the end of the duct. The two troopers fell to their knees either side of her, covering the exit with their guns. Lee ran up from behind. He took one look at the grating blocking their way and realized this was no time to attract attention by blasting it with a pulse gun. "Right," he said. "Electro."

Had the control center security array survived the limpet blast, a perimeter light would have been flashing its socks off. Within half a minute Harkes had arced an opening large enough for them to squeeze through.

"Go!" said Lee.

Harkes climbed out first, then the others. Lee brought up the rear, stepping out to find the raiding party back-to-back in a defensive stance against shadows cast by the blazing processing plant on the hill above. Lee glanced at flames splintering the sky, then stalked slowly around, peering into the dark for a friend—or an enemy—that could come from anywhere. He whistled softly. His low-pitched, two-note signal immediately attracted an echo.

From out of the shadows stepped a black-clothed figure, a getaway driver extraordinaire; his blackened face grinning with joy that all four of his comrades had made it. He nodded in the direction of perimeter duct twenty. "Bit of a commotion back there, huh?" he said, then gestured for the raiders to follow him.

Lee had set a small decoy charge at the entrance to duct twenty just after Harkes had arced her way through it with the electro. The decoy was enough to leave a trace of a flicker on the perimeter light up in the control center. The security guard and his chief were hoodwinked into believing that the clandestitutes would exit the way they came in. In fact, they had surfaced, as arranged, half a kilometer away at perimeter duct twelve.

The skimsub had been camouflaged under bushes. With the raiding party aboard and firmly in harness, the getaway driver pressed the sealing button and engaged forward motion. The torpedo-shaped skimmer rolled seaward on small wheels. Taking off downhill, it gradually increased speed until it flew off the edge of the cliff.

"Brace yourselves!" shouted Lee as the G-forces of freefall engulfed him and everyone else aboard the sub.

The reinforced glass-plated nose of the skimmer dipped toward the Caribbean. Down, down, it plunged into the blackness of a small cove. It hit the sea with a dull plop rather than a grand splash. It straightened and climbed toward the surface like a high-diver after a perfect entry. This diver was different—it straightened out again just below the surface. The wheels flipped over, morphing into stabilizing fins. The propulsion unit went full ahead as the skimsub pulled away from the coast at increasing speed.

Keeping always two meters below the surface, it made its way out into the vast haven of the Caribbean. Neither boat nor plane, leaving neither wake nor radar trace, the skimsub darted beneath the waves, carrying Lee and his comrades out into the Gulf to rendezvous with a freighter that would ferry them away from danger.

Chapter Seventeen

Waiting never comes easy. Not when hard news breaks—especially if it's guaranteed to provoke an angry reaction from the boss. Elie Sacchard stared at a passing triggerfish. Somewhere in the dome above the coral walls of his home, Ronald Carver descended from his astronomer's nest. Sacchard lost interest in the fish and stared instead at the reef behind it, at coral that once ran red with a map showing worldwide Bio domination. A wry expression played on his lips. He turned to walk across the room.

The door opened.

"Well, Elie?" Carver was red-eyed from too much stargazing. "What is it?"

Sacchard took a deep breath. "Trouble in the north, sir. We have reports of a rebel attack on Vancouver Base. NORWESCOM flyers defected to the clandestitutes. They're . . ."

"NORWESCOM defected?"

"Yes. At least two wings attacked the base at Cape Scott. They also . . ."

"Two wings! Call a meeting at SMB right away. Inner Chamber and strategic commanders to attend. Emergency session—now. Is your flyer on standby out there?"

"Yes."

"I'll take it. Stay here, Elie. Coordinate the lot. Get

them to SMB in thirty minutes. Use my flyer then, as soon as you've called them all in."

"Right away, sir." Never lacking reverence for Carver's quick-fire leadership, Sacchard found himself admiring yet again that clarity and decisiveness which had returned for the first time since the Central Council meeting at which Carver had ordered the elimination of the five military leaders. That upturn in Carver's spirits had been a false dawn. The man had quickly withdrawn again to his introverted, isolated state. Now his mood had swung once more. For a moment old emotions stirred in Sacchard's mind, but one look at the dreariness, the lonesome haggardness, the emotional disarray on his leader's face and Sacchard knew he had made the right choice in Helga Wren.

"This is too much," said Carver. "Coming so soon after that raid on our Gulf Coast geminizing unit. They've got to be stopped. Snap to it, Elie." Carver spoke with the dominant tone Sacchard had heard so little of in recent times. He felt like saying something to dispel Carver's sense of isolation, but thought better of it. Someone would have to convince the man to look after himself, to get more sleep, to . . . This may have been the place to say those things, but it certainly was not the time.

Carver did not speak to Sacchard's pilot on the flight to the State Militia Building. He paid no heed to the city lights below, and ignored the stars above, as the flyer came in low over the Bay. He ruminated on the five Council members eliminated in March. Military men all, their ringleader had been commander-in-chief of NORWESCOM. Carver recalled the last time he had seen him: white-knuckled, ashen-faced, bouncing a laser pencil up and down nervously. Carver thought he had got rid of him at that final, fatal Central Council meeting. But the C-in-C had come back to haunt him in the shape of two wings of flyers loyal to their executed leader. The raid on the geminizing plant had been bad—this was worse.

SMB Command Center was a hive of table maps and plasma screens. Early in the emergency session Carver learned that the guts of three wings were involved. Forty flyers had come in low and fast over Queen Charlotte Sound, strafing Vancouver Base out of existence. A daring raid, its source was a clandestitute fastness probably in the Yukon Territory. Two other bases, in Alaska and Alberta, were also in flames.

Conflicting reports were coming in about the status and allegiance of Bio wings all over NORWESCOM. No one at SMB knew what to say, though everyone knew these were flyers loyal to their former C-in-C. If anyone at SMB thought it through to its logical conclusion, they would have realized that Ronald Carver, in eliminating five military leaders, was ultimately responsible for the chaos. If anyone dared think that way, they kept their counsel to themselves.

Elie Sacchard thought like that. So did Helga Wren. They had confided to each other more than once that Carver had erred tactically in condemning the military leaders. Together they had whispered of a future hitherto unthinkable—a world without Carver. But as the night wore on and Bio's strategic commanders began to make sense of what was happening, Sacchard found not only a changing future, but a changing Carver.

Like a man reborn, the head of Bio commanded the thick of things—questioning, evaluating, ordering. Gone was the creeping malaise that had enveloped him since his closest associate had ditched him for Wren. There was clarity in his eyes that had been undetectable this past while. He bore the look of a man hungry again with ambition. One glance at that face and Sacchard knew that this was no trick of the light—Carver's skin seemed to have tightened along with his resolve.

One look across the crowded Command Center and Sacchard knew that Helga Wren was thinking along the same lines. She too knew that Carver was back doing what he did best: commanding. In her eyes Sacchard saw a look he recognized—a gladness that the head of Bio had tossed off the malaise that had hung about his neck for too long. In that moment of mutual recognition, Sacchard realized that Carver was a man who thrived on confrontation and that the world of Bio could survive only on a confrontational and repressive level. Once inertia sets in, it falls apart. Now that its leader had blown away the symptoms that had debilitated him, Bio might finally stir itself and rid the world of these troublesome clandestitutes. Somewhere in the back of his mind Sacchard entertained the thought that Carver might have deliberately, perhaps subconsciously, provoked this confrontation by fomenting a military coup against himself. Whichever way it had happened, it was working like electric shock therapy—and the patient was responding.

Once more Sacchard looked across at Wren. Her lips played a slender smile. He knew how she was reading the situation. Their eyes met again and were lit up by sparks of joy. Carver was the boss—and their happiness was unconfined at seeing the boss back in charge.

At the far end of the command console, Ronald Carver III orchestrated the introduction of martial law.

At precisely that moment Xiao Qi Ching stepped onto a gravel path somewhere on the banks of a fast-flowing Mississippi. His security men breathed a sigh of relief as their leader walked from the hover to the marble-columned porch of an Association safe house. Bio's most wanted clandestitute did not travel much—his enlarged skull made him the most conspicuous man on the planet. He spent most of his time indoors, traveling only when necessary. Top-level meetings posed immense security risks—Association members were glad to see him beneath a safe roof, away from Bio surveillance.

Ching walked with his companion through the porch into a large hall. The dark-skinned woman by his side was fifty-ish. Her sharp eyes took in everything. She was enthralled by the opulent surroundings of the big old house. The broad staircase, the copious chandeliers and marbled floor were just as she had imagined them to be. This was the sort of white mansion where centuries previously her ancestors had been treated as slaves. She and Ching were escorted by a sergeant-at-arms through the hall toward the door of a large drawing room where a gathering of clandestitutes awaited their leader.

The sergeant was about to open the drawing-room door when Ching put a hand on his arm and said, "Take us to Leandro Vialli."

"Yessir." The sergeant released the doorknob. "He's waiting for you down this way, sir."

Two doors down, a small parlor. "Leave us," said Ching, and the sergeant obeyed. The dark-skinned woman stood and waited in the corridor as Ching opened the door and entered.

Lee was on his feet and moving as soon as the old man set foot across the threshold. Ching embraced him by the shoulders, then held him at arms' length and looked closely at the tell-tale flakes on his forehead, like tiny peels caused by too much sun on fair skin. "Your face is beginning to peel. That ethnic implant needs renewal. I told you to get it seen to."

"Yes, sir."

Another brief embrace, then Ching said, "That was an excellent report you wrote on the pharmaceutical raid. Some interesting observations, too."

"There were plenty of holes in the organization of that mission."

"Your report was right," said Ching. "You should never have repaired the storeroom grille on the way in. It was a poor percentage shot; the chance of it delaying your retreat was greater than the risk of maintenance workers discovering it. The photographic plasma gun was too effective—a flaw in its application must have attracted a security guard's attention, thereby causing the shutters of the control center to be opened. The four of you were lucky to get out alive. Having read your report, and having interviewed the other personnel involved, the Association has come to the conclusion that the raiding party would have perished were it not for some quick thinking and decisive action on your part."

"Thank you, sir." Lee hoped his hard-hitting report might lead to a reappraisal of who was to lead the attack on the wombship *Catalina*.

As if on cue Ching said, "We were impressed by your leadership—not least by the guts you showed in submitting that report. Matter of fact, it made us reconsider certain things . . ."

Ching paused to look out the window. Lee held his breath.

"I know how much you would like to lead the assault on the wombship—that mission has been rubber-stamped now, by the way—but on account of your report we have decided to give it to Harkes."

Lee could have sworn that the heel of his shoe scooted up off the floor, hitting him hard in his own backside. Harkes had spent three years working cluster station *Pacifica.* If anything, that qualified her more than him to lead the mission. Lee's glowing recommendation of her in his own report had tipped the scales in her favor. He smiled ruefully at the way the report had backfired on his own chances.

Ching caught the smile, guessed its cause, and said, "Not to worry, Lee. We have something special planned for you. Two things, actually, which we have decided since I saw you last. Perhaps your memory of that visit to my lodge is a little . . . hazy?"

Lee smiled again at the recollection of all that wine. Hiding his disappointment at missing out on the wombship mission, he said, "Too much Fukien makes one hell of a hangover."

"We're planning a spectacular strike deep at the heart and soul of Bio," said Ching. "Beyond that I can say no more. The matter will, I hope, be given the green light at today's meeting. I'll pass on details to you as soon as they are ratified." Turning to the door, Ching added, "They are waiting for me. I'd better go."

"You said that they were two things," said Lee. "Another raid?"

"One raid."

"And the other?"

"It concerns your twin."

Lee put his hand on the door, determined that Ching should not get away without telling him more. "My twin? What about him?"

"We have decided to let you make contact with him."

Lee grasped Ching's hand. "Do you know what this means to me?" he said.

"Of course." Ching shook Lee's hand firmly. Then he reached for the old-fashioned doorknob.

"Tell me before you go," said Lee. "Is he in any danger?"

"No, not at the moment. There's someone . . ."

"Is he a prisoner?"

"No."

"An Association member?"

"No," said Ching. "If . . ."

"You mean," interrupted Lee, "that he's an ordinary member of society? But . . ."

"Actually, he's a gynecologist."

Lee felt as if he was an inflatable mannequin on which someone had pulled the plug. "A what?" he said.

"You heard." Ching turned the doorknob. "Take your hand away from the door, Lee. I want to open it. There's someone out here who knows a lot about them."

"Them?" Lee's look of incredulity and disgust was replaced by one of confusion.

"Yes, them. His girlfriend figures in the equation. We think she's also ready to come over to our side."

"I suppose if he's a gyno, she must be a member of Bio's Inner Chamber," snorted Lee.

"Not quite," said the old man. "But close. As a matter of fact, she's an enforcement officer."

"Yeah, and my name is Ronald Carver. Know something, Ching? Your sense of humor isn't up to its usual high standards today."

"I was not trying to be funny. Your twin *is* a gynecologist—and his girlfriend *does* drive an enforcement car. Outside this door is a lady who will fill you in on all the details. Although your twin does not know it, this lady—she's his receptionist, actually—has been like a guardian angel to him for the last few years. Now, if you will excuse me, I have a meeting to address."

Lee's arm had gone limp. Ching opened the door without difficulty, enjoying the stunned look on Lee's face. As soon as he left the room, the woman who had been waiting outside walked in. She held her hand out and said, "Pleased to meet you, Mr. Vialli. May I call you Lee?"

Violet Harding's first impressions were not what she had expected. Lee was not at all like Max. Because of the ethnic implant, facial differences were to be expected. Slight personality changes could be put down to varying background input in the formative years. But this, well, she was not prepared for this. Lee was so *different.* She could not get over the gulf in personality between him and Max.

As she answered more and more of his questions she began to notice that the differences, including personality, were external. It reminded her of a fantasy she sometimes indulged in. For all she knew, other people indulged in it, too. Take a man. Take a characteristic in him that is, say, objectionable (according to Violet, most men have at least one objectionable trait). Reverse that characteristic. Imagine him then. Different personality, same man. Lee was like that: an obverse Max with different qualities. An inverted version of the same person. She shook her head in disbelief.

Chapter Eighteen

Violet placed her ebony hand on the console table. Leaning in close, she spoke softly, her voice a whisper—but not so soft it could not be amplified by the Surveillance Bureau's eavesdropping equipment.

The surveillance booth was dimly lit, consisting of one master console, a desk, a chair and two screens. Elie Sacchard adjusted the booster-signal apparatus. Tuning in carefully, he eliminated the white noise until Violet's words were audible. He heard her say, "Mrs. Chapman appears a little apprehensive today, Doctor. I think she knows."

The receptionist's face was turned sideways as she spoke. Grant Maxwell's back was turned to scanner one, but Sacchard could see his face on scan two. He heard the doctor reply, "Well, that's good. The bad news won't come as a shock."

Sacchard examined both monitors carefully. All of the gynecologist's office was visible onscreen except for one small blind spot down near the keyboard where Violet's hand was hidden from view. Sacchard yawned and rubbed his eyes, then fast-forwarded the tapes. He saw Max stand up, turn sideways, and walk to the window. The receptionist left the office.

Sacchard studied the onscreen caption. *March 31*. He pressed the pause button and leaned back in his chair. Five times the scanners had captured the doctor and his receptionist speaking in low voices. This last time had been three weeks ago. Each time the whispers had been innocuous, usually referring to patients in the waiting room. Sacchard could figure out no pattern to the messages—except that they were the nearest things he had to subversive behavior on Max's part. It struck him as odd that Violet always took up the same stance, leaning on the console table, but he was so busy trying to find hidden meanings in their conversation that he never twigged to the fact that her hidden hand could deposit something—a note, for instance—in the blind spot by the keyboard.

A whispered 'return' sent the vidfile scurrying back to its place in the Surveillance Bureau memory banks. Sacchard leaned further back, hands joined behind his head. He straightened his legs and pushed himself up on his heels until the hind legs of his chair had almost reached the point of no return and the knuckles of his clasped hands brushed against the cool metal of the wall behind him. He tried to organize his thoughts, telling himself for the umpteenth time that, as far as Bureau records could tell, Dr Grant Maxwell was cleaner than a womb-cot capsule. He smiled, amused by his comparison. And yet . . . And yet there had to be something. If what the boffins said about concordance was true, then Geminizon-induced twins should have identical personality traits. Given that Maxwell's twin had been born and raised in an Association stronghold, and that he was now most likely a clandestitute activist with an altered face, was it not logical—despite the vast differences in their upbringing—that his brother would also have subversive tendencies?

Sacchard sat bolt upright, the front legs of his chair hitting the floor with a smack. So what if the gyno was so

189

clever that the Bureau could never pin anything on him—
the same could not be said for his girlfriend, Mandy
Ullman.

Ronald Carver sat in a glass-paneled anteroom in the
bowels of the State Militia Building. Through a one-way
wall he could see the feverish activity of his generals in the
main chamber of the Command Center. He had taken to
living in SMB now that the threat to Bio was so serious.
NORWESCOM flyers were not the only arm of the military
to support the clandestitute cause. Pockets of resistance
were springing up all over. Putting them down was a full-
time job, but Carver was glad of the challenge—and delighted that he had moved out of his coral-walled home. He
had been a prisoner of his own device in that high castle of
architectural innovation. It was not the real world—his astronomer's nest at the top of his dome had not been the real
world, either. Now he was out of it, and out of himself. The
change had done him good, made him feel like a new man.
He took pride in his appearance again and took time out to
shower each morning.

Sacchard smelled the aftershave the moment he opened
the door. It made him marvel at how a newfound sense of
purpose could work wonders for Carver's self-esteem.

"Yes, Elie?" The head of Bio was helping himself to a
cup of freshly ground java at the coffee dispenser.

"I was hoping, sir, that we might discuss my original
brief as Surveillance Bureau Chief."

Carver's brow furrowed, as much in puzzlement as an-
noyance that Sacchard should call him 'sir'. The Surveillance Chief had always addressed him formally in work
situations—even in the old days when they still had a relationship. Once a private joke, the title now served only to

remind Carver of the distance that had grown between them. He forced himself to be civil. "What's that, Elie? I don't get your drift."

"I'm talking about the Maxwell business, sir. The twin of the Sulawesi boy."

Carver's forehead cleared. He sat down. "Has there been a development?" He pointed at the chair in front of his desk.

"Yes," said Sacchard, taking a seat. "Some days ago we received a report concerning an enforcement officer who had, apparently, displayed subversive tendencies. Her name is Mandy Ullman, born in San Andero '117."

Carver was about to sip his coffee, but stopped.

Sacchard went on, "As a result of the tip-off, I researched her and discovered that she had been doing some unauthorized digging into your background. In fact . . ."

"When did you say she was born?"

" '117. She's been researching the Enders Gang. San Andero, '132. She accessed files on Jim Chawke and Charlie Tully—and interviewed them both."

"How do you know this?" Carver planted his plastic cup on his desk.

"I had both men brought in yesterday. A little persuasion and they both squealed. It turns out that Ullman's best friend was Reggie Brooks. Both were classmates, San Andero High, '132."

A ghost flashed in front of Carver's eyes, a ghost he thought had been buried a long, long time ago in a gully off the West Coast Highway. "This Ullman," he said. "I presume she's a clandestitute?"

"I've looked for a connection, but there doesn't appear to be one. My conclusion is that she's working on her own."

"A lone crusader." Carver blew the heat off his coffee.

191

"Just what has this got to do with Grant Maxwell?"

"She lives with him."

Once again the cup stopped a hair's breath from Carver's lips. He blew on it again and took a sip, then put the cup down. "Elie," he said. "Are you telling me that this woman, this so-called officer, is Grant Maxwell's lover?"

"Yes."

"Then he has to be in on it as well. Two people working together are a conspiracy. Conspiracies smell of clandestitutes. They must have got to him."

"I don't think so, sir. I dug up everything we have on Maxwell. I spent the night fine-combing all available records. There's nothing to indicate a clandestitute connection."

"I hope so, Elie. Your initial responsibility in the Bureau was to keep tabs on him. I'd hate to think the clandestitutes got to him without you finding out."

"You have my word on it, sir." Sacchard glimpsed a look in Carver's eyes—a look he hoped never to see again. Knowing his boss's fondness for occasionally interrogating suspects, he sought to placate him by saying, "Do you wish to interview Officer Ullman personally?"

Carver stood and walked to the side of the anteroom. He looked out at plasma screens aglow in the Command Center. Activity had died down a little—the clandestitutes were obviously losing ground this morning. "No, I don't wish to interview her," he said. "You deal with it. Report to me immediately after you've disposed of her."

"And Maxwell?"

"Bring them both in." Carver did not turn around. He kept staring into the main chamber. Then he added, "We should have disposed of Maxwell a long time ago."

"Right away, sir." Sacchard was on his feet, heading for

the door, remembering that it had been he who had recommended years previously that Maxwell be let live. He opened the door praying that Maxwell was not a clandestitute. Before he stepped out of the anteroom Carver spoke again. "By the way, Elie. Who tipped you off about Maxwell's lover?"

"A duty sergeant at the enforcement building where she's stationed."

"An operative of yours?"

"No, nothing to do with the Bureau."

"Then why did he report her?"

Sacchard shrugged. "I asked around about that. It seems he and Officer Ullman didn't pull together very well."

"You mean he reported her for spite—for not letting him screw her?"

"No, it wasn't that. They just didn't get on. Personal animosity, I guess."

"You're saying that this sergeant failed to spot anything subversive in her behavior?"

"That's right. I knew from our files about her connection with Maxwell. That's why I investigated further. Otherwise, it would have gone down as one officer making a vindictive report against another. Do you want me to pursue the duty sergeant's involvement in this?"

"No," said Carver. "Get rid of him. His conduct was unprofessional. An enforcement officer should not report a fellow officer simply because of a personality clash."

Carver stared again through the one-way partition. This time it was neither plasma screens nor table maps that grabbed his attention. It was Sacchard. Elie had never let him down—personally maybe, but never professionally—yet there always was a first time. Carver's eyes bored down on

Sacchard's strong back and smoothly cropped hair as the Surveillance Bureau Chief disappeared around the Command Center exit. Deep down, Carver heard two voices in his head. One said Elie would never make a mistake—the other said God help him if he did.

Sacchard walked past the sensors and the plasma screens. He was tempted to turn around and look back but subliminal sensors of his own told him that Carver's eyes were on him. He left SMB praying that he had given Carver the right advice fifteen years previously when he had advocated letting the Maxwell boy survive as bait to lure the runaway teenager from Sulawesi.

The Surveillance Bureau hoverpark was packed, as usual. Sacchard pulled into his reserved slot near the entrance and rode the executive elevator down to basement levels. Within minutes of entering the Bureau he was back in the surveillance booth he had used earlier that morning to view the tapes of the gynecologist Maxwell and his receptionist, Violet Harding.

He ordered up the current whereabouts of Enforcement Officer Ullman. According to the enforcement log she was off-duty, so he called onscreen the apartment she shared with Maxwell. The bedroom scanner showed her sitting on the bedside, talking on the vidphone. She wore a negligee so short Sacchard pursed his lips in admiration of her thighs. Ample just about described them. He called up both vidshots.

The onscreen image split in two. On one side Mandy's head and shoulders—the other face was that of Grant Maxwell. An onscreen caption indicated that he was calling from his office. Some kind of argument was in progress. Sacchard switched Mandy from vid to scanner so that he could admire her legs again. Leaning back in his chair, he heard her say, "Why are you ringing me at this hour, Max? I'm only off-duty since four—I didn't hit the sack until five."

"I thought you were finished at two."

"No. There were riots down town. The curfew was broken again all over East Side. No one was let off-duty until four. As a matter of fact it was nearer half four. It's only ten o'clock now. That's way too early to call someone finishing a late night shift."

"I never heard you come in so I didn't know you were so late. You should have left a note. Anyway, you told me you could survive on six hours' sleep."

"That's when I haven't been on a goddamn ten-hour riot shift."

"Look, Mandy, I've had a rough morning, too. Another patient lost her cool. She damn well bit my face off. I was going to suggest lunch. Forget it—you'd better catch up on some sleep."

"Fat chance of that now. Where do you want to eat?"

"That place down Petty Street. One-thirty?"

Sacchard lost interest in the remaining conversation. At his command the screen fell silent but the picture stayed. He spoke into his lapel mike: "Interrogation squad ready at the double. Monitoring and recording equipment, the works. No need for a sergeant, I'll take personal control."

Mandy switched off her phone-screen and swung her legs up onto the bed. The vidcall had blown the sleep from her mind, but it was too early to get up. She lay back, stretched herself languidly, kicking the top sheet onto the floor. She maneuvered herself down the bed until her head was off the pillow and her negligee was riding to her hips. It was warm today, no need to cover up. She spread her legs slightly.

It was equally warm in the surveillance booth. Little sweaty droplets broke out on Sacchard's brow at the sight of her dark bush peeping out from beneath her negligee. The beat of hot blood pounded in his head. He stretched back in his chair to give himself room. Loosening his collar, he zoomed the hidden scan-lens in for a close-up. The squad upstairs could wait. This was better than any interrogation.

Chapter Nineteen

Max needed room to think in a faraway place where burdens might fall. For him the nearest faraway place was two kilometers away, but he chose not to take the hover. By the time he got there, the walk had blown some of the deadwood from his shoulders.

It was not just the argument with Mandy on the phone that had him in this pensive mood. There had been another uncomfortable encounter in his office, a more animated replay of the Mrs. Chapman incident. Two arguments—one personal, one professional—were more than enough for one morning. At least he had no more appointments until the afternoon. A glance at his watch told him it was nearly eleven o'clock. Two and a half hours to kill before meeting Mandy for lunch.

Max's destination was that wooded inlet down from the restaurant where he and Mandy had dined the night she had told him of Carver's involvement in the rape of Reggie Brooks. Max walked half a kilometer out to where the Bank Walk dropped into the high-tide mark. There the path petered out into a small cove. He remembered a carafe and a half of wine and the rough bark of a tree that night with Mandy. Storm clouds had been gathering then. Now a heat-haze descended. On the other side of the cove the path reappeared and puffed itself up into the Far Bank Walk—

which was hardly ever used. Most people turned back or went right and returned to town via an old asphalt path.

Max liked the other side. It was far enough away to be appropriately called the Far Bank. From there he could see the islands. The tide was out. Mud banks glistened beneath their slimy coating. The distant sea was flat calm and larks hovered overhead. He never could figure out how anyone, poets most of all, could be attracted to their noisy twittering.

The Bank Walk became more estuarine. The larks never shut up, but Max was too preoccupied to hear them any more. No more path now, only a small grassy headland. There was a seat, a lovers' bench. He sat but did not want to sit. He felt restless and compelled to keep moving. He stood up knowing he would not go back the way he came.

The headland was thumb-shaped. Half a kilometer wide, one kilometer long, its slopes carpeted in furze so thick that to walk around the other side was impossible—except down on the shore below the high water mark. It was muddy down there, *very* muddy. Previous experience had taught him that he would emerge on the other side with shoes covered in slime and filthy brown tongues of mud licking his trouser legs. Boots—waders—were essential but he was wearing shoes. Grown men, he told himself, did not do this sort of thing, least of all gynecologists of repute. But this was that special place and there would be no one here to recognize him. Hell, it just didn't seem to matter.

He straddled his way down the grassy slope before stepping out into the mud. Bladder weed popped and squelched underfoot. Though the mud was soft and slippery, he felt no fear of sinking. Or rather he did, but was too caught up in his thoughts to care. He considered a paper he might one day write—a paper he had wanted to write for some time. *The Cumulative Effect of Grief over Lifespan.* Yes, that might make a good title. He stood on an exposed patch between clumps of oar weed and sank to his ankle. "Shit," he muttered, pulling his shoe up out of the slime.

It was tiresome, plodding through this blancmange of clinging mud. Max was beginning to regret his decision not to return the way he came. His consolation was that he was halfway to *terra firma.* He looked around to check how far he had come.

In the bushes something stirred.

It was a movement so subtle it was gone almost as he noticed it. But he had seen something—an animal, perhaps. He knew that goats lived out here, though the glimpse of whatever he had seen just did not square up with a small quadruped. He turned and trudged on, his nagging doubts dispelled by further ruminations on the state of things.

Five minutes later he came within ten paces of a marshy field leading back to that old asphalt path out of town. The end of mud, at last. He turned around and once again something plunged out of sight into the bushes. A two-legged creature, he was sure of that. It had reacted quickly to his backward glance and was gone almost as soon as he caught sight of it. He had seen enough to know that he was not being followed by a goat.

He turned around as if he had noticed nothing. He plodded his way to the field and clambered up the muddy bank toward the road. Stepping gingerly on soft grass, he veered slightly to his right until he was out of view from the shoreline. Then he ran for cover behind an enormous furze where he squatted down to wait.

No irritating exaltation of larks now, only a menacing silence made pregnant by its length. He heard the first squelch in the mud, followed by another and another.

More silence.

Whoever was stalking him stood less than twenty meters away, where the muddy foreshore metamorphosed into the marshy field. He could almost hear the other breathing and was tempted to crane his neck, but was afraid he might be seen.

Unmistakable sounds of exertion reached his ears; the grunts of an invisible ogre climbing the muddy bank from estuary to field. Spongier footsteps now, ten meters away. Though the bush was ample cover, Max was certain his own heartbeat would betray him. He blinked nervously and could wait no longer. Curiosity compelled him to raise his head, despite the consequences. Fearing for his safety, he half-expected to meet a massive militia thug twice his size and strength. Slowly, his line of vision ascended until his forehead cleared the topmost layer of protective furze. His eyes peered through a jumble of yellow petals and focused on the figure opposite.

His pursuer was not twice his size. Matter of fact, his build was identical—so was his height. Color of hair and eyes were different, as were the lines of nose and mouth. The skin on the face was flaky, as if badly sunburned, and covered in spots. Yet Max knew instantly who it was. He gasped in shock and stood bolt upright, head and shoulders above the spiky yellow bush.

The noise of his gasp carried over the furze, alerting his twin brother—who turned with a start. Both men stared at each other silently for several crazy-frozen seconds. In the instant that their eyes met, Max saw his life halved as surely as if a hundred years had disappeared down the gullet of some great time-consuming monster. It was like looking into his own eyes in a hall of mirrors, and seeing that all he had lived for had been one gigantic lie. He felt the hairs jump up on his head. It crossed his mind later that each of those hairs must have turned the palest shade of gray; a hundred whitening for each year lost. He could no longer feel his heart beat. He swallowed the lump in his throat and tried to speak, but his twin spoke first.

"Are you surprised to see me, Max?"

The voice sounded different, but only slightly. Max's legs began to move of their own accord. He was barely aware that he was walking because his limbs seemed hollowed out and filled with jelly. Fear of the unknown, rather than fear of confrontation, pervaded him now. He found himself standing on the far side of the bush, facing a man who wore a strange half-smile—the kind of smile a father wears when he looks at a child who asks an awkward question. It took Max a while to get his tongue out of shock to say, "I don't . . . How . . . ?"

"My name is Lee. I'm your twin. I think I owe you an explanation."

"That might be right." Max tried to sound nonchalant, though his mind reeled as a thousand chaotic thoughts raced inside his head.

"Okay. I'll try not to leave anything out." Lee had rehearsed this speech many times in recent days, yet found it difficult to remember now. For some reason his mind seemed loose, vacuous and vague—as though extraneous thoughts had seeped in from somewhere. He forced himself to concentrate. "Thirty-one years ago we were separated at Deliverance. I was never placed in the womb-bank. I was smuggled out of Chicago where our biological parents were then living and raised in an inaccessible place away from Bio, away from the militia."

Max broke eye contact with Lee. He looked out over the

muddy estuary, then back at his twin brother whose words washed over him like the incoming tide, unstoppable and irreversible.

"I was informed of my illegality as soon as I could understand the concept. My parents—my foster parents, that is—told me. From that moment I've been committed to the Association . . ."

Max held up his hand. A thousand questions bubbled in his mind. "Hold it, hold it. Let's go back to the beginning. Who took you from the clinic and how could a Deliverance fetus, at only twenty weeks, survive without being placed in the womb-bank?"

"My foster mother snatched me. Through Association contacts she had access to a high-tech incubator and safe houses. Smuggling a three-hundred-gram fetus across the Pacific was not that difficult, believe me."

Max believed it. When he was starting out, the medical profession was rife with stories of baby smuggling and the mysterious disappearance of equipment. Nowadays such rumors were mentioned in whispers for fear of career intervention.

It was as if his brother had read his thoughts. "I know my appearance comes as a shock, Max. It's like being told that your life is cut in half, like a death sentence. But you are in danger. You know that, don't you? They know about me and they know about you. Do you realize what that could mean for you?"

"An accident?" Max exhaled sharply. For the first time he saw his brother's face break into a grin he thought exclusive to himself.

"We reckoned you'd have it all figured out." Lee spoke warmly and extended his arms to embrace his brother.

Max raised both palms to block him. "Listen, I need

time for this. It's all too much."

"Yes, of course." Lee shrugged in mute apology. "It's too much to expect anyone to take it in so soon." He paused momentarily. "If you're like me I guess you want to hear all the facts before making your mind up, right?"

Max could not prevent the corners of his mouth from breaking into the tiniest of smiles. "Go ahead," he said. "I'm listening."

"Let me start in the present tense and work my way back. My apologies for creeping up on you through the mud, but this is just about the safest place for us to meet. I couldn't risk making a direct approach in town. Too many people, too risky. I had to follow you around to find somewhere safe to talk. Do you think we're safe here?"

"Absolutely. No one comes here. If this isn't safe then no place is—unless someone followed you."

"No one did."

"Fine," said Max. "Tell me more."

"I've been tracking you for three days, hoping for a secure location to make my move. I guess it's a case of desperate measures. Look, I once spent six months working in Hokkaido. A colony of children—activated fetuses, as Bio calls them—exists there. It's been there for decades, like an adventure playground, a summer camp. There are plenty of facilities to keep the children happy. Thousands of them live under the thumb of Bio. It's not only Hokkaido. What used to be Taipei, Borneo, the South Island of New Zealand—they've all been turned into colonies. And that's just in the Pacific. Have you any idea what such places are like?"

"No," said Max, though deep down he knew.

"Ever hear of Disney World, turn-of-the-millennium Florida?"

"Of course."

"Well, it's like that. A huge theme park, except for the chamber of horrors awaiting each child at the exit door."

"Why are you telling me this—Lee?" Deep down, Max knew the answer to that, too.

"Because we need you. A man like you could do much for us. We can protect you by getting you out in time. There are places beyond the reach of the militia—we have our own womb-banks, batteries of them—places where your skills are badly needed."

"You're taking one hell of a risk. I could turn you over to the authorities right now."

"Your own flesh and blood, Max? We researched you. We know about Mandy and that she feels the same way as you do. She could be in danger, too. We know how you both feel about the world situation and your personal involvement in it."

Max turned from his brother and walked to the edge of the marshy field. He stood on the shoreline facing the islands, the brown monotony of the mudflats broken now by incoming streams glistening like silver webs in noonday sun. The estuary was filling up, but Max did not notice. Instead he saw all the Mrs. Chapmans of this world. Most of all he saw Mandy. He turned to his twin and looked into a pair of eyes that might once, in seventy years time, have been his. In those eyes he saw his brother, he saw himself. Instinct told him to reach out, to embrace, but . . .

A hovercar careered down that old asphalt path out of town. Lee turned and saw it, too. He reacted first, grabbing Max by the arm and pulling him behind the furze bush. They crouched and watched the hover slow to a halt near the edge of the marshy field.

It struck Max that there was something familiar about that pale blue color. Not many models like that these days.

As for the driver hunched behind her guide-stick, her dark face barely visible through the tinted windscreen, there was something familiar about her, too. Her dark face? Max craned his neck and strained his eyes to see if it was . . .

"Violet!" He knew instinctively that something was seriously wrong. He jumped from behind the bush and ran across the field. "Come on," he shouted back at Lee. "It's okay. Run!"

Lee followed and soon caught up with Max. Together they squelched through the grass, racing for the hover. The door opened as soon as they reached the asphalt path.

"Get in, quick!" hissed Violet.

The hoverdoor closed as Lee squeezed in after his brother. Both men sat in the back, catching their breaths. Then Max said, "What's up, Vi—why the panic?"

"They're after you. I guessed you'd be out here—I got away just in time. Your office was raided by the militia. So was your apartment and . . ."

"Did back-up tip you off?" asked Lee.

"Yep. They were keeping an eye on Max's apartment. They saw an interrogation squad go in and reckoned the office was next. They were spot on, Lee. Militia arrived just as I got in the hover. Missed me by . . ."

"Hang on just a minute." Max grabbed hold of the driver's headrest as the hover swung off the asphalt onto flyway 22. "How come you know his name, Vi? Do you two know each other?"

Violet glanced in the rear view mirror. For a moment her eyes caught Max's, then Lee said, "I'll explain. Concentrate on getting us out of here."

"We better move fast," said Violet. "They'll find out from Mandy that you were on the Bank Walk."

"Mandy—they've got Mandy?"

"Don't worry," said Lee. "They'll just interrogate her to find out where you are. They have no interest in her."

"That's what you think," said Max. "She's been snooping into Surveillance Bureau files—if they know that, she's in trouble."

"Shit," said Violet. "Are you sure she's been doing that?"

" 'Course I'm sure. Why else would I be saying it? Look, we've got to get her out of the apartment!"

"Right. Calm down," said Lee.

"I will not calm down. We've got to . . ."

"Shut up!" barked Lee. He turned in his seat and pointed a finger directly at Max. "Do as I say—calm down."

One look at the threatening finger and Max fell momentarily silent. He glanced in the rear view mirror. Violet was looking back again, this time at Lee. "Back-up?" she said.

"Okay, call 'em. There's only three, but they've got weapons." He looked his twin in the eye. "I guess if your enforcement officer friend is in trouble we better do something about it, right?"

Chapter Twenty

Sacchard hoped that Mandy Ullman might still be wearing her revealing negligee. Unfortunately from his point of view she had dressed in the fifteen minutes that had passed between him leaving the surveillance booth where he had been peeping on her and his arrival at the door of her apartment. Clothes did not matter much now anyway—he had seen enough to mentally undress her the moment the interrogation squad smashed their way in.

She was wearing a sleeveless turquoise blouse and white cheesecloth jeans with sneakers to match. She stood at the far end of the apartment, half-looking out the window, half-rearranging a pair of potted geraniums. When the door burst open she turned quickly, knocking one of her plants off the sill. Before the pot hit the floor the restraint officer was crouched in front of her, stunset aimed directly at her head, and firing.

The cerebral wavelength dazed her. Disoriented and docile, she swayed from side to side and would have collapsed but for the M&A (monitoring and appraisal) men. They grabbed her by the shoulders and sat her on the sofa. Sacchard pulled up a chair as his officers attached diodes to her forehead. By the time the stun wore off, the M&A equipment was connected, ready to interpret and record.

For Mandy Ullman everything appeared two-dimensional and detached. Then her vision reclaimed a shaky grasp of perspective and depth. She saw five men—surveillance officers, by the looks of them—one on either side, sitting her down, touching her forehead, attaching things. Another pocketed a stunset, a fourth man pulled up a chair. The fifth, in the murky distance, seemed to be closing the door. Everything was three-dimensional now, like virtual reality. After virtuality, reality comes no more real than a slap in the face.

Sacchard hit her cheekbone hard, where it stings. That brought everything sharply into focus.

"Why were you accessing unauthorized files in the State Record Department?" he demanded, his face looming large before her.

"Wh-what files?" she mumbled.

Another slap, harder than the first. It knocked her head to one side. Out of the corner of her eye she noticed a wild fluctuation in the liquid display unit held by the officer to her right. Black with pain, it must have registered at least 7.5 on the M&A scale.

"Know what that is?" Sacchard indicated the display unit.

Mandy nodded.

"Just testing to see if it works," he smiled. "Want to see how high it goes on the pain scale?"

She shook her head so furiously the diodes nearly flew off.

"Okay, then answer me. Charlie Tully, for instance. Why access him?"

Fighting hard to keep the panic down, she said, "I dunno why. I used manual. I wanted to key in Rully. Typed T instead of R."

"Typological error?" That sneer again.

A Satsuki rhododendron sat on a shelf behind Sacchard. It was an elegant bonsai with small, glossy, dark green leaves. Mandy concentrated on it for all she was worth. She knew that if she could use it as a stabilizing entity, her emotional response might fool the M&A unit.

"Y-yeah, typo," she said. "Can easily happen," she heard herself say.

"Of course," nodded Sacchard. "Now explain why you called up Tully 218 instead of Rully 38."

Mandy was afraid to glance at the M&A. She prayed it showed indigo—for confusion and panic, purple even—for terror. Anything but green. The game was up if they knew she was lying. The miniature branches of the Satsuki were so delicate. "I don't know . . . I can't . . . I wasn't feeling well . . ."

"Sure, sure," said Sacchard. "It could happen to anyone. Of course, a subversive might use the old manual method to call up a file knowing that its appearance onscreen could be put down to a series of typological errors."

"Maybe," said Mandy, concentrating hard on the Satsuki, glancing occasionally at Sacchard, hoping her thoughts would not prompt the wrong color in the liquid display.

"So you weren't feeling well? I guess you weren't the best two weeks previously either, huh?"

Mandy was genuinely confused, though only for a moment. Then Sacchard brought up her previous unauthorized break-in. "Is that how you called up Jim Chawke, too? By accidentally typing C in front of Hawke, the surname you had been authorized to access?"

That Satsuki was late this year. Its deep pink flowers should have been out by now. They were a couple of weeks late. It might blossom before the month was out. It occurred to Mandy that the plant might see more of the month than she would.

"Well?" Sacchard leaned in close, raising the back of his hand. "Well?" he shouted, demanding an immediate response.

"It was an accident!" Mandy blurted it out, closing her eyes, bracing herself for the broad sweep of his hand. It never came. She opened her eyes and glanced again at the Satsuki. Its shiny leaves were the deepest green she had ever seen.

Sacchard glanced over his shoulder and saw what she was looking at. He got up off his chair and laughed as he walked to the shelf where the plant stood. "Think this is the only green thing in this room?"

Then Mandy realized that the M&A men on either side of her were laughing, too. When she saw the liquid display unit she realized why. No rain forest ever contained an emerald so bright. The liquid crystals registered 9.5—a big round whopper.

"Know what, Mandy?" Sacchard held the twelve-year old miniature upside down. It was a perfectly shaped plant, a thing of beauty, pruned and re-potted by her only days previously. Its moist loam clung to the pot, preventing it from falling out too quickly. Sacchard tapped the rim off the shelf until the plant came loose. It hit the floor with a soft thud. "You really enjoyed yourself this morning, after Max called, didn't you?"

Mandy watched him grind the roots of the Satsuki into the carpet with the sole of his shoe. The slender branches disintegrated with a soft crackle. Her mind was all splayed out like the roots of a trodden plant. She heard him say, "We have a vid scan in your bedroom. That was quite a display you put on."

Like a rainbow now, Mandy's LDU ranged from green through indigo to black, then a perfect ten in deep, deep red.

She was on her feet before the M&A men could react, her forward momentum whipping the diodes off her head. It was an instinctive lunge—no forward planning, just rage. Sacchard was startled, transfixed. Her fingernails caught him on the side of the cheek, gouging four crimson trails down his face.

He pushed her aside. An M&A man pulled her by the shoulder, away from her target.

She was ready to lunge at Sacchard again, but the restraint officer locked arms on her, holding her rigid.

Sacchard felt the side of his cheek. His face ran red with Mandy's scrawls, matching the color of the crystals. He took one look at the drops on his fingertips and cracked his fist off the side of her head, knocking her unconscious.

Awareness returned with a rhythmic motion that washed over her like waves. In the ebb and flow of her mind she saw Sacchard towering over her demanding to know where Max was. Prickly circles of heat played on her temple like miniature concentrations of heat. An extractor diode was sucking her mind. *If he's not at his office, where is he?* She was too dazed to resist the questioning. Anyway, the M&A men could hoover her brain regardless of will. In the distance she heard a voice, her voice, muttering something about the Bank Walk. Then the heat eased on her forehead, Sacchard's face pulled out of her hazy vision, and her consciousness ebbed back into the void.

When she came to, she was crumpled over on the couch. Her eyes opened; otherwise she resisted the urge to move. Sacchard was on the vidphone, barking at the militia, ordering them to comb the Bank Walk area again. She heard something about a pale blue hover on an old asphalt path. An enforcement car had spotted it. Two minutes later the enforcement officer had heard the alert on his comm—by then the hover was out of sight.

Agitated that Max was still on the loose, Sacchard turned once more to Mandy. He ordered the M&A men to sit her upright and re-attach the LDU to her forehead.

He asked about the Association. Her denials of clandestitute involvement did not elicit the violent blows she expected, at least not initially. Sacchard and the M&A men seemed genuinely puzzled by her answers. The LDU equipment obviously told them that she was telling the truth.

Hard as it was for Sacchard to take, he had to believe the diode readings. Growing increasingly frustrated, he grabbed her blouse and pulled her so close he could smell the hot flush of her breath in his nostrils. Her irregular panting, warm and nervy, turned him on. Soon she would breathe no more. The power of death, especially the power of death over women, was always a turn-on for Sacchard. That and the sweet scent of fear were guaranteed to get him going.

"Okay," he said, drawing her so close their noses touched. "Tell me exactly why you accessed classified information."

Little sweaty beads broke out on Mandy's forehead. She could feel the dampness under her hairline and around the warm diodes. The sickly stench of her ragged breath rebounded off Sacchard, making her nauseous. She hadn't felt so scared, so helpless, in thirty years. Not since the day her mother had called her out of school to tell her that enforcement officers wanted to talk to her about Reggie's last whereabouts because something dreadful had happened. She had never experienced such a gut-carving feeling since.

One look at Sacchard's face and she knew there was no way out of this.

"Answer me!" he roared with such controlled intensity that he gently head-butted her.

His face was so close it filled Mandy's vision with a large round flesh-colored blur. She did not care about focusing now—there was no point. Her eyes were stinging from the pummeling and the threats. Her heart was beating frantically. Her mind was racing, grasping for something, anything, to rescue her from what she knew to be inevitable. Her arms were rigid by her side. Her fingers dug deep into the sofa as if seeking to tunnel their way out of the apartment. Max was right all along; her private digging had been too risky and now too costly. She braced herself for a sudden movement of the face looming into her—a jerky twitch or pulling back of the head to make room for an incoming slap or a sharp punch.

She glimpsed the movement she expected, though it did not herald an assault on her. Sacchard's face pulled back, his hands let go of her blouse. Her eyes snapped shut in anticipation of a stinging blow. None came.

She opened her eyes to a crescendo of noise. Now she saw Sacchard clearly in profile, staring sideways, pulling back, standing up, arms raised in self-defense.

In the periphery of her vision, the bulbous nose of a pale blue hovercar smashed through the apartment window. The noise was deafening. She crouched down on the sofa, covering her head from the glass fragments that showered down like sleet in a blizzard. Another noise filled the air. Pulse fire. The front half of the hover was in the room— guns pointing out from either side, spraying the apartment with deadly rays.

The interrogation squad had little time to react. The restraint officer let off a few rounds but his stunset was useless. With no time to aim correctly, his efforts rebounded off the hover's metallic nosecone. A pulse blasted him off his feet into the wall. Rays from the other gun took care of the two M&A men in one fatal sweep.

Sacchard dived for cover but the deadly rays caught him just above the elbow, spinning him across the floor with such force that his arm was nearly wrenched off. He lay in a heap alongside the crumpled body of the fifth surveillance officer, who, like the others, had had no time to react to the lightning raid and had been taken out by the first wave of pulses.

The hoverdoor opened. A man bounded across the glass-strewn floor. "Mind your feet," he shouted, grabbing Mandy by the arms, pulling her across the floor.

A crystal forest of pointy glass sprouted from the carpet. Eyes down, she tried to avoid the larger chunks. Before she knew it, she was bundled into the hover.

"Lie down!" barked her rescuer as he pushed her into the back seat. He barely had time to get in himself before the hover slammed into reverse with such force it threw him on top of her, pinning her to the seat.

Mandy and her rescuer were thrust up against the roof of the hover as it plummeted three flights to ground floor level. They were thrown down again onto the seat as the driver abruptly stopped their freefall less than half a meter above the tarmac. They were on the hoverway then, driving against the flow, riding around and over oncoming cars. Mandy and her backseat rescuer were tossed around like ninepins. Sideways G-forces, upside down G-forces, downside up G-forces had them caroming around the insides of the rear compartment. By some miracle, their heads did not crack off each other. The clandestitutes in the front seat were harnessed, safe from the worst excesses of the ride.

The hover leveled off leaving a roller coaster of wreckage on the hoverway behind it. In the correct lane now on a route parallel to Gemini Boulevard, overtaking at breakneck speed, they prayed no enforcement cars would block them off or get close enough to keep on their tail.

Now that she was being buffeted sideways, and not upside down as well, Mandy had a chance to glance at her rescuer. He was holding onto a headrest, staring straight ahead. A profile in concentration, he shouted instructions at the driver, then glanced back to see if they were being tailed. Satisfied that they were not, he looked at Mandy. She noticed that his skin condition was spotty and flaky like a bad case of adolescent acne. He looked at her face with some distaste, too—as if she also had bad skin.

"Your cheek," he said. "Don't touch it. There's glass in it."

Mandy's hand was millimeters from feeling the glass in her face when he roared, "Watch out!"

They were about to crash the lights at an intersection. From out of nowhere the cab of a huge rig came bearing down across their path. It was almost on them before their driver swerved the hover to one side and tried to pull ahead of the converging vehicle. The rig jammed on its brakes, swerved, and screamed past just behind them. It came so close the paint on the rear of the hover bubbled and blistered in the searing heat of passing metal. The front of the cab brushed off their back fender with the lightest of kisses. Horns blaring in a fury of sound and speed, the rig went into a spin and crashed into two enforcement cars that had been waiting for them at the other side of the intersection, demolishing them both in a tornado of twisting metal.

"Jesus!" said the hover driver. "That motherfucker was

going too fast!" Slamming the guide-stick to one side, he jerked the hover back into the correct lane just in time to avoid a head-on collision with an oncoming bus.

"Hang a left!" barked Lee. Mandy was once again tossed against the side door as the hover right-angled into a side street. More swerves had her careering around as they avoided oncoming traffic. Then one final heave as the hover sideswiped the corner of an apartment block. Down into an alleyway they flew. The walls were so narrow and near they appeared to be going faster and faster. In reality they had slowed considerably. Then one more turn and an alleyway even narrower. Finally, they slowed to a crawl. A door opened invitingly in the side of a warehouse. In they hovered, the door closing behind them.

As soon as Mandy had dragged herself out of the hover, Max raced forward and took her in his arms. "Mandy!" he said, "Thank heaven you're . . ."

"Don't." She pulled back out of his embrace. "My face, it's . . ."

"Hold it," Violet intervened. "I see it. It's a small piece."

"Violet!" roared Mandy. "What are you doing here?"

No answer came. Violet produced a tweezers from her pocket. "Now hold still and this won't hurt."

Mandy winced as the glass came out. Then Max took her in his arms again and said, "I thought you'd never get here. It was like eternity waiting. They wouldn't let me go to rescue you."

"Damn right." Violet fixed several folds of paper to Mandy's cheek to stop the bleeding. "No untrained personnel on missions. Association rules. You got to wait until you've had training. There, that should hold the flow until we get bandages."

Mandy started to tell Max about the raid on their apartment and Sacchard's interrogation, but Lee intervened. "Come on," he said. "There's no time for pleasantries. Let's go."

They thanked the hover driver and the back-up team for rescuing her and took the stairs three at a time. Six flights of steps later they were breathless but delighted to see a hover ready for take-off on the roof of the warehouse.

"You two in the back," said Violet, as Lee took the controls.

Slowly they lifted off the roof and drifted eastward on a homing beam out of the city. Once they were locked onto their route, Lee turned to his backseat passengers. "I never thought the day would come when the Association would use its resources to rescue a gyno and an enforcement cop," he said.

Mandy thought that there was something vaguely familiar about Lee, though she could not quite put her finger on what it was.

Violet looked around, too. "The paper has stemmed the bleeding. Any bandages aboard?"

"I don't think so," said Lee. "Sorry."

"I knew you were sizing me up," said Mandy, leaning forward.

"What?" Violet turned around again.

"The day Max introduced us in that twentieth century pub down Petty Street, remember? You were asking questions, trying to pigeon-hole me, suss out my views, right?"

"Was it that obvious?"

"Hey," Max butted in. "As soon as the riots got bad that day you left. You wouldn't come with me and Mandy."

"I told you I had a date."

"And we believed you." Max looked down at the city. Then he looked at Violet. "The day you saw two militia men tailing me and Mandy down by the pier, you also said you were on a date. Some date. I bet you were tailing them tailing us."

"You guys are bright for a gyno and a cop," quipped Lee.

Something in his voice did not appeal to Mandy. "Oh yeah?" she said. "Who the hell are you—Flash Gordon?"

Lee glanced at the source of sarcasm behind him. She may have been an enforcement officer but she was well trained—her rapid recovery from the ordeal the interrogation squad had put her through, not to mention the helter-skelter ride in the hover with glass in her face, testified to that. Besides, she was fiery. Lee liked that.

Mandy leaned forward, staring at him with an intensity which telegraphed that she was sure she had seen him somewhere before. "Haven't we met?" she asked.

Lee shook his head in amazement. So much for the ethnic implant. She was obviously eagle-eyed to boot. "Okay," he said. "Vi, you're the only one here who's already met everyone else. It seems to me you're best qualified to do the introductions."

She was. And she did.

Part Three

Chapter Twenty-One

Fifteen key personnel attended an Association meeting in Xiao Qi Ching's hunter's lodge at the foot of Mount Whitney. With great good humor they squeezed themselves into Ching's modest parlor and settled down for the meeting to begin. They knew that they were going to hear good news. Lee found himself seated beside Harkes—the diminutive figure who had beaten him to the cluster station raid. He chatted amicably to her before the meeting began.

Ching did not disappoint his top operatives. He told them that whole divisions of Bio forces had defected following the NORWESCOM raids. In announcing that the Association now had enough air power to engage the enemy in major confrontation, he looked directly at Lee and said that an air battle would shortly be combined with a daring raid on one of Bio's most sensitive facilities. Switching his gaze to Harkes, Ching said that Carver was now directing most of Bio's resources to the Mars project. Consequently, operations on cluster station *Pacifica* could become vital should Carver try to flee to Mars when—Ching did not say 'if'—Bio collapsed.

Lee's heart skipped a beat when he heard that. No one, least of all Ching, had spoken before with such certainty of outright victory. Lee was sitting close to Harkes, so close her arm touched him. He felt a frisson of excitement rush through her—maybe it was a shiver of trepidation at the realization of how important her assignment on *Pacifica* would surely become.

When the meeting had ended Ching took Lee to one side and asked, "How is your twin?"

"Different," said Lee.

"That's only surface dressing." Ching smiled. "Ultimately you're both the same. You have to be, given the Geminizon factor."

"Same ingredients, maybe," said Lee, "but the mix is different. We're like chalk and cheese."

"At the moment," said Ching. "Give it time. Where is he now?"

"In the Rockies, training."

"When will you see him?"

"I'm going north tomorrow."

"Good," said Ching. "Make sure you give him my regards."

Summer comes high in the Rocky Mountains. It comes with a welcome breeze that cools the sweatiest, most ardent brow, and makes even the hardest military course seem bearable.

Max jutted his jaw into the breeze. Balm-like and refreshing, it caressed his face—which was sweatier than most. Though he had been sitting in a cleft in the rocks for two whole minutes, his pulse still raced. That was only to be expected considering how unfit he was—or had been. With some satisfaction he ran a hand over his hardening calf muscles. A few more thirty-K marches would make him as fit as the best of them.

The others in his half-dozen strong training group sat side by side on a rocky ledge, their legs dangling into the valley below. Max wanted to sit with them but hung back in the cleft because the uphill jog had left him breathless—and he did not want his lack of fitness to be so obvious. Now that he was getting his wind back, he stepped past a clump of what looked like azaleas and walked to the rocky ledge. He shuffled his way past the other trainees, making sure to keep his breathing under wraps as he passed behind the drill sergeant's back. He perched himself on a boulder at right angles to the six of them and muttered something nonchalant about the view.

Looking him in the eye, the drill sergeant said, "Good on ya. Now it takes only three minutes before you're able to speak."

"Pass me the oxygen tank," laughed Max, making sure to guffaw louder than any of them.

Base camp consisted of a series of long abandoned missile silos—late twentieth century, he had heard someone say. The array of underground silos had been inter-connected by a series of passageways tunneled out by Association sappers. Off the passages they had carved out dorms and living quarters. The arrangement was primitive and warren-like; but no one expected a holiday home, not even Max, for whom this was his first time away from the comforts of twenty-second century life.

The camp was just below the tree line where pines provided cover from prying overhead sats. A soft carpet of crumbling needles and decaying cones made an ideal surface for an assault course and shooting range. There was even a recreation zone through which Max passed on his way to silo hatch number two.

In a remote spot like this, where PseudOzone cover was scant, the best protection was underground. Once below Max wiped the UV blocker from his face and hands and lay on a bunk to do some reading while waiting for Mandy.

Because of her background she had been allocated the shorter five-day physical training course. That completed, she had been assigned to Tactics. Today she was studying two units of clandestitute theory: Subversive Technique and Military Stratagems.

She finished her training a little later than Max. By the time she had showered away her UV screen it was dinner call. When eating was over, darkness fell.

"Let's take a hike," said Max. "You-know-who is waiting for us up on the ridge."

They made their way under a milky moonlit sky, walking hand-in-hand beneath silvery pines. Up a steep hill they trudged, the light of the moon and the hooting of owls keeping them company.

Lee was waiting on the ridge, a heatcone at his feet to keep the cool mountain gusts at bay. "Take a seat." He indicated a storm-damaged pine by his side.

The view from the ridge was compelling—a rugged manifestation of summit and valley, stark and ethereal in crisp night air.

With his boot Lee maneuvered the heatcone nearer to the pine-seat. When he sat they spent a while talking about base camp training. Then Lee told Max he would be part of an upcoming raid. As yet details were classified. It was an important mission—he would reveal more information nearer the time. He told Max not to be unduly concerned about the raid—his involvement would be purely observational and not involve any real risk to his safety. After some small talk the conversation drifted to Lee's earlier life.

He told them about Sulawesi, recounting in graphic detail the deaths of everyone who had ever meant anything to him. In the telling Mandy put her hand in Max's and held on tightly. For her it was a harrowing tale. For her lover it proved hauntingly familiar. Lee was describing how he had sealed off the corpses in Camp Agrina after the condenser raid when Max butted in: "That's what the dreams were!" He stared wide-eyed at Mandy. "That's what they were."

"That's what what were?" asked Lee.

"I used to get recurring nightmares. In them I've seen the people you've described."

Lee shrugged and said that the dreams may have been a manifestation of sibling telepathy, nothing more. He looked out over the valley. Something winged its way out of the mountains into his consciousness. A childhood image flitted across the sky. The drogue bird again—that fake kingfisher in all its deceptive glory, its cam-eyes swiveling as it flashed by, its plumage brilliantly guilt-ridden in the Sulawesi sunlight. Mechanical wings beat out their familiar rhythms: *If only you hadn't gone fishing, if only you hadn't gone fishing . . .* He clutched at a small engraved stone in his pocket—the talisman he had found at the salt spring minutes before the condenser attack. If only he hadn't gone fishing, the drogue bird would not have seen him and Bio might never have discovered the Sulawesi hideout. He felt the stone in his pocket and remembered Zenga, that fine old Polynesian, telling him to keep it for luck. Some luck.

One look at Mandy and Max, at the way they were holding hands, and Lee felt old emotions, familiar pangs, rising in his heart. These were emotions he did not want to stir—they did not even bear thinking about.

For a moment there was silence.

Mandy got up and stood near the heatcone, arms folded. "Everyone's got their own private hell, Lee. You've been to finishing school when it comes to pain, but that doesn't mean you hold the franchise."

"I never claimed to have a monopoly. I'm just showing you what it's like on the other side of the tracks."

"Well, it's not all roses this side, either."

Lee said nothing. He stood and walked to the ridge overlooking the valley. Again he saw that winged something flap its way between the pines. It was no drogue bird—it was a bat, a harmless bat high up in the branches.

Mandy sighed and said, "One of the reasons I came over to the Association was because of the Bio decree that twins of those with mental histories were to be destroyed. I figured that my mental problems when I was younger would probably mean termination for my twin."

Lee looked surprised. Before he could say anything Max intervened: "Hang on, Mandy. That wasn't classified officially as a breakdown."

She sighed again and touched the heatcone with her foot.

"What breakdown?" Lee stared hard at her.

Max wanted to get up, to comfort her in the telling, but she was standing and he was sitting. Her folded-arm stance was a picture of self-sufficiency, so he sat and listened as she recounted the 'Dero Diner incident and its aftermath, leaving out nothing from the moment she first realized what had happened to her friend Reggie to the night she forced Charlie Tully up against a factory wall and squeezed him until he coughed up all he knew about Ronald Carver III. She went into detail about how the loss of her friend had affected her teenage years, culminating in a nervous breakdown.

Max had heard it all before. His gaze wandered to the other side of the valley to moonlit mountains where—outlined against the peaks—he saw Lee in silhouette, hanging onto Mandy's every word.

Max studied his twin's expression and saw in it a darkness wrought by more than the night. He looked at Mandy and realized that she too had experienced a dark side he could never fully comprehend. In their shared and mutual understanding Max felt suddenly apprehensive. The cold night air whipped up from the valley floor. Despite the heatcone he felt alone and strangely shivering.

Chapter Twenty-Two

It took some time to put Elie Sacchard's elbow, arm and shoulder back together again—what remained of them. Bionic implants replaced muscle and bone destroyed by the pulse gun in the raid on Mandy Ullman's apartment. For three weeks they kept him under medical care. Though his body rested, his mind did not. The first inkling that all was not well came when Helga Wren did not visit. No calls, no candy, not even a get-well card. Nothing. She was not there to hold his hand as he walked through the clinic gates. Nor was she in the apartment to greet him. There was no trace of Wren or her belongings. It was as if she had never existed. Not that Sacchard was overly distraught about her disappearance from his life. Things had not been so good between them in recent times. Perhaps she had simply abandoned him in favor of someone else. He was not unduly upset by the loss of her affections and knew there would be plenty of surrogates to take her place.

He stood in the middle of his apartment, head-scratching with his one good hand. Then he saw the message on his porta-vid. It told him that he was relieved of all duties until sent for. In the meantime he was confined to city limits.

He hovered to the Surveillance Bureau hoping to ride the elevator to his office, but they would not let him in past reception. His pass was no longer valid. He tried the State Militia Building. Same tune, different lyrics: *Sorry, sir—SMB is off-limits to unauthorized personnel.* His secretary, Esther Varnia—she of the designer face and firm thighs—could not be raised on the vid, nor could any of his departmental personnel. They had all been seconded to in-service courses, he was told. When he asked for the Surveillance Bureau Chief, they said information regarding that department was classified. It was a strain for him not to yell down the vid that *he* was the chief. But he knew better than to stir things up.

For days he hung around, head-scratching some more, trying to figure out why he had been sidelined like this. He hoped that the raid on the Ullman apartment and the death of his four colleagues had led merely to a temporary reorganization at SMB. Things were changing so fast these days. Maximum security prevailed—the less one knew, the better. Those porta-vid orders had probably been intended for his benefit: rest and recuperate for a few days; don't exert yourself by straying outside the city limits; we'll send for you when we need you.

To pass the time between porn holos and visits to rent-boys and hookers down East Side, Sacchard outlined a report suggesting ways to combat the clandestitute threat. Sometimes, in the days and nights that crawled by, little doubts sprouted in his head. They pointed up at him, spiky and prickly like the sharpened ends of poisoned bamboo, as if they were deadly *punji* stakes at the bottom of a mantrap, waiting for a careless victim to step over the pit and fall to an impaled death.

Every time he looked in the mirror he saw scars to remind him of Mandy Ullman's fingernails gouging four pink trails down the side of his cheek. They were like four tracks pointing down—down to that mantrap he had stupidly stood on. Each time he saw those trails he remembered Carver's skepticism and unwillingness to accept that Ullman and Grant Maxwell were not clandestitutes. He remembered even more vividly the veiled threat of what Carver might do to him if he was wrong, if it turned out that they had been Association members all along. But they were *not* clandestitutes. Surveillance told him so, monitoring and appraisal equipment told him so, gut instinct told him so, everything told him so. And yet . . . If he thought about it for too long, the ground he was standing on felt soft and spongy, and the *punji* stakes glinted up at him, pricking him just hard enough to make him uneasy.

Seven days out of the clinic, a message on his porta-vid summoned him to SMB.

Carver was sitting at his desk in his glass-paneled office at the far end of the Command Center. Sacchard could see him from the moment he walked nervously into the long chamber. He made his way to the office, edging carefully between banks of sensor indicators and plasma screens. Strategic commanders and their minions scurried between table maps and databanks, brushing against him, adding to his anxiety as they constantly evaluated, updated and changed things. Sacchard walked up the three steps to Carver's door and knocked as firmly as he could. He swallowed hard and walked in as he knocked, trying to look casual.

Carver was on his feet now, away from his desk, standing where the coffee dispenser had been. In its place stood an aquarium—a meter-long tank containing a small brown-spined creature Sacchard immediately recognized as an antimis fish. Alongside it was a mineral water dispenser, which bubbled as Carver filled a cup.

"There have been some changes since you last visited." Carver motioned his former Surveillance Chief to a seat. "Take, for instance, this fish tank. There used to be a coffee machine in here but this looks much better. Coffee's bad for you, Elie. You should try clean water instead."

Sacchard sat on the edge of his seat and recalled the last time he had been here. It had been warm then. Now he felt strangely cold. The frosty look in Carver's eyes did not help—it had been there from the moment the head of Bio had turned to him as he walked through the glass-paneled door. No friendly enquiry as to the extent of Sacchard's injuries, no *sit down and take it easy, Elie;* not even a vaguely supportive word.

Carver returned to his desk and sat well back from it, his right leg crossed over his left. Sacchard could see through the transparent desktop that Carver's leg was swaying with a pendulous motion. To and fro it swung, as if in time to an inaudible tune. Sacchard recalled those slow-motion knee jerks from the day Carver had dealt with Colonel Art Reynolds in the aftermath of the Sulawesi raid. Recollection of the colonel's subsequent suicide served only to make Sacchard even more nervous.

Carver handed over one of two plastic cups he held in his hands. He drank from the other. "The best Madagascar Spring. Knock it back, Elie."

Out of fear of not holding the cup steady he swirled the contents around and took a sip, all the while wondering why Carver was inviting him to sit down and tickle his taste buds when more serious matters needed to be discussed.

"You let me down, Elie. You let me down badly."

Holding the cup firmly in both hands, Sacchard managed to say, "What do you mean?"

"You know exactly what I'm getting at. The Ullman-

231

Maxwell affair. Both were clandestitutes long before you raided their apartment."

"With respect, they were not members of the Association. Sir, everything we have on them suggests that they . . ."

"Elie, how do you explain why they rescued her from the apartment? Or that Maxwell went missing the same morning? And his receptionist?"

"I . . . I don't know, sir. All I know is that the files don't lie."

"Elie, in the time that you've been recuperating in the clinic and in your apartment, your replacement has done some digging. Maxwell's receptionist, Violet Harding, has been up to her neck in the clandestitutes for years."

Wishing for something stronger, Sacchard swirled the contents of his cup again and drank some more. He felt queasy and thought that the shock of his professional demise was making him nauseous. A replacement, his own replacement—un-prefaced by the forgiving word 'temporary'—was the last thing he needed to hear. "Ronald," he said. "I don't know how it happened. I don't know what to say except that I sincerely believed Ullman and Maxwell to be free of clandestitute involvement."

"You can hardly deny it now that our latest intelligence confirms that they are both full-time activists."

"Yes, but . . ." Sacchard tried hard to find some way of extricating himself out of this. "You know me, Ronald. Over the years I have never given less than one hundred per cent. If they fooled me, they could have hoodwinked anyone. You know me so well you know that's true."

"No use groveling, Elie. You should have done that a long time ago—instead of wasting your time fooling around with Wren."

Mention of her name was like a switchblade to the back of Sacchard's neck. The way Carver had spat it out cleared any doubts as to why Helga had disappeared. "What did you do to her, Ronald?" he said.

"Let's just say there was one woman too many in the Inner Chamber. Now there are none at all, which is the way it should have been right from the start. Maybe then she wouldn't have enticed you from me. And maybe now you'd be addressing me by my first name not as an act of groveling, but as a token of your sincerity."

Sacchard considered mentioning the report he had been compiling on anti-clandestitute tactics. He thought about mentioning it for less than half a second. Carver's own misogyny was largely responsible for his condemnation of Helga Wren—more so than any regret that she was the one who had wooed Sacchard away from him. It was too late now, he knew. Making a play for a second chance would be like trying to pull the wool over King Solomon's eyes. No way, baby. No use appealing to Carver's better nature, either—what little remained of that had been clearly subsumed into this crazy war against the clandestitutes.

"What are you going to do to me?" he asked.

"Want to know what this fish is?" Carver stood and walked from his desk to the aquarium.

Sacchard placed his half-empty cup on Carver's desk and rubbed his brow. He was feeling shivery now. Feverish, almost. He tried to nod in reply to Carver's question but his head disobeyed and shook itself instead.

"It's an antimis, Elie. One of the most poisonous creatures on the planet. It comes from the warm waters of the Indian Ocean. One of my sidelines at our research station at Flok Island has been to develop a method of extracting its poison and convert it to clear liquid. Its characteristics when distilled are similar to pure vodka—no taste, no bouquet, no color—just like spring water."

Sacchard heard but did not want to hear. He believed yet did not want to believe. It was his stomach that finally convinced him Carver was not joking. In a momentary remission from the illness that engulfed him, he saw the irony of Carver extracting poison from a creature he professed to love, an endangered species, and then using it to kill the only person who had ever come close to loving him.

"That's all you're capable of," Sacchard heard himself say. "Poisoning everything." The dizziness returned. A burning sensation welled up in him like hot coals tumbling through his bowels, but he forced himself to go down fighting. "This is all you've ever done, poisoning . . ." He tried to spring off his chair, to lunge, to strike out, but succeeded only in lurching forward. He fell to his knees and saw that Carver was sneering.

Knees rooted to the floor, unable to move, face contorted in pain, venomous tears streaming down the four channels gouged out by clandestitute claws, Sacchard's vain attempts to get up off his knees made him look like a beggar pleading for a handout.

"It's no use, Elie. You're just like all the rest. You don't deserve any better. And you're right, everything is poisoned—not by me—but by those who stand in my way. That's why the new world up there," Carver pointed skyward, "will be so much better."

Sacchard wanted to scream that he was not groveling, that it was the poison that had him on his knees, that he would throttle Carver there and then if only he could—but his stomach had been demolished—liquidized by the white heat of the antimis. The burn erupted from the pit of his stomach and flooded into his throat like hot gushing magma. It turned his eyes to jelly. The last thing he saw was the floor dissolving in a tearful haze of anguish and pain. The poison ripped through his veins, down his arms and legs, to his fingernails and toenails, where it turned around and came back ten times stronger. The mother of all iron maidens embraced him in her suffocating grip, winking out his lights one by one until nothing was left except darkness and void.

Chapter Twenty-Three

For Max, five days of small arms drill and guerrilla tactics had been telescoped into three. He was released from his final forty-eight hours of base camp training to attend a secret summit meeting of the Association in that marble-columned Mississippi mansion where Lee had first met Violet. Mandy's shorter training course had already ended, so she accompanied him south from the Rockies in a stealth flyer invisible to Bio surveillance.

The moon was out. They came in low over a broad arm of Mississippi that lay glittering beneath them like a golden lunette. Their pilot set them down on a lawn so perfect it had to have been tended by a master gardener. The lush grass yielded to their feet as they stepped toward the marble columns where an Association overseer showed them to their room.

Early the next morning Max attended a conference chaired by Xiao Qi Ching. Seventeen other Association members were also present. All came from medical backgrounds. Topics raised included the dismantling of Bio womb-banks; how to deal with or dispose of stored fetuses; what to do with the colonies of activated children; and how best to convince the world's population to back the Association in whatever action it deemed correct to follow.

Max contributed little to the proceedings. He was

finding it difficult to concentrate—his thoughts flitted all over the place and a dull ache brewed up in the back of his head. At one p.m. Ching adjourned the meeting for lunch. Max hoped food might dissipate the light-headedness and the aches that had cloaked his brain, but as he walked to the dining-hall he was told that someone was waiting for him down at the jetty. When he saw who it was, or rather who was *with* him, his headaches grew worse.

Lee picked up a flat stone and skimmed it across slack brown water. The Mississippi had been so flattened by the dead weight of Southern heat that Lee's projectile skipped nine times before sinking beneath the surface beyond the jetty.

"Well done," said Mandy, who had been sitting on the grass alongside him. "Nine hops—that's a record."

Lee held out a small wedge of dark stone. He was about to ask her to have a go when something distracted him. He turned and saw his brother walking toward them. "Want to skip rocks?" he directed his hand away from Mandy, offering the stone to Max.

"No thanks. I haven't time for brotherly games."

"Brother*lee*—is that a pun on my name?"

"Very funny. They told me you wanted to see me. I presume it's about this mission we're going on."

"That's right." Lee motioned Max to sit on a mound under the shade of an old lime tree. "Is your conference over now?"

"It resumes at two. Ends at six."

"Good. We fly out at three a.m." Then, to Mandy, "Make sure he's fixed up with sleep inducers by seven p.m."

Mandy nodded, sitting cross-legged on the grass before them.

"Where are we going?" asked Max.

"Flok Island, South Carolina. Bio's number one development lab. It's time we shut it down. You won't have any actual input into the raid, but I'd like you to come along as an observer so you get a feel for what these missions are like. It'll make it easier for you later when you take a more active role in some of our plans."

"How dangerous is the raid going to be?" asked Mandy.

"If everything works as planned, and we take them by surprise, there shouldn't be any problem. Flok Island's got no defenses worth speaking of. Don't worry, we'll have him back in one piece by 7 a.m."

Mandy said nothing. She plucked a blade of grass and curled it between her fingers.

"Have you two been down here long?" asked Max.

"About an hour. I've been trying to teach this sister of mine to skip rocks."

"Sister?" Max looked quizzically at Mandy, then at Lee.

"Yeah, well . . ." Lee could see what his twin was thinking. Mind reading never came as easy as this. He shuffled about on his makeshift seat. "Now that I've found my long lost brother, I guess that makes Mandy my sister-in-law. Or sister, depending on how she skips rocks from now on."

Max stared out over a parabola of Mississippi mirror—the calmest surface he had ever seen. That light-headed feeling was still with him. So was the headache. He looked sideways at Lee. In the midday glare, his brother's face was as pockmarked as a cratered asteroid.

Lee caught his gaze and said, "I haven't had a chance to get the implant recharged yet."

Mandy grimaced.

"Don't worry. It won't fall off."

238

"Your hair's turned lighter in the past month," said Max, searching for something civil to say.

"It'll revert to its natural color—same shade as yours. But my eyes are still brown—at least they were this morning."

"They still are," said Mandy.

"Why haven't you recharged it by now?" said Max.

"I keep putting it off. With things happening so fast nowadays there just doesn't seem to be time. Maybe, deep down, I want it to revert to its natural state."

Silence ruled for a few moments. Then Mandy said, "A couple of years ago you would have had no choice but to re-construct your face, for Max's sake. Now that Bio's breaking down, maybe you two can afford to look alike."

"Oh, give me a break!" Lee roared with a laugh that Max did not share.

"Have they decided what to do with the womb-banks?" asked Mandy, rather quickly.

Max shrugged. "Yeah, we discussed it this morning. Termination on a grand scale is a possibility."

"I figured that," said Mandy. "Logistically, it's probably the only way. Eliminate Geminizon and the twinning process in one grand sweep. Return the world to its pre-Bio days. It's not a very pleasant prospect, but it's understandable."

"You could call it 'century deprivation,' " quipped Lee.

"Eighty and ninety year old first-lifers won't like that. How would you feel about losing your twin, your second life?" Max asked her.

"I don't think I have one to lose. It may have been termi-nated under the mental defective decree because of my breakdown, remember?"

"Suppose we find your twin fetus still womb-banked. What then?" asked Lee.

"I reckon it's a question of balancing everything," said Mandy. "It would be nice to live another hundred years, but what needs to be done needs to be done. I've no problem with abortion—before they're born. It wouldn't be so bad for me. I'm forty-four. Another fifty or sixty years ought to be enough. You may have difficulty persuading the older generation. People who are months—days, even—away from Transposition won't take kindly to outright Association victory."

Lee sighed. "There are no easy solutions. What do we do with newly transposed teenagers, for instance? When we release the children from the colonies, how will their elder twins react? Like you said—it's a mess. Main thing to remember is: nothing has been decided yet."

At eight p.m. Lee crawled into his bunk, glad to lay down his head and grab some sleep. He rubbed his forefinger along his left temple, unable to remember the last time he had experienced a headache as bad as this. This was no migraine like the ones that had plagued him in his youth on Sulawesi; this was different—*something* was interfering with the smooth running of his brain. He closed his eyes, shielding them with his arm. His mind was full of thoughts scurrying in and out like rats skulking behind tombstones. These strange extraneous thoughts that crawled around inside his head refused to go away. If only he could shield his mind as easily as his eyes. Maybe then he might find it easier to relax.

Stressed out, he told himself. He hadn't felt like this since the day he first met Max down by the muddy estuary. He remembered then the thoughts that came from nowhere and rambled across his mind as he tried to explain to Max who he was. Then, he had succeeded in shaking off his lack

240

of concentration. Right now his mind resembled a sieve. Visions—mainly of Max, also of Mandy—paraded up and down in his consciousness. He had no control over them— they came and went like unwelcome mantras in his mind. He rubbed his tired head again, wondering if what he was experiencing might have anything to do with the twin sleeping soundly less than ten meters away in a room on the other side of the corridor.

A wingful of hypersonic Association attack craft, stealth deflectors raised, flew in low over the archipelago. Their speed and power reverberated through the islands, waking the children of the colonies to a bright new dawn. They rushed to their windows and looked with exuberance at the early morning skies. The sight before them filled their youthful eyes with awe. It filled their guards and overseers with fear. The angels of the Apocalypse were in battle formation, riding overhead.

Behind the attack aircraft, an armored personnel carrier kept its distance. Lee and Max sat behind a bulkhead aboard the APC, waiting for the initial assault to soften up the target before they moved in. Lee rubbed his forehead— what a time for his mind to go walkabout again. Max sat beside him, looking pale.

"Are you okay?" asked Lee.

"Just a headache," said Max. "I get them from time to time."

"Don't worry about it." Lee put it down to pre-attack nerves. "You're not the only one. We'll be going in in a minute. Stick to my heels and you'll be fine."

"Attack craft engaging," said the APC pilot.

Lee poked his head around the bulkhead and looked at the horizon-display screen in the cockpit. It was strange that he, too, should feel so nervous. This was a well-planned mission—there was little danger of exposure to real combat. He forced himself to concentrate on the rhythmic progress of green dots on the APC's display screen, hoping to dispel the fear that kept edging into his mind.

Ignoring the colonies of children, the attack craft made for the target land mass. Six kilometers long and banana-shaped, Flok Island filled their gun sights invitingly. Slowing down now, deflectors lowered, they targeted the area around Station Hill.

An array of ground and airbursts destroyed the hoverstation, the research center, the womb-buildings and the so-called leisure complex where thousands of fifteen-year-olds had spent their last day. Half a minute it took, then the assault craft were gone and the southern half of the island—including Station Hill itself—lay flattened by a barrage of blast bombs.

Over on the northern shore, up from a sandy strip of beach, Bio's development lab remained intact—though its staff had been dispatched by a small condenser wave (half a kilometer radius) dropped by an advance attack craft. Twenty seconds after that lethal assault, the APC landed vertically on the shingle beneath the lab. A dozen men in combat dress jumped out, taking the steps up from the beach two at a time. Eight of the men were clandestitute troopers. They crouched on guard as the four others, including Lee and Max, stormed into the building. Knowing exactly where to go, they made for the data files and memory banks that they knew could only be accessed from Doctor Ambrose's office.

The doctor was still there, in body if not in spirit. He lay prostrate on the floor. His pair of gold-rimmed ornamental spectacles had smashed into his nose—which had also broken in the fall. The two clandestitutes with Max and Lee went straight to their task—extracting information from the files. Visions of Sulawesi corpses flashed through Lee's mind as he put a boot under the doctor's shoulder and overturned him so that he lay face up on the floor. "Dr Daniel Ambrose, Bio's head boffin." He noted with satisfaction the ashen look on Max's face. "This is how my family died on Sulawesi. Condenser attack. The whole lot, sixty-nine of them—sixty-two children, seven adults—all like this."

Max swallowed and looked away from the corpse to the datamen beavering away at the lab's main terminal. Thirty seconds later they had what they came for.

"Let's go," said Lee.

The four men spilled out into the salt-laden air. With the eight troopers covering, they took the steps down to the beach three at a time, except for Max. He raised his visor and stared into the distance, transfixed by clouds of smoke billowing from the island's devastated southern shore.

"Jesus H. Christ!" hissed Lee when he saw his brother standing in the open. Ordering the troopers to board the carrier, he bounded back up the steps and grabbed Max by the collar. "Bio'll be here in a minute. Want to stay and say hello?"

"I thought I saw . . ."

"Get the hell outta here!" Lee hauled his brother down to the beach. The APC was already in motion, its four legs retracting as it hovered a meter above the shingle. The two twins were last to board, piling in as the carrier pulled away. They sat behind the bulkhead again, out of earshot of the others.

Five seconds later a crewman pressed a button. A flap opened in the fuselage down by the undercarriage. The

APC banked to the left, dispatching a homing blast bomb in its wake. Within seconds it had found its target, Ambrose's office, and destroyed the entire lab in a spectacular groundburst. The fleeing APC soon reached top speed, leaving behind the scene of devastation on Flok Island.

"Bio flyers approaching from the coast!" shouted the navigator.

"Stealth on!" urged the co-pilot.

"Deflectors already engaged." The reassurance in the pilot's voice had a calming effect on onboard personnel, including Lee who turned to Max and said, "Okay, now that we're cloaked we go back to base. Via a circuitous route," he added for his brother's benefit.

"I hope so," said Max. "We're hardly headed back the way we came."

Lee said nothing. He was surprised that Max could be sardonic at a time like this. He peered around the bulkhead. The cockpit display screen was brimming with green Xs approaching from the Carolina coast. The dots representing Association flyers seemed hopelessly outnumbered by the threatening Xs. He turned around again, hoping the cloaking would work—the APC could do little to defend itself if a Bio attack craft slipped through.

The brothers sat a while in silence. Then Lee asked, "Did you see something move out there before we boarded?"

"I think so. It might have been a bird, then again it might not."

"The condenser range was 500 meters. It could have been Bio troops moving in from out of range," said Lee.

"It could have been someone needing medical attention."

"There are no half-measures with the condenser. That's

the beauty of it. It leaves no wounded, just fatalities."

"The *what* of it?" Max shook his head. Before he could say anything else, the navigator shouted, "Bio flyer approaching! Seven o'clock."

"Shit." Lee glanced at his brother. "Brace yourself," he said.

Max's complexion reverted to a shade that reminded Lee of that old white mansion in Mississippi. What price a safe house now, he wondered.

The APC lurched to one side. A Bio missile came out of nowhere. Confused by cloudbursts of metallic confetti, it missed by a matter of meters. The missile was confused for all of two seconds. It turned and homed in on them again. The pilot pressed a button to release another burst of spoilers. The APC right-angled to starboard. Again the missile whizzed by, closer this time, rocking them with its turbulence before turning to attack once more.

Roller-coasting across the sky, the APC twisted and turned as it dropped confetti by the bucketful. Its harnesses somehow held, preventing onboard personnel from being tossed around like pinballs. Max was numb with fear, certain he was about to die. Lee broke out in a cold sweat. Death was toying with them before moving in for the kill.

Knowing he could not shake off that missile forever, the pilot was about to give the order to auto-eject everyone aboard when a shadow flitted across the cockpit. An Association attack craft came out of the overhead clouds. Like an angel of mercy it strafed the missile out of the sky, then swooped to engage the Bio flyer.

The APC pilot steadied his craft, intent on putting as much clear air as possible between him and the ensuing dogfight. Seconds later he heaved a sigh of relief: the Bio flyer was down and cloaking was now one hundred per cent effective. Resounding with cheers, the APC hurtled to safety at supersonic speed.

"What's the matter?" said Lee to Max. "Before we were attacked you seemed okay—now you look anxious and depressed. Seems to me it ought to be the other way around. Now that we're hidden from their radar, and there's no one on our tail, you should be happy and cheering and roaring and shouting with the rest of us. In fact, you ought to be on a high after the success of our raid."

"On a *high?*" chortled Max sarcastically. "If you think there's beauty in killing, that's your problem. You forget that I'm a doctor. I'm supposed to prevent death, not revel in it."

"Oh come on," said Lee. "For a medic you should be better at pulling the finger out of your own tight ass. It's obviously jammed so far up there you're scared to admit the truth. Geminizon is supposed to have made us the same, but in many ways you're totally different. It makes me wonder what Mandy sees in you."

"Leave her out of it. The less she has to do with you the better."

"You arrogant little shit." Lee pulled off his harness straps and got to his feet. "You think you're better than everyone else, that you're really something special. Too good to be involved in a war—might get your hands dirty. Well, Mand—"

"Shut up and sit down!" ordered the pilot. "There'll be no rows up here. Save your fighting until we've landed."

Lee glanced at the cockpit. The pilot and co-pilot were staring at him; the look in their eyes was clearly one that would brook no argument. He glared momentarily at his brother, who had also stood and was squaring up to him. Muttering something profane under his breath, Lee ignored his brother and strutted to a spare seat near the troopers. He strapped himself in alongside them.

Max sat down behind the bulkhead. He turned and looked out. The azure sky that filled his vision ought to have been dark and bleak to match his mood. With the passing miles his emotions became confused. Were they so completely different, like opposing versions of one person? Was his twin a mirror of something lurking in his own psyche? Another, darker side of the same Geminizon-minted coin? Yes, he had felt a surge of adrenalin on Flok Island. He had put that down to the fear and excitement that had coursed like rocket fuel through his veins in the moments before they had landed. What if Lee was right? Maybe that rush had come because he had been genuinely turned on by the thrill of it all. It was not easy, living on the edge like this after a cushy lifelong existence. It was not easy, accepting criticism from a more dynamic version of oneself.

Meanwhile, Lee sat alongside the troopers, glaring occasionally at the bulkhead that separated him from Max. Confusion reigned in his mind, too. Another voice was in his head and all his old certainties were faltering, making him see things differently. That voice said his brother was right—there was more to life than war and revenge. A second voice—more familiar, more stubborn—said he was falling under the influence of the wrong people: gynos and cops, for instance.

Once they had landed safely in clandestitute territory, and disembarked from the APC, Lee apologized to Max for his outburst. The stress of war, he said, made everybody uneasy. Let's call a truce, he suggested, and they did.

Both men transferred to the Mississippi safe house where Mandy ran to meet them, delighted that they had made it back. She at once noticed something different—a tension worse than the one she had noticed before, despite their truce.

As he held her in his arms that night, Max again mulled over the arguments between Lee and himself. He wondered if indeed they were twin versions of the one, crazy, mixed-up self. Then he thought that if Mandy loved him for what he was, might she not see in Lee a deeper, darker, ultimately more alluring version of the man she already loved? The more he thought like that, the closer he held her.

Next day Lee felt his mind slip occasionally into that different way of seeing things. Old perspectives about who he was, and what he believed in, were definitely gone. His defenses were down. He thought about seeing a shrink but decided not to. Instead, he told Mandy over lunch about how confused he was. When the meal was over, and Lee had returned to the shooting range for firing practice, she called Max out of his military theorems lecture and mentioned Lee's symptoms. Max recognized them at once and insisted on seeing his brother immediately.

Both men spoke at length about their symptoms. With the speaking and the sharing came an understanding of what might have been causing the dreadful tension between them. They concluded that it may have been a hitherto unknown side-effect of Geminizon which had remained undetected in the normal course of events because twins did not usually live contemporaneously, never mind in such close proximity. With this newfound understanding of what might be happening came an easing of tension—though both agreed it would be better if they stayed away from each other's immediate company until the war was over. Then they would let the doctors figure out a way of preventing their minds from melding.

Chapter Twenty-Four

Ronald Carver's coral-walled home stood deserted in noonday sun. The bright light of summer tried hard to penetrate its dome-like structure, but the opacity of the walls defeated the daylight rays and rendered the interior dark and sullen—an atmosphere befitting its newly abandoned status.

One part of his home that Carver did not abandon was the astronomy nest that had once adorned the apex. Now atop the State Militia Building, Carver had had the little dome, complete with rotating floor and reclining chair, transferred shortly after he had taken to living at headquarters in the wake of the NORWESCOM raids. He visited his nest most nights to stare in fascination at the vastness overhead—most of all to study the small red planet he craved so much.

Everything on Mars was almost ready. The twin towns were boomtowns. Terraforming of the desert was set to begin within six weeks. There was enough water in the Martian poles and enough vapor in the clouds to convert eighty thousand square kilometers. Colonies of activated fetuses were already well established—the womb-banks were almost full, too, and the wombship *Catalina* was ready to service its last load. From then on Mars would truly be its own world. Transposition capabilities were up and running, and research facilities as well as a small development lab had also been built. As yet, these were barely operational. Most development work, particularly on the achievement of multiple lifespans using third party fetuses as backup, was still carried out on Flok Island.

Carver retired from his Mars-gazing at three a.m., leaving instructions that he was to be woken at eight. He got less sleep than he had bargained for.

The 'bot that roused him at five-ten a.m. did not have any emotional make-up to render it nervous about its task, but the officer with the responsibility of informing him of what had happened certainly did.

Carver rode the elevator down to Command Center where early morning plasma screens and sensors flared with disturbing regularity. A timid, weasel-like general attempted to gloss over the raid. "The buildings below Station Hill were not that important, sir," he said. "We have dozens like 'em all over. I'm afraid the loss of the lab was the most serious blow."

Carver held himself in check. It was not the uniqueness of the leisure center, the womb-buildings or the research complex that was important. Neither was it that this was where Carver himself had been transposed. Rather, it was the symbolism of Flok Island—that's what mattered so much. How do you explain symbolism to a weasel? How do you get it into his thick skull that these were the first such buildings? Therefore, in clandestitute eyes, the most important? Destroy them, destroy the foundations.

Carver tried to be patient as General Reeves whined on in that high-pitched tone of his, attempting to justify the rebels' escape. Carver listened to some nonsense about Bio flyers chasing phantoms and then let his attention wander to the effervescent screens and ever-changing table maps.

Personnel scurried about trying to keep everything updated. The general was nasalizing about some satshots taken of the raiding party—at least the man had enough low-life cunning not to mention lack of defenses, thought Carver. He sighed and looked again at the screens. No one had ever warned him it could come to this. One of Bio's sacred places, site of the leader's own Activation and Transposition, razed to the ground. If things were this bad, maybe SMB itself was vulnerable. Perhaps Carver was next on the hit list. That thought prompted him to think again that maybe it was time to cut loose, to . . .

"Sir?" The weasel again. "The satshots, sir. They're ready for your inspection."

"What!" hissed Carver. "Do you think I have the time or the inclination to study clandestitute terrorists in action?"

"Begging your pardon, sir." General Reeves' eyes darted about like rabbit's eyes searching for cover until the predator had passed. "Some of them were not troopers. The files have come up with the name Maxwell, sir, and his twin. If you come with me to the AV room, I'll show you."

They went into the small room where Elie Sacchard had once used a light-stick to point at a boy in a school uniform, Grant Maxwell, and a boy on the banks of the Ludese River. It seemed so long ago. More than fifteen years in which much had happened and much had changed. With a growing sense of *déjà vu,* Carver listened as the AV operator explained the significance of the satshots.

"Twelve personnel were involved in the raid. Eight troopers in guard-mode plus four others—two of whom we think were technicians. As you can see from enhancement, they appear to be carrying software and other technical equipment that they probably used to ferret the files in the lab. As for the remaining pair, one of them was inexperienced—he made the mistake of removing his visor to stare at something in the island landscape, thereby revealing most of his face."

Carver strained forward. An overhead view of a face filled the screen. The image was grainy: nose, cheekbones, blond eyebrows—a lock of hair peeped from beneath the helmet. The AV man went on, "Super-enhancement techniques enable our telemetry program to build a three-dimensional copy." Carver watched as a 3-D drawing of a man filled the screen. "Even from an overhead view we can calculate height. From the way clothing cleaves to the body we can construct the physique. All we need is a small part of the body and face, from any angle. Our computers then take over and correlate everything; height, weight, body-build, hair coloring, facial evidence—in this case: nose, forehead and cheekbone structure. From all this we get an accurate picture which makes identification easy. In this case we had more than enough information for a quick match-up." The 3-D figure dissolved to a photo-image of Grant Maxwell. Carver leaned back in his chair and sighed.

"Now this is where it gets interesting." The AV man re-called to screen the overhead view of a visorless Grant Maxwell. "If we move the image on a bit—there, hold it right there—we can see another individual—not one of the troopers, not one of the technicians, but the twelfth member of the party. See, he moves forward and grabs Maxwell, pushing him down the steps to the beach where the APC is taking off. At this point our scanners raised an alarm, as they're designed to do when they spot two persons with body structure so identical they're bound to be twins."

"Can you be sure it's his twin?" Carver was leaning forward again.

"His face is covered. Using telemetry, we can eliminate

boots, socks and helmet, thereby calculating his height to be exactly that of Maxwell's—right down to point zero zero one of a millimeter. There are no essential differences to body or bone structure other than those brought about by dietary intake or physical exercise. The computer calculates that the chance of them being twins is over ninety-five per cent.

"One other thing," said the AV operator. "Using height and build, we correlated the man on the left, the one pushing Maxwell down the steps, with one of the raiders who attacked the Gulf Coast geminizing unit last month. In fact, from vidshots taken of the raiding party as they ran to their escape duct, we calculate from his behavior that he was their leader. From the evidence on Flok Island, he almost certainly led that raid as well."

For the first time since entering the AV room, General Reeves spoke. "Sir, from information at our disposal we are in no doubt that Grant Maxwell's twin is one of the clandestitute's top terrorists. We have matched him to one of the raiders who killed four surveillance men in the raid on the Ullman apartment—also last month. As you may recall, we were fortunate to have a vidscan in place that captured the entire raid. He's had one of these implants to change his features, but now we know his face since he made the mistake of not covering up during the apartment raid. This is a major breakthrough for our surveillance people. It should make it easier for us to eliminate him. Chances are that if we locate Maxwell or his cop-girlfriend, we will also find the renegade from Sulawesi."

Carver stared hard at the onscreen image of a man in his early thirties, fifteen years younger than he was himself. "Did I hear you say *chances*, General? And *if* we find him? I don't want ifs. I don't want percentage shots. I don't want games of chance. I want Maxwell's twin and I want him alive. You have seven days. Understand?"

"Yes," said the general, swallowing hard.

Later that night Carver paid his customary visit to his astronomy nest. He needed to see Mars up close. The day's events had taken a toll on whatever patience and tolerance he had left. He gripped the eyepiece firmly and studied the Martian surface. The more he thought about the raid that had destroyed Flok Island, the more determined he became to make the Mars project succeed. Up there, in the purifying vacuum of space, a whole new world was waiting.

Next day Carver stood on a small beach and stared at his coral-walled former home. Time for one last lingering look. Advisers had warned him that it, too, would be a probable clandestitute target—it was too far from the center of Longevity City, too inaccessible from the western suburbs to protect it properly. Nothing was safe these days—anywhere beyond city limits was liable to be attacked. But Carver would not let them get his dream home. No sir, he was going to get it first.

The coral walls had morphed from dream to nightmare, painfully transforming his home into a metaphor for all that had gone wrong in recent months. Within those encrusted walls Carver saw things he did not want to see. Endangered species were now the epitome of a failed Earth. Attempts to conserve wild animals were a throwback to his father—a tugging of the forelock to a man he had always hated. Carver did not know whom he detested more: his father, or himself, for conserving and embellishing the legacy of a man he ought to have long since disowned. All this pent-up agony against a planet that had refused to co-operate, against a parent who had abused him by fathering him only in name, against a people who had rebelled—all this rage he now concentrated in one direction—his coral-walled home. In its domed shape he saw a doomed planet, its teeming waters encompassing all the creatures of the Earth.

The Bio tech-unit had installed the necessary explosives earlier that morning. Carver pressed the button on the remote he had been holding in the palm of his hand. His house detonated with an ear-splitting roar. Its opaque dome lifted off the ground like a mushroom cloud rising above a groundburst. It splintered as it rose, ten thousand tentacles splitting and slithering across its surface. Within milliseconds, though it seemed like ages to Carver, the gray dome collapsed in on itself. Then the entire structure erupted again. This time there was no exotic roof, just a ball of coral and glass and fish and water exploding in all directions. Though they were out of range, the tech-men crouched instinctively for cover. Carver did not even blink. He stood upright, getting wet. It was raining now, raining bits of fish and coral.

Triggerfish and butterfly fish, worms and mollusks, cones and cowries, all came tumbling down. Dead or dying, they littered the sand with their broken bodies. Some species, like great clams and burrowing crabs, did not look out of place on the beach, though now their shells were cracked and their claws would burrow no more.

A catfish head plopped onto the sand, centimeters in front of Carver's feet. He recognized it as the last of its kind, the only surviving specimen of a species he had been trying to breed for years. Though the body had been blown off, the head still lived. It seemed so appropriate, watching it vainly struggle to breathe its last. Its fishy eyes looked up pleadingly. Then it gave one last gasp and died.

Carver looked down on the catfish. A mawkish grin stretched across his face. Though he was standing on sand, he felt as if his feet were levitating off the ground. All the hates, all the frustrations, that had swirled around inside his head had dispersed with the disintegrating dome. His fingers and toes tingled. So did his brain. Decision day had arrived, and he had not been found wanting.

Chapter Twenty-Five

Fighting spread across the Pacific. The first islands to be liberated were the Aleutians in the north, followed by the New Hebrides in the south. Then a string of islands in between: the Solomons, the Carolines, Guam and the Marianas. Sulawesi was liberated on July third. In the week that followed, clandestitute troops spread through Japanese Kyushu and Honshu. In a classic pincer movement, another rebel force came down from Sakhalin—their objective: the enormous colony of children that was Hokkaido.

Association policy was to free the children and destroy all Activation and Transposition facilities. This was achieved in a mammoth five-hour ground and air assault. Seven wings of attack craft swooped in low, leaving a trail of destruction behind them. Guards' barracks and overseers' quarters were devastated by blastbombs. Womb-buildings and storage facilities were vaporized, their contents sacrificed to the expediency of the Association war machine.

Lee led the first assault by ground attack troops. He made sure to be far enough ahead of his brother to be out of range of the mental interference they had experienced in the safe house and during the Flok Island raid. Mandy and Max came with the second wave—a mopping up operation that encountered little opposition. The remaining Bio troopers were mostly dead or captured. The overseers who had not fled were surrounded and taken prisoner. The only danger that Mandy and Max encountered came near the entrance to the children's colony at Azing Baru. A Bio trooper who had survived the initial attack and who was unwilling to surrender cut loose with a blast of pulse rays that killed five clandestitute soldiers and wounded eight others.

Max reacted quickly to the trooper's sudden spray of gunfire by pushing Mandy into a crater, then diving in after her. A stream of pulses arced harmlessly over their heads. Max stood up, leaned on the rim of the crater, and unleashed a blast from his own gun. His may not have been the only weapon firing on the hut where the enemy was pinned down but it seemed that way as he looked down the gun sight at his own pulses streaming to their target. Within seconds the Bio trooper had been silenced. "Got him!" exclaimed Max as he dropped back into the crater, breathing hard, a broad grin on his face.

All the children had been liberated by nightfall. Few were casualties—the initial bombing had been so accurate that the colonies themselves were spared almost any damage. Whatever innocent victims there were had been caught in crossfire. That the children were not directly targeted did little to assuage their terror during the initial attacks. Realizing they were to be spared, their fear soon gave way. Some of the older ones, who had figured out what lay in store for them under Bio rule, quickly recognized the clandestitutes as liberators and welcomed them with wild cheers. Association troopers found themselves giving history lessons, explaining that Bio would have killed them all at age fifteen. In the new order they would be free to live out the rest of their natural lives. By ten p.m. the huge island was under Association rule. Not a pocket of resistance remained anywhere. No gunfire, no fighting—just the joyous sound of many young voices cheering, dancing and singing. The release of the children was not welcomed by the elders who had been queuing at Transposition for a second life and instead found themselves left with nothing except chronic old age. Their semi-senile screaming continued into the night, but they may as well have been howling at the moon for all the good it did them. Most fortunate of all those rescued were the birthday boys and girls about to be anaesthetized in the Transposition chamber. They sang and laughed loudest and longest of all.

Mandy heard their cheers. As the night wore on she joined in with them. The more she thought about their predicament and how lucky they had been, the more emotional she became. In their young faces she saw her own image when she was younger—and that of Reggie Brooks. It was impossible to understand whatever it was that ordained who should survive, and why. It occurred to her that the cutting edge of fate knew no conscience and was something that did not bear thinking about, yet she could not help but dwell on it. She looked at them laughing and clapping and singing, and realized that they were all her children now. She wished Max could be by her side so they could talk about it, but he was working in the Activation facilities where his expertise would be needed throughout the night. At ten-thirty Mandy excused herself from the celebrating youngsters and stepped into the dark, leaving them to carouse the night away with the other soldiers.

She walked along a path that led to the shore. Stars glittered above her head. In the silver-shaded light she saw a shadow sitting on top of a dune. Lee. She trudged her way up the steep sand. When she sat down alongside him, she saw that he had been crying.

"What's wrong?" she asked.

He shook his head and said it was nothing.

"Tell me," she said, and saw him shake his head again.

They sat in silence for a minute. Sensing that he might open up if she said the right things, she spoke about her own feelings at what had happened that day—how it had affected her to see the children, particularly the older ones who would have been dead by now had they not come to set them free.

Lee shifted slightly. Something made her stop in mid-sentence. A tear rolled swiftly down his cheek and fell to its silent death in the sand. She put her hand on his arm and said, "Don't keep it bottled up. Tell me what it is that's troubling you."

He stayed silent.

"It's better to talk about it." She gently squeezed his arm.

He shook his head again.

"I'm your sister, remember?"

He lifted his head and stared at the white waves breaking on the invisible beach. He glanced at Mandy, looked up at the stars, then glanced at her again. "I'd better tell someone," he said. "Though I'm not sure if I should. I don't know if you'll understand why I did it—or forgive me for doing it."

"Try me."

He swallowed and said, "I spent six months working here in Azing Baru Colony as a camp overseer. All the while I was working under cover, info-gathering for the Association. I told you that already, I think, but I didn't tell you about this girl. To keep track of all the children they used a restricted number of standardized names with numbers added. She was the three thousandth eight hundredth and ninety-second female white Caucasian named Melinda to be activated in '143, so they christened her Melinda FWC 3892 A2143."

Looking out over the dunes, he said, "There would have been no problem if we hadn't fallen in love. Not that Mel and I were actually lovers, she was only fourteen, but I couldn't sleep nights thinking what a beautiful woman she'd grow up to be. Know what obsessive love is? What it's like to have someone imprinted on your brain? To know that there's one person in the world you'd do anything for?"

One glimpse into her eyes and he saw Max staring out. "Yeah," he said. "I guess you do. Anyway, there still isn't a day goes by . . . It was five years ago. Then one day I saw her—only she wasn't Mel any more. Some one-hundred-and-five-year-old-bitch had taken over her body. Know what I did? The Association had refused to let me rescue her before Transposition—they said it would blow my cover. 'The greater good of our long-term campaign takes precedence over the good of any one individual'—the usual bullshit. Being the good soldier, I obeyed.

"A week before her time was up Mel asked me why Bio placed more emphasis on physical rather than intellectual or emotional education. She looked me dead in the eye and said it was as if her body counted for more than her mind. I told her a barefaced lie—I couldn't take the idea that she might know what was going to happen, but she knew. Then I couldn't bear to see her any more, so I didn't—until the week was up and her time had passed. I secretly hoped that after Transposition her mind—like her body—would somehow be the same—that it would be the same Mel. Then, the day after Transposition, she came looking. A lot of new elder teens do that. They get these young bodies so they celebrate with a good fuck."

Mandy tightened her grip on Lee's arm. He went on.

"There's these beaches—not this one, beaches further up the coast—that were off-limits to the children until their minds were transposed. First thing they'd do, if there wasn't enough of their own kind to go around, is grab the nearest overseer. I know it's not possible, but some residue of Mel must've been left in her brain because she actively sought me out and suggested a walk along the beach, so I went. It was like walking with Frankenstein. She took my hand and there was I hoping it was her, and then she put her other hand in my pants. I just stood there flummoxed, looking into what had been a beautiful, idealistic, innocent face—and there was this cynical, self-centered bitch leering up. So I . . ." Lee paused and glanced again at Mandy. She was staring hard at him, oblivious to everything but his story.

". . . When she grabbed me like that I just lost control. I couldn't help it. She started to scream so I caught her by the throat and strangled the life out of her. Then I ran into the night. Next day the Association got me away from Hokkaido. As far as Bio is concerned, I'm on the wanted list not just because I'm the twin of one of their gynos, but because I'm a murderer."

Mandy kept her hand on his arm. She had also loved a fifteen-year-old to whom something terrible had happened. She wanted to hold Lee close and tell him that she understood his pain, but somewhere in her head a voice told her to hold her emotions back, to keep them buttoned up.

A mist rolled in from the sea. Lee stood up and said, "That's unusual for this time of year. It doesn't normally get foggy along this coastline at night. Guess we better get back."

"Yes," she said.

He took her hand to steady her as she got to her feet.

262

When she was standing he did not let go.

"Please, don't." She forced her hand from his grasp. She turned and sidled down the dune. In the dark night, with the mist rolling in from the sea and her back turned, he could not see the tears on her face. He wanted to run after her, to take her in his arms, but something held him back. She was his brother's lover and therefore unattainable. And yet . . . These past weeks in Mississippi and the Rockies had wrought in him emotions he had not felt in the empty years since Mel. Right now the last thing he wanted to do was to hurt Mandy—which he knew he would do if he forced her to choose between his brother and himself. He did not want to hurt Max, either. He wasn't such a bad guy. So what if he was a gyno and a wimp—Mandy loved him and they both were happy. Jesus, why was life so damn complicated?

Lee's head and heart fought their own private battle on top of the dune, and his heart won. He could no longer help himself—he had to tell her, had to tell her now. "Mandy!" he shouted, propelling himself down the side of the dune. "Mandy!"

She turned and saw him scampering among the dunes. She knew why he was running to her and for a moment did not know what to do. She was standing near the top of a dune two hundred meters from the gates of Azing Baru. She glanced at the colony. Max would be at work in the Activation center, perhaps wondering where she was at this very moment. There was no way she could betray him. She . . . Her thoughts were distracted by loud voices from the camp. There was something different about them now—a raw urgency in place of the celebration that had been there before. Then she peered at what was happening within the gates and saw people running about. No more singing and cheering, only screaming. Desperate, high-pitched screaming. She turned to Lee.

The look of alarm on Mandy's face stopped him ten paces from her. She was staring back, not at him but around and above him. Her eyes were wide with terror. He heard a deep, deep rumbling from behind and turned on his heels. "Oh shit," he muttered at the sight that rose before his eyes—a sight so awesome it rooted him to the spot.

From out of the night came a Mark Two Vindicator. Its camouflaging mist dissipating, it came in off the sea, rising from the shadows between the dunes. Its sheer size blotted out all the stars above. Its powerful engines reverberated deep into the ground, shaking it beneath Lee's feet, whipping up grains of sand like a desert storm. Lee shielded his eyes and crouched beneath the metal underbelly of the monstrous war machine passing overhead. He saw Mandy still standing—until the guns started firing. Then she too dived for cover behind a clump of sand and grass.

The Vindicator hovered over Azing Baru. All guns blazing, it strafed the colony with deadly pulses. Clandestitute troopers had little time to react—their radar had broken the enemy's cloaking code less than thirty seconds before its arrival. There had been time only for panic. The children who had been screaming and trying desperately to flee were mown down without mercy. The Association troopers who did manage to grab their guns found themselves with puny weapons compared to the heavily armored angel of death hovering overhead.

Within a minute most of those on the ground had been killed. The Vindicator then switched from blanket fire to irregular bursts—no need now for saturation coverage; the attrition rate had been so high that most of the Vindicator's turrets began to shut down. Those still operational covered the entire colony, sniping at anything that moved.

Mandy crept stealthily toward the gates of Azing Baru. Lee urged her to hold back, telling her she was crazy to go in that way—but she was determined to find Max. "Look up!" he hissed. One look at the Vindicator overhead and she saw the sense in Lee's suggestion that they avoid the gates. Instead, they jumped through a hole in the perimeter fence and dived into a bunker where a clandestitute trooper was taking cover.

"What's happening elsewhere?" asked Lee.

"Don't know," said the trooper. "Except that it's bad. Took everyone by surprise. Last thing we heard on the comm, the only thing we heard, was that they were dropping condensers all over, though for some reason not here."

Mandy was halfway out of the bunker. "Max!" she screamed, her voice lost amid the deep rumble of the Vindicator's drive system. The sound of gunfire and the screams of children hiding and dying in the wreckage of dormitories and recreation buildings also made her voice inaudible—but not to the man running out of the shadows of what was left of the Activation center.

He sprinted in zigzag fashion across the grass, jumping over charred and maimed bodies. Somehow, through the dark and the smoke and the panic, Mandy had recognized him even when he was but a silhouette against the bright flames of the Activation building.

"Max!" she screamed, one foot out of the bunker, ready to run—Lee grabbed her and held her back. "It's him!" she yelled. "Max! Over here!"

A pulse-burst hit the grass centimeters in front of Max. He tumbled to the ground and rolled over twice. On his feet again he sprinted straight for the bunker.

"Zigzag for Chrissake!" roared Lee, but Max could not

hear him through the din. On and on he ran, getting nearer and nearer.

Mandy could hear the thunder of his boots in her ears—but her worm's eye view from the bunker had foreshortened the distance between them.

A pulse from the Vindicator caught Max high up in the chest and sent him sprawling. He fell forward, face downward, less than two meters from the edge of the bunker. This time there was no holding Mandy back. Lee went with her as she clambered out to haul Max in. They grabbed his arms and pulled him along, expecting a pulse gun from above to shoot them at any moment. None fired.

A glint of metal a short distance away caught Lee's eye—Max's gun. As soon as they had pulled him to the edge of the bunker, and the trooper reached up to grab Max, Lee ran for the gun, snatched it off the grass and dived back into the bunker, again expecting to be shot—again getting away with it.

All thoughts of why they had not been fired on were banished from Lee's mind when he hauled himself to his knees in the bunker. Then he saw Max. The hole in the chest was deep, wide and squirting blood. Mandy tried to stem the flow with what was left of his shirt but it was like trying to stop a flood with paper. She held him in her arms then, sobbing quietly. Max stared glassy-eyed at his brother, then turned his pale sweat-soaked face to Mandy.

Lee did not know what to say or do. He felt like a stranger intruding in a very private moment and wished he could be some place else, anywhere else. His mind was like a slow-motion jackhammer thrumming with wave after wave of anguish. Time seemed to stand still. All the noises now—the hum of the Vindicator, the sounds of gunfire, the screams of children—were blotted out by the intimacy of

Mandy holding Max. Lee heard no sound except his brother's ragged breathing and Mandy's quiet sobs. Lee looked up at the Vindicator's callous underbelly. It seemed so cold, so unreal, so oddly two-dimensional. It was like looking at an old-style overhead movie screen. Beyond this bunker the world ended. So did reality. Lee wondered why a weird thought like that should enter his head at a moment like this. Something brushed against his midriff.

Max's hand reached up. He tried to say something but the sound he made was the gurgling of blood in his throat. From the corners of his mouth came a frothy liquid. It varied in shade from clear to crimson, and alternately spurted and trickled down his chin. The hand reached almost to Lee's heart, then trailed down forlornly across his ribs. With each passing rib, Max's life edged slowly away. Lee grasped the hand and held it tightly.

Max looked at him. Then his eyes rolled over to Mandy and back again. Once more he tried to speak but his throat was full and his chin awash with blood and saliva. He looked up at Mandy and his eyes blinked languidly before closing for the last time.

He went limp, a dead weight in Mandy's arms. In that moment Lee's body shuddered as if a thousand volts had seared into his brain. He felt as if he had been riveted to the side of the bunker; his whole body racked by something interminable that throbbed and rattled up his spine. His mind went blank. His eyes went blind. The spasm ended as quickly as it began, and Lee's body and mind were restored to normality as the world intruded again.

The Vindicator was revolving slowly above the colony. People resumed screaming. Pulse-bursts and gunfire started to fill the air once more. Mandy cradled Max's corpse as Lee stared hatefully at the death-bringer overhead. He knew that its scanners must have recorded Max's run from the Activation center. They must have seen how they had hauled him into the bunker. Why then the delay in targeting them? Realizing that there was no time to lose, Lee grabbed Max's weapon and barked instructions at the trooper. Then he turned to Mandy. "Go with him—I'll cover you," he shouted as he climbed out of the bunker.

He ran a crooked line, firing at the Vindicator as he went. He fell and rolled over. Glancing back, he saw an obedient trooper pulling a reluctant grief-stricken figure away from the bunker toward the perimeter of the camp. There was a chance that they would get away if he could distract the war machine overhead.

Still no pulse rays came at him, or anywhere near him. "Fuck you!" he cried, unleashing his paltry weapon at an enemy that seemed to be playing with him the way a cat plays with a mouse.

The stun-ray hit him like a bolt to the brain. It knocked him out before he even hit the ground. Within seconds, a spindly retrieval arm had him in its all-embracing grip, lifting him high in the air, straight into the arms of Bio.

Chapter Twenty-Six

Lee came around gradually, painfully. The back of his head lay on a cold hard surface—metallic, by the feel of it. His body lay horizontal, shoulders and buttocks pressing down on that same cold metal. Beyond his torso and head, tactile awareness ceased. Limbs no longer existed. He tried to raise his head but could not, mustering only enough energy to turn his face perhaps ten degrees maximum to either side. His eyes, though, roved freely in their sockets.

It was hard work trying to peer into the dark. Dim walls rose in the blackness on either side. A ceiling loomed low overhead. Concentrating on his other faculties, he tried to make sense of his surroundings. Taste and smell told him nothing except that wherever he was lacked air-conditioning. Through the texture of his sweaty back on the table on which he lay—perception led him to believe it to be some kind of raised slab or table—he sensed vibrations normally associated with drive systems. Big drive systems. His ears informed him of a vaguely audible hum equivalent to the deep rumble of a Mark Two Vindicator—except that now he was hearing it from the inside rather than the outside, and a pleasing sound it did not make. Logic whispered *prisoner* in his ear. Memory reminded him of that white flash that seared his brain as he had tried to distract the Vindicator with Max's puny pulse gun. He thought of his brother then. Dead. Other memories flooded in. Mandy. He wondered if she had made it away from the Vindicator's deadly wrath. Then he knew why Bio had dropped condenser bombs all over Hokkaido but not on Azing Baru. It was for the same reason that the Vindicator's pulsers had not shot him dead in the bunker alongside Mandy and his dying brother—because they had wanted to take him alive all along.

Gravity tugged his head gently to one side. The huge ship was banking to the right. A swelling in his ears hinted at descent—a vague suggestion of a jolt somewhere far beneath confirmed that the Vindicator had touched down. The cabin door opened and a halo of light hit him hard between the eyes. He forced his eyelids to remain open. Within seconds, the pain of bright light had abated. Two guards lifted him off the table and placed him on a trolley. No harness had held him in place during the flight. Straps were not needed—the absence of feeling in his limbs confirmed that he was totally immobile, capable only of turning his head as they transferred him from the Vindicator to a waiting hover.

Half an hour later they delivered him to the Surveillance Bureau—he recognized the building by its daunting portals, an image he had often seen in Association recon photos. By now he could tell that the stun was wearing off because he could lift his head a little. They wheeled him down into the last place he wanted to go. Knowing from clandestitute intelligence what lay in the basement of the Bureau, he watched with trepidation as the elevator numbers counted down. With each passing floor, a blood-knot of dread and impending pain tightened in his stomach.

The guards left him lying on a trolley in a corridor in the deepest bowels of the building. He forced his head over to one side, took one look at the sign on the wall, and swallowed hard. It read, *Monitoring & Appraisal Division—Main Chamber.*

Lee had heard of this nightmare place. It was Bio's central M&A unit, their number one interrogation chamber. He knew that it was buried as deep beneath the ground as it was possible to go in the Bureau. Here all truth accumulated, no lie remained undetected. This was the sump of all Bio surveillance; the place where no knowledge, no information, no *dis*information, could hide. Appropriately underground, as far as Lee was concerned it was a tomb.

As time wore on he began to feel again what it was like to have fingers and toes. With a little effort he could imagine himself wiggling them about. That did little to console him. He was wondering why they had left him out in the corridor when he noticed jerky little movements in the diaphragm of the scanner peering down at him from the ceiling. It was taking images of his face for analysis. Lee wanted to shake his head in disbelief—he probably would have, if it weren't so much of a physical effort. Stills analysis meant that they were scanning the files for match-up. He hoped the ethnic implant might fool them into thinking that he had no twin, not that it mattered much now that Max was dead, but when the time came for them to hoover his brain he could at least die with the consolation that the knowledge of who he had really been might shock them.

After what seemed like hours during which he dozed off, Lee stared up at the scanner. Its diaphragm had ceased moving. By now he could feel movement returning to his hands. Arms by his side, the back of his right hand rubbed against something hard in his pocket. It took him a moment to figure out that it was the stone talisman from the Sulawesi salt spring. The Surveillance Bureau scanner

would never have failed to spot it unless it had been inadvertently shielded by the back of his hand . . . It would not
make a great knuckleduster but anything was better than air
between his fingers.

A door opened and a pair of M&A men stepped into the
corridor. They grasped both ends of the trolley and steered
it toward the interrogation chamber. As they wheeled him
in through the open door he heard an elevator hiss open
over by the far wall. A man in military uniform stepped out.
"Place him on the slab," General Reeves ordered the M&A
men. "Clamps on."

They lifted him bodily off the trolley, carefully posi-
tioning his ankles, wrists and neck over five metal slats set
strategically into the slab. Then an M&A man stepped to
the side of what seemed to be a huge medical scanner. He
looked down at Lee and pressed a button. The slats
whipped up, grabbed him tightly, fastening him to the slab.

The officer who had activated the clamps pushed the
trolley away. His colleague adjusted the scanner so that it
pointed directly at Lee's head. "Make sure those clamps are
secure at all times," warned the general. "His stun is beginning to wear off."

Lee stared up, convinced that from this moment he
would no longer be in control of his own brain. The only
thing that gave him hope was the clamping—why bother if
they were going to turn him into a vegetable—or even kill
him, as they most certainly would. Maybe they were not
going to suck out his mind just yet. Perhaps they were going
to let him survive. But for what? Lee felt that he was
grasping at straws. It had to be death or a brain-wipe—and
it had to be now.

As if reading his mind General Reeves stood over him
and said, "The stun wears off in a matter of hours, though

we may need to keep your body and mind together a little longer than that. You may have a visitor—a very important visitor. These clamps ought to do the trick, huh?"

Lee had never felt so trapped. He could not move at all except to breathe. What did it matter anyway, if the end of his life was only hours away? Christ, it had to matter—he had to convince himself to keep hoping. "What are you going to do?" he hissed, his throat rubbing painfully against the hard metallic neck-clamp.

The general reached for a button at the back of the scanner. Before pressing it he said, "We're going to revert your face to its natural state—turn you back into Dr. Grant Maxwell." With that, Reeves engaged the button.

Lee closed his eyes and clenched his teeth and fists. So the bastards had known who he was all along. He told himself not to look at the scanner or machine or whatever the hell it was. He tried to make himself concentrate . . . Keep concentrating . . . What's the use in concentrating when it's your skin and bone they're after? He opened his eyes and promptly shut them again. In the instant that they were exposed he felt his eyeballs quiver beneath the piercing white assault waves of Bio's machine. Keep them shut or they'll dissolve your eyeballs, he told himself. Something was happening to—or was it beneath—his face. "Open the neck-clamp," he heard the general say. "Revert that area as well."

His skin crawled, literally and figuratively. A million tiny grubs shifted about under his flesh. He clenched his fists even tighter, digging his fingernails into his palms, desperately seeking an alternative pain. His palms bled, warm and sticky-moist with sweat and blood which he gratefully welcomed as a distraction from what was happening to his face. Ching had been right—he should have got it renewed.

Maybe then they would not be able to revert it. On the other hand, it might have made it even more painful . . . His cheekbones were changing, compressing, as if a vice was closing in around his jaws. The grubs were marching the goosestep now; his mouth was caving in slowly; his skin twisted and turned like a scalp rotating on top of his skull. Mucus and crumbling bone streamed from his nostrils in a heady cocktail of blood and gristle.

He wanted to open his eyes—he wanted to keep them shut. His brain yelled 'Scream!' but the terror of where the grubs might go if he opened his mouth, and what they would do when they got in there, kept it firmly shut. His lips were alive, crawling with snails defecating the filthiest slime. Their excrement seeped into his mouth and smelled and tasted like the shit it was. He was going crazy. The weasels in his brain, the grubs in his brain, grew ever larger and more repulsive like giant slithering slugs. Got to keep them out, he told himself. Got to keep the slugs out.

He shook his head, furiously trying to shake off his skin, his face. He *was* shaking it off too, as if it was vile and reptilian. It was no use—the grubs clung on no matter how fiercely he shook. Something slimy crawled out of one ear, then the other. This time he opened his mouth and tried to scream. A deep low grunt came out. The grunt built up until it climaxed in a noise so loud his entire body shook, racked by a huge spasm. Losing consciousness, he plunged into a disturbing world where grubs and slugs and all things creepy-crawly slithered through tunnels, avoiding corpses and walls caving in. He tried to reach a light but it was fading fast, getting dark, and he could not breathe . . .

The next day was not a good day in Longevity City—for Bio. Bad day at the war office, too—for Ronald Carver III.

Wings of clandestitute flyers came in off the sea. Rebel armored divisions rolled west from the Great Nevada Basin, north from the Gila Desert, south from the Cascades. Advisers and strategic commanders milled about in Command Center. Fear lit up their eyes with what their sensors and plasma screens told them. Table maps were redundant now—nobody bothered to update them after they had run out of clandestitute flags. Rebels were everywhere: north, south, east and west. They were in the sea and in the air. They were tunneling up from under the floorboards and were lining up in the woodwork, ready to crawl spitefully out.

Yesterday, Bio defenses had downed all incoming missiles. Today, some rockets were getting through to targets in the city. Defensive positions were being whittled away. Law and order was standing at breakdown's edge. Eastsiders rampaged through the streets chanting pro-clandestitute slogans, demanding the head of Carver. Whole units of Bio forces were surrendering—or turning their weapons on those still loyal to their leader.

Some of Carver's Command Center staff had not turned up for work, opting instead to hide or flee or defect. Carver's frantic impulses told him to lash out, to destroy, to kill—but he subjugated his anger through force of will. With weary calculating eyes he made the decision that his whole life had been leading up to—the decision which had always been inevitable. He chose to take with him one loyal servant who, thus far at least, had not botched everything up like all the others. But before he left town with General Reeves, there was one person Carver wanted to see. Someone who amounted to the manifestation of all that was evil in the clandestitute cause; the one single rebel who had been more of a thorn in his side than any other; the man who had led the attacks on the Geminizon-producing factory on the Gulf Coast and the Flok Island research center—he was waiting over in the basement of the Surveillance Bureau, and it was time to pay a visit.

Lee came to with a start. He had been sleeping, but was now awake and badly disoriented. He blinked several times in an effort to focus his eyes. He desperately needed to rub them, but the clamps still trapped his limbs. When he felt their steely embrace he remembered what the general and the M&A men had done to him. The urge to touch his face was overwhelming, the restriction of the clamps unbearable. He flexed his body to check if the power of the stun had worn off. It had. The scanner had been moved to one side, out of his line of vision. In its place was a face he instantly recognized.

The face grinned at what it saw. Once more Lee tried to feel what the rays had done but the clamps held. "What do you want?" he said, his throat again caressing the cold restraint of steel wrapped once more around his neck.

Carver raised his arm and pointed it at Lee. In his hand was a pulse gun, already primed.

"What do you want?" Lee felt the crazy urge to pinch himself, to check if the most powerful man in the world really was aiming a gun at him. Perhaps it was all dream or nightmare, but of course he could not pinch himself. Not that the clamps quenched his amazement or his curiosity that Carver should come to see him. He reiterated his question in a desperate bid to buy time. "Is it information you want?"

"No. Just vengeance. I have all the information I need about you and . . . Max, isn't that what he called himself? Of course, Grant Maxwell is dead now, isn't he? We don't need information from you, Lee. We know all we need to know about you and your twin." Carver paused, then said, "Even though you're his brother, your name is not Maxwell, is it?"

"I ca-can't . . . talk with this . . . cla-mp."

"Oh really?" Carver raised the back of his hand, ready to draw the hard stock of the pulser across Lee's face. Something made him stop. Lips curling in distaste, he withdrew his arm and said, "What's your second name, Lee? Is it Armitage, after Haria and Raul? Is it Ching?"

Lee wanted to hit Carver, to strangle him with his bare hands, but he couldn't even pinch himself, never mind attack someone else. He felt a slight tremor. He looked at the ceiling. It seemed to shimmer ever so slightly. There came a noise like the sound of a dim and distant thud. He felt another shudder and guessed its nature. "Are things getting hot up there?" he asked with a grin.

Before Carver could even think about venting his anger, the chamber door burst open. "Better go, sir," said a Bio trooper. "Clan . . ." A blast of pulse-fire from down the corridor riveted his last syllable to the wall.

Carver sprang behind the scanner casing and backed toward the elevator. Its half-open doors provided perfect cover as he pointed his gun at the other side of the chamber. To the left of the main entrance, the prisoner lay on his slab. To Carver's right, the bulky scanner. Anyone trying to get at Carver would have to come between the two—right into his gun-sights.

Lee wanted to shout to warn onrushing Association soldiers but knew that Carver would blast him to bits if he did.

A shadow sprang across the doorway, pulse gun ready, seeking opposition in the chamber. The doorway made a small and easy target, framing the clandestitute attacker the moment he rushed into the room. Carver unleashed a stream of pulses, killing the clandestitute instantly. Then a man dived full length, tumbling like an acrobat across the opening. Carver's fire was quick, but not quick enough for the acrobat.

Lee strained his neck to see what might happen next—two clandestitutes would doubtless take both sides of the door simultaneously. He was right. Two men dived in—one rolled left, the other rolled right. A pulse from the elevator shaft took out the soldier on the left—the one to the right rolled for cover behind the scanner housing. Carver's eyes darted from doorway to scanner, waiting for a clandestitute gun barrel to flare.

The soldier shielded by the scanner glanced at Lee, who thought for one fleeting second that he saw a look of disgust in the man's eyes—probably something to do with the state of his face. The clandestitute soldier glanced in the direction indicated by Lee, saw a button, and looked back.

Lee tried to nod furiously, like a woodpecker in cartoon bondage.

The soldier reached forward and pressed the button with the muzzle of his gun.

The clamps whipped open, distracting Carver. The soldier sprang to his feet and fired a pulse, but missed. The doors to the elevator shaft began to close.

Carver rolled from one side of the elevator to the other, cutting loose with a burst of his own through the doors, taking out the soldier and two others as they plunged into the chamber.

Lee was in the act of sitting up, ready to jump from the slab. The elevator doors were closing but Carver had time for one parting shot. He lined up his pulser with Lee's chest. Lee's arm was in motion, hurtling something through the air.

Carver was about to pull the trigger when Lee's projectile distracted him. The small, engraved stone flew through the narrowing split between the doors. It passed by Carver's head, nearly grazing him, and bounced harmlessly off the back wall of the elevator. The flight path of the lucky charm had been enough to disrupt Carver's concentration, throwing his pulse just off line, making him miss his target by millimeters.

The elevator doors closed.

No amount of clandestitute pulse fire could penetrate the reinforced doors of the elevator shaft. By the time explosive charges would be set, Carver was bound to be on the roof, or damn near it.

"Cover all doors to that shaft—up to and including the roof, understand?" Lee shouted. He was standing on the floor now, stretching his aching limbs. The corporal taking his order glanced at him momentarily, then looked away and repeated the order into his lapel mike.

A sergeant stepped forward ready to attach explosives to the elevator door. "Save your plastic," Lee advised him. "We'll get our man upstairs."

Lee touched his face. It felt raw and moist, like meat coated in vegetable oil ready for the pot. He was looking for a reflective surface in the chamber when a voice crackled on the comm. "No car in the shaft. Repeat, no car in the shaft."

Lee was incredulous. He grabbed the corporal by the collar and yelled into his lapel mike: "There has to be a car. We saw the doors close. It went up. This is the bottom deck—it has to have gone up." The corporal strained his neck back. Lee's face was so close it was almost rubbing

279

against his cheek. Lee held on to his collar, waiting for a reply from the voice in the mike. He could see the corporal's nose all screwed up with fear and disgust. Pity about him. Lee was breathing hard down his neck when the voice crackled again. "No car. Repeat, positively no car in the shaft."

"Then the car's jammed!" Lee let go of the corporal's collar. "He's stuck right behind those doors! Sergeant," he yelled. "Blow that door."

Ten seconds later the elevator doors buckled in the white heat and deafening noise of plastic explosives. A dozen pulse muzzles trained on the shaft, ready to fire their deadly load into the stranded car.

There was no car.

Lee raced into the shaft and looked up. The voice on the comm had been right. There was no evidence of a car anywhere above.

"Sir?" It was the corporal, staring down at Lee's feet. At first Lee thought this was a ploy to avoid looking him in the face. The way he felt now, he was about to berate the corporal for avoiding eye contact when addressing an officer. Then he looked down and realized where the car had gone.

It had not gone up. It had not jammed. They were standing on its roof.

Chapter Twenty-Seven

Lee spoke into the comm. "Our information was not correct. There was a passageway beneath the bottom floor. It led to a hoverpark two blocks away. He could have gone anywhere. If only we had blown the elevator door sooner, we . . ."

"Don't worry," said Xiao Qi Ching. "The main thing is that he is on the run."

"I want to go after him. I want to . . ."

"We'll find him. What is your current position?"

"I'm on that grassy headland overlooking the bay. We can see the entire city from here."

"Good," said Ching. "Watch SMB."

Lee turned to a soldier and asked, "Where's SMB?"

"That massive bunker over there, sir—the State Militia Building." The man pointed to a large squat structure that seemed to grow out of the soil like a monstrous gray slab dropped from the sky. Its dirty-white roof was adorned by a small dome-like structure housing some sort of gun or telescope. Lee was trying to figure out what it was when a flash streaked across the sky and into the building. As soon as the missile found its ground floor target, SMB disappeared in a groundburst so violent that even the grassy headland where Lee stood shook from the explosion.

The comm crackled into life again. "Like that?" said Ching.

"Yeah. Where are you?"

"On the other side of the cit . . . hold it."

As he wondered what was distracting Ching, Lee held the comm in his hand and looked out over the city, trying to make sense of it all. Smoke hung low over Gemini Boulevard. Buildings burned everywhere, especially down East Side. He looked out over the western suburbs where blazing fires had breached the boundaries of the rich. Somewhere in the distance, the roof of an exclusive school. Maybe it was Golden Gate High, where Max had attended.

Ching was on the comm again. "We have just received information about Carver's whereabouts."

"Where is he?" Lee was no longer interested in the smoky cityscape.

"He took off in a shuttle some minutes ago. What's left of Bio's air defense is protecting him. We may not be able to down that shuttle."

"I've got to go after him, sir."

"We already have personnel on station cluster *Pacifica*, as you well know."

"That may not be enough."

"He's on the run and won't be coming back. We have enough personnel detailed to cover the situation."

Lee leaned on the side of the jeep and spoke resolutely to Ching. "Sir, the man was determined enough to enter that elevator shaft alone, determined enough to take on our soldiers in face-to-face combat. If he gets to Mars, it will result in unnecessary violence and a prolonging of the war. He's got to be stopped on *Pacifica*. We can't afford to let him board the wombship *Catalina* and flee to Mars. He's crazy enough to try anything. We need backup on *Pacifica*, sir. I saw the look in his eyes less than an hour ago. He won't be easy to stop. Believe me, we need backup."

282

Lee bit his lip and waited. Static gurgled on the comm. Absence of an immediate response was, he hoped, significant. He looked at the sky and sighed. Station cluster *Pacifica* was up there somewhere, five hundred kilometers above the Earth. He looked down at the comm and caught his reflection on the control's silver casing. It was the first time he had seen his new face. It stared up at him, purple and wrinkled like a rotten potato—or a newborn babe.

At its widest point, the spidery web of *Pacifica* measured 2.2 kilometers in diameter. The web's threads, wide as redwoods from the forests of long ago, made up the station cluster's framework. Studded along the outer rim of the web were service pods accessed by maintenance vehicles or by workers operating from within the threads themselves. This man-made membrane connecting the component parts of *Pacifica* provided a ready-made series of walkways, rendering maintenance vehicles redundant—except for odd jobs at the web's extremities.

The maintenance vehicle hovering at Pod 23 was ostensibly there to repair a meteorite-damaged antenna. In reality, it was there to communicate secretly with Association HQ on Earth. The diminutive figure piloting the vehicle was Commander Harkes, the clandestitute who had fought alongside Lee in the raid on the Gulf Coast geminizing factory back in April. Things had come a long way in the intervening months. The balance of power had shifted on Earth, and Harkes was back on *Pacifica* where she had already spent three years working and spying for the Association. If anyone was well acquainted with the cluster station, it was the dwarfish figure now listening to reports of Bio's collapse. News from the home planet was good—Harkes' hazel eyes were wide and bright. She looked at her second-in-command and smiled. Then came news of Carver's escape and his flight to *Pacifica*.

"What will we do?" said her companion, a burly Mexican in his mid-thirties.

Harkes stared out of the maintenance vehicle window as if Carver's shuttle might come looming up from Earth at any moment. It was too early for that, but not too late for planning. "He's going to take the wombship. We better get the Censurer," she said. "Call in the others. Meet on the platform two viewport in ten minutes."

The Censurer line was a series of short-haul hunters initiated at enormous cost in the 2150s in response to a convenient aliens scare invented by Bio's propaganda machine. This provided an excuse for constructing sentinel craft to protect the two cluster stations. In reality, the Censurers were there to protect *Atlantica* and *Pacifica*, not from aliens, but from any future dissident threat such as the clandestitutes.

Ronald Carver's shuttle was now less than four minutes away, and plainly visible through the station's viewport. Harkes could see it—a clearly defined dot growing perceptibly as it reached up from the ocean below. She could also see the wombship *Catalina* hanging by its nosecone from the space-dock framework. Fuel lines were hooked up, filling it with cryogenics for the journey to Mars. The leading edge of the wombship wing seemed to sway—probably caused by the crew testing retros prior to embarkation. Harkes studied closely the configuration of the *Catalina*'s airframe. Its hundred meter-long design may have been based on the old supershuttles, but some of its turrets and torpedoes were highly innovative, adapted from the Censurer program (Carver had also used the alien pretext to adorn the wombship with a deadly arsenal).

"What will we do now?" the Mexican whispered to Commander Harkes as they stared out the viewport window. It had been the second time in fifteen minutes he had blurted out that question.

Harkes did not think such behavior was good enough from her second-in-command, but she did not hesitate to reply. "I have an idea." She stepped back from the viewport, leaned on the catwalk rail and looked down into the docking bay. The catwalk was one of a series criss-crossing the circular docking area at a height of thirty meters. Reception and departure facilities were networked by a maze of overhanging walkways. Because of the overhead view of vehicles coming and going, plus the exterior view of Earth and the stars, the catwalks were popular with off-duty personnel.

Harkes hoped that she and her three colleagues could make their way unnoticed to the Censurer. It was large enough to accommodate four, of that she was certain—but she was not sure if it was capable of successfully engaging the wombship. Still, it was a damn sight better than any other plan she could come up with. If it worked, she and her colleagues would have a ready-made escape craft back to Earth.

Ronald Carver also had plans for the Censurer. He saw it as a useful escort vessel in the event of attack from Earth. The Censurer's outer range was one hundred thousand kilometers—once that far out the wombship would be safely out of clandestitute reach. Just to make sure, he was toying with the idea of destroying both cluster stations on his way out of Earth orbit.

Carver looked down on his home planet. From this height above the Pacific, the Earth took on a strange hue: a pastel half-world almost entirely blue, the monotony of ocean broken here and there by wisps of unfurling cloud. Tiny islands gleamed like wet stepping stones in sunlight. The weather was good except for a depression over Tahiti. There were a lot of reefs down there, Carver thought, like the one he had destroyed the previous day.

Not that reefs interested him any more. He had other matters to think about. The old planet was dead, long live the new. He turned from the Earth, relishing the control he would exercise over his clandestitute-free world on Mars. He looked up at a different shade of blue, not pastel but deep and dark, tending to blackness, generously interspersed with stars and planets—a view superior to any he had seen through his old telescope. Directly overhead, through the shuttle's transparent roof, he could see the gangly shape of a cluster station hanging like a chandelier above a world to which he wished never to return. The moment he saw the silvery web of *Pacifica*, he made up his mind to destroy both station clusters. It seemed to him as though it would be a fitting gesture—a final severing of the umbilical before leaving the mother planet forever.

The marshal at Jula Airbase looked down from Tower Control. One of the three Earth-bound Censurers stood ready and primed for launch on skyway two. "Remember," the marshal addressed the pilot through his mike, "you're in a state-of-the-art machine designed to respond instantly to oral commands. It's a cinch to fly."

"I'll try to tell it that." Lee tightened the harness around his shoulder.

"What you have to do," the marshal said, "is to state your instructions clearly, without hesitation. Onboard controls will do the rest. Datascreens are there to show you all you need to know. Cluster station homing beams will assist your docking. Should anything go wrong and you need to eject, press the airbutton on the left side of your helmet—it will give you a twenty-minute oxygen supply. Controls for your backpack retros are on your belt. Good luck."

"Thanks," said Lee. He braced himself for take-off and looked up, knowing that Commander Harkes and her three-man team were the only Association presence on *Pacifica*. He hoped that whatever they might be doing right now would render his flight a simple there-and-back mission to the cluster station five hundred kilometers over his head.

Harkes was not prone to panic, neither could she lip-read, but from her catwalk view it was obvious that the first thing Carver did after stepping out of the docked shuttle was to inquire about the Censurer's flight status. She could see him gesturing plainly toward the attack craft. That, plus a flurry of activity around the Censurer, sent fear waltzing up Harkes' spine as surely as if she had seen her own death-mask. She had counted on being able to sneak aboard the attack craft in the aftermath and general confusion of Carver's arrival, then bide her time until the wombship was underway.

Depending largely on surprise, she hoped to engage the Censurer's thrusters, batter her way out of the dock and destroy the wombship. Simple, she kept telling herself, but the view from the catwalk told a different story: a three-man crew made their way to the changing area to ready themselves to man the Censurer. Harkes looked down despondently; her original plan in ruins, but when she thought about it she realized that Carver might have inadvertently done her a favor. Now the Censurer could depart calmly without arousing suspicion. Flight-suits would provide a perfect disguise. In fact, they were so bulky that Harkes and her team might be able to carry weapons with them in case they were discovered before boarding the Censurer. The only trouble was how to deal with Carver's intended crew . . .

In the end, it seemed it might be easier than she dared to hope. Carver's arrival had caused consternation. The advent of the head of Bio would have had an unsettling effect at the best of times. Now the cluster station was alive with rumor and intimation that insinuated its way into every man and woman on board. Within minutes, *Pacifica* was infested with confusion, doubt and fear. Some said the Earth was in turmoil, others said *shut up or face a death squad.*

Carver stood on A-deck, halfway between the docking bay floor and the viewport catwalks. As he waited to board the wombship he could see the signs, and knew it would not be long before this place also became unsafe. Despite its handpicked crew, clandestitutes were bound to have infiltrated *Pacifica.* While all around him confusion and rumor reigned, Ronald Carver kept a vigilant eye, ever watchful for an enemy that might show itself at any time.

Security personnel were too caught up in trying to figure out what was going on to notice that the Censurer crewmen who had come out of the changing area were not the three who had gone in. Sidetracked by the day's events, they did not even notice that the crew had increased to four and that one of them had, in the space of five minutes, shrunk by half a meter and grown breasts.

Carver leaned on the A-deck rail. It was not Commander Harkes' physique that alerted him, but the complexion of her second-in-command. Carver could not recall seeing a Latin-looking crewmember enter the changing area, certainly none with such glistening skin. He caught a glimpse of the sweat-soaked face behind the visor, and also saw that the man appeared to be stocky—too stocky if the girth of his waist was anything to go by.

"Stop that crewman!" Carver yelled.

The four clandestitutes stopped in their tracks and looked up. When Harkes saw who had shouted at them from A-deck, she froze. Three security men stepped forward.

"Oh shit," hissed the Mexican, his visor clouding over with vapor from his panicky breath. "What will we . . . ?"

"Shut up!" muttered Harkes.

"Frisk him!" shouted Carver, pointing at the Mexican.

Harkes knew that it was all up now. Breathing hard, she looked at the Censurer. It was close, tantalizingly so, but there was no cover. At least they were carrying weapons and would go down fighting. "At three," she whispered. "One . . ."

The security men were close enough to hear 'two'. Before they could react, she said 'three'.

The two clandestitutes behind her and the Mexican in front broke from single file. Peeling off in different directions, pulling guns from their cumbersome flight-suits, they sprinted in zigzag patterns to the Censurer.

They never stood a chance. Security men with weapons pointing from shoulder straps reacted quickly, getting off several bursts before the clandestitutes could take proper aim. Up on A-deck, Carver ducked for cover. The two men behind Harkes were mown down in a single sweep. The Mexican got to within arm's length of the Censurer before a pulse splintered his shoulder, spinning him to the floor. He pulled his trigger as he fell, unleashing a burst that sprayed uselessly overhead. He hit the deck never needing to know what to do again.

Harkes was last to die—a round pulped her kidneys. She

fell to the floor and rolled over twice. Looking up, the last thing she saw was a sleek black nosecone directly overhead. She pressed the detonator on her belt, taking the Censurer's front undercarriage with her as she went.

Carver had hidden behind a transom when the fighting began. He got to his feet now, immediately demanding a damage report—not that one was needed. The craft in the docking bay, its nosecone rent in half and pointing at the floor, was clearly out of commission.

He spent the next five minutes on the *Catalina*'s bridge supervising its embarkation. The ship's nerve center was small and cramped, with barely room for three. Carver sat in the middle—to his left the wombship navigator, to his right General Reeves. In front of them a viewport shielded now until they were underway. Below the viewport a bank of screens indicated their current status. One monitor showed the *Catalina* shedding its remaining fuel line. Another showed the mooring link, the only physical contact between the wombship and *Pacifica*. Between screens, a computer graphic displayed a Censurer-class attack craft climbing through the stratosphere.

"Disengage nosecone," the navigator spoke into his mouthpiece.

Carver's fingers drummed non-stop on his armrests during the unhooking operation. In the moment of final severance, his stomach lurched satisfyingly, confirming that they had indeed broken free. The sensation of drifting was short-lived.

"Retros firing," said the navigator who glanced sideways, hoping to impress Carver with his efficiency, but Carver was preoccupied by the readout of an attack craft pulling clear of the atmosphere and heading straight for the station cluster.

Fuselage retros maneuvered the wombship vertically out of range of the hook-up area. A hundred meters out, the *Catalina* was ready for the next phase of its embarkation procedure.

"Do we have to turn through ninety degrees?" asked Carver.

"Afraid so," said the navigator. "Otherwise we'll collide with the docking area."

Carver sighed as the *Catalina*'s thrusters fired a short program of measured bursts, slowly turning the ship from upright to horizontal. Cartwheeling majestically, its poetic motion betrayed no forward momentum at all. Dipping its nose and raising its tail, midships turned on a precise mathematical axis. Silver and silent, and loaded with five hundred capsuled fetuses, the ship executed its maneuver in less than a minute. Carver glanced back at the capsule-batteries in the main fuselage. Their twins were living back on Earth, where the head of Bio hoped they would remain. Once on Mars, these new arrivals could be brought to term and birthed as potential breeding stock for Bio's new civilization on the red planet. Behind the cargo area, hidden from view, was the engineering section manned by a maintenance crew of two who were in constant voice contact with the *Catalina*'s bridge.

By the time the *Catalina* was pointing directly away from the cluster station, the Censurer was ten kilometers off the far side of *Pacifica*'s maintenance wing.

It turned to face its target.

For anyone with eyes to see, the *Catalina*'s onscreen graphics showed a pair of streaks shooting from the Censurer's bows. Carver saw the telltale streaks, but his navigator and his general were too busy maneuvering the *Catalina* to notice. Carver leaned forward and studied the three-dimensional image of the attack craft that had come up from the planet below. He saw it veer so fast to starboard it almost went off-screen. At the same time, an urgent message came through from the cluster station. The two men beside him listened carefully to the words. Carver did not need to—he had seen the evidence for himself.

"Censurer torpedoes launched! Repeat, Censurer torpedoes launched!" barked the voice from *Pacifica*.

The navigator and the general were in the middle of assimilating what that meant when Carver said, "Reverse thrust!"

The navigator again looked sideways at him, his brain still not at the far end of the assimilation process.

"Reverse thrust, you fool! Get us behind the station!" Carver shouted with such force that the navigator remembered all his training and instantly obeyed.

Carver knew from onboard data that the Censurer had just cleared the cluster station's far side. He also knew that its torpedoes would pass close to maintenance wing en route to impact. If the *Catalina* reversed quickly enough, and if the torpedoes were not smart enough, they might adjust angles without realizing what lay between them and their intended target.

Marrow solidified in Carver's bones as the *Catalina*'s thrusters went into overdrive. The wombship may once have been little more than a glorified long-haul freighter, but its drive systems had been souped-up to match its revamped status.

The ship shuddered and lurched back with such force that the contents of Carver's stomach jumped to his larynx. His face broke out in sweaty bubbles; his hands clung to the sides of his chair. For some reason he had time to wonder if this gushing nausea was caused by G-forces or by the fear of death. Then he wondered if time itself was on his side.

It was, but only just. Micro-whiskers on the torpedo heads detected a sudden shift in the wombship's position.

"Damn!" hissed Lee. Graphics showed torpedo number one heading straight for the pod at the far end of the maintenance wing. Number two might have slipped through the angular tubing leading to the pod, but it was caught up in number one's explosion. Both torps detonated in a spectacular display of silent pyrogenics.

Lee brought his fist down so hard the control panel nearly jumped out of its casing. "Jesus," he muttered, at the audacity and speed of the wombship's maneuver.

The moment the torpedoes exploded, a relieved navigator used his initiative to bring the wombship to a halt just in time to prevent it re-emerging beyond the far end of the cluster station. One glance at the head of Bio sitting alongside him and he thought better of any further independent action. "He's flying a loop pattern," he said to his boss, "far side of *Pacifica*. Procedure?"

Carver leaned forward, face covered in sweat, clammy-handed. His heart, thumping with dread only seconds before, soared now from a mixture of fear, relief—and joy that from this moment every beat was a bonus stolen from the clandestitutes.

The wombship was behind the far end of *Pacifica*, a full two kilometers away from the damaged maintenance section. Readouts showed that the navigator had halted the *Catalina*'s reverse thrust with meters to spare—its tailpiece was just hidden behind the cluster's outer rim.

"Forward thrust," said Carver. "Take us along the path

we just reversed. Fire at him as we pass behind maintenance wing."

General Reeves said, "Sir, he's well armed with torpedoes and quantums. It's a top-of-the-range Censu . . ."

"Execute maneuver!" With a wave of his hand Carver
dismissed the general's advice.

Drive systems at full throttle, quantums blazing, the
wombship swooped from behind the wreckage of the maintenance wing.

Lee saw it coming on his screens and took evasive action
immediately. A zigzag roll pattern brought the Censurer
back to safety behind the cover of *Pacifica*. He put the skids
on then, but not before unleashing a quantum burst at
Carver's vessel.

"Incoming!" shouted the navigator of the *Catalina*,
swerving his ship to starboard to avoid a direct hit. Luckily
for him, the quantum burst glanced off the wombship's
tough outer shell. "Damage report!" he roared, turning the
Catalina into a tight roll that brought it safely back to the
far side of the station.

"Superficial," a voice from engineering section responded on the comm. "Outer fuselage only."

"Where's the Censurer now?" demanded Carver.

"Directly opposite," said the navigator. "On the other
side of *Pacifica*."

"He's programmed a shielding operation," said the general. "He's using the station as a barrier."

"So are we," said the navigator. "Whoever's over there is
a clever bastard."

Carver, chastened by the indirect hit off the fuselage,
forced himself to agree. "Yes," he said. "Hold position until
we see what he does."

For two minutes both craft stalked each other: the wide spidery web of *Pacifica* was large enough to accommodate and shield quite some maneuvering. Each time the wombship changed position, the Censurer did likewise.

"He's programmed his drive system to mirror our movements," said the navigator.

Frustrated by this game of cat and mouse, General Reeves glanced nervously at Carver. "We can't stay here forever," he said. "If another Censurer comes up from Earth the two of them together will turn us into that." He pointed at the mangled wreckage that had once been the maintenance wing.

Carver's eyes lit up. "That's it!" he said.

"Pardon?" The navigator's brow furrowed.

"Take us behind the dormitory wing," said Carver.

The navigator's forehead corrugated again. "The dorms?" he said. "Why?"

"Just carry out orders." Carver shook his head tiresomely. As usual, he was the one to come up with solutions.

Five swift retro burns brought the wombship into position.

"Lock all torpedoes and quantums on the enemy," said Carver.

The navigator looked at the general, and in the moment of looking he read Carver's intention. "But," he said, "there's people . . ."

"Shut up and do what you're told," said the general.

The dutiful navigator swallowed his spittle. Then he swallowed his conscience and programmed the weapons.

"At my signal," said Carver. "Fire three torpedoes. Then another three, plus all quantums, one-point-five seconds later. Do you understand?"

"Yes," said the navigator.

"Good," said Carver. "Fire."

Lee could not believe what happened next. The dormitory wing of station cluster *Pacifica* disintegrated in a starburst so bright it briefly outshone the sun. Whole sections of sleeping quarters were ripped apart, the poor souls within dispatched by the severity of the explosion. The tubular mainstays that formed the lattice framework interconnecting the dormitories buckled and fragmented in the lethal heat of Carver's torpedoes. A brief fireball engulfed the wing, incinerating metal and flesh with consummate relish—and equal ease.

Lee was dazzled. The explosion lit a supernova in his cockpit, washing out all his graphics. When the white light faded he looked at his screens and saw to his horror that three torpedoes were speeding through the gap where the dormitory wing had been.

One-point-three kilometers and closing.

Again his cockpit blanched as one of the torpedoes caught some stray piece of solid matter and detonated in yet another brief fireball. As the glare faded Lee looked at his screens and turned pale from the realization that the other two torps had got through the debris and were headed straight for him.

One-point-one K and closing fast.

The Censurer rocked from side to side in the slipstreams of passing quantum fire. Lee did not need to think twice to know that Carver had outsmarted him. No time now to attack the wombship. With not a hint of strategy other than mere survival, Lee ordered the Censurer hard to starboard, hoping that maximum thrust might enable him to outrun the torpedoes. Somewhere in his subconscious an idea germinated—put enough distance between him and the incoming torpedoes. Maybe then he could do a U-turn and blast them first. He could not risk shooting at them now, not with what was left of *Pacifica* in the way, but before he knew it the Censurer shipped a quantum burst on the port side.

Lee's bones jumped in their sockets. So did his eyes. For a moment everything went out of focus. Alarms wailed, screens blinked in panic—the quantum had deflected the Censurer off its starboard course, destroying a vital stabilizing fin. The hit was so severe it knocked out the drive systems. The Censurer drifted and began to rotate in a slow spin. Lee watched, helpless, as his world turned upside down in a death waltz that was sure to be very short-lived.

Zero-point-six K

A hail of quantums rushed past. Miraculously, there were no more hits. Lee glanced again at the flashing graphics.

Zero-point-five K

He was terrified. The crippled Censurer was drifting like a sampan in the eye of a hurricane.

Zero-point-four K

Death could only be seconds away. To hell with *Pacifica*, to hell with everything. "Fire all torpedoes, fire all quantums," said Lee, praying that luck was on his side.

"He's firing, sir," said the navigator.

Carver glanced at the screen.

"He's used all his torpedoes, sir. Scanners indicate they're not even programmed—they're heading straight for what's left of dormitory wing."

Zero-point-three K

Carver chuckled. Unprogrammed torpedoes would be easy to dodge.

The throbbing of departing torps quickly subsided. With the firing of the last one, Lee felt his quantum guns vibrate as they too dispatched their load. Rapid though those vibrations were, they struggled to keep up with his heart rate. He glanced at the warning screen.

Zero-point-two

Zero-point-one

Once again the sun was relegated to second place. Both incoming torpedoes exploded simultaneously, or so it seemed to Lee. Whatever delay there might have been between the two—there must have been some—was infinitesimal to human faculties. In the moment his quantums met the torpedoes, Lee was certain he would perish, the explosion was that close. Shockwaves of quantum and torpedo spun the Censurer back, head over tail.

Carver watched the Censurer somersault once, twice.

"Sir," the navigator spoke. "I'm getting reports of two Censurers—both terrestrial and climbing toward us. And sir," the navigator listened intently to information coming through from what remained of *Pacifica*.

"Well?" said Carver.

"Sir," the navigator swallowed. "They're both hostile."

Carver looked at Reeves. "We've got to move—and move quickly," he said.

"If we pull away now," said the general, "maximum thrust ought to take us out of Censurer range and beyond their outer limit."

"What about the other Censurer?" said Carver. "He's not dead yet."

"Scanners indicate that he's badly damaged," said the

general. "He's used all his torpedoes. It would be suicide for him to take us on."

"Very well," said Carver. "Navigator, take us clear of the station. Maximum thrust for one hundred thousand K."

Lee took several deep breaths. At least the Censurer's airframe was holding despite the rigors of quantum hits and nearby explosions. It was drifting aimlessly, nosecone at right angles to the station cluster.

The voice on the comm startled Lee almost as much as the incoming torpedoes had. It said that the remaining terrestrial Censurers were in clandestitute hands, and climbing rapidly. Lee exhaled slowly, a trace of a smile on his lips. He leaned forward and peered out through a viewscreen scarred by torpedo and quantum debris. He could see the cluster station off the starboard wing, its dormitories notable by their absence. Soon, he told himself, he would see the back-up Censurers. Then he saw a sight that froze his lungs.

From off the far side of *Pacifica,* a wombship loomed. The *Catalina* looked almost beautiful, a thing of grace— and, as far as the world was concerned, profound in its implications if it made its getaway. Lee did not need to hear a voice to know who was aboard, or where it was going. Neither did he need anyone to tell him that, given a head start, it could outrun the other Censurers.

"Forward thrust," he said, amazed at how calm his own voice sounded.

The Censurer did not budge out of its slow drift.

"Shit," he said. "Go to oral response. Repeat, oral response. Confirm oral mode."

Oral response confirmed, said the onboard computer.

Lee whistled a low note of slow relief. "At least something works around here," he said, glancing at the readouts. The wombship was seventy-one degrees to starboard and at an elevation of twenty-two.

"Hard starboard seventy-one degrees, elevation twenty-two degrees," said Lee.

After what seemed an age, the Censurer responded.

"Confirm ejector status," said Lee, his voice a whisper.

Command inaudible, said the machine.

Lee repeated himself—louder.

Ejector status functional, it replied.

"Forward thrust," he said, his pulses thundering blood through his veins like never before. He said it loud, he said it clear, hoping that an authoritative tone might kick-start the only thing that stood between Carver and a new beginning for Bio.

The navigator could hardly believe what his screen was showing him. "Sir, the . . ."

"Fire all quantums," said Carver. "Fire now!"

"He's committing suicide," said General Reeves. "He's . . ."

". . . coming straight at us!" said the panic-stricken navigator.

"Hard to port!" roared Carver. "Hard to port!"

The Censurer was accelerating so fast Lee's weight glued him to his seat. Graphics flashed again. Incoming quantums—another readout told him that the wombship was adjusting its position.

"Five degrees starboard!" Lee shouted. He did not need readouts to know how rapidly the Censurer was eating up the vacuum between it and the wombship. He could see it looming ever larger in his viewscreen. He could also see quantums shooting from its turrets. One look at them and he could wait no longer. "Eject navigator," he yelled. "Eject nav—" The rest of the word stuck in his throat as the ejector apparatus responded.

It rocketed him a hundred meters into blackness. Everything was a dark blur. Darkness turned to blue—a blue world spinning around and around in front of his eyes. The world slowed down as his retro-pack automatically engaged. It fired a series of short bursts that took him out of his spin and brought him to a halt. He got his bearings in time to see his one-winged Censurer spinning away from its target, freefalling harmlessly.

One-winged? Lee blinked his dazed eyes and focused on the wombship. Its tail was missing—the Censurer must have got very close before the *Catalina*'s quantums found their target. The impact of its departing wing must have taken the wombship's tail clean off, such was the force of the explosion that had blown the Censurer apart. Lee blinked again. The wombship *Catalina* was not only tail-less, it was foundering, cartwheeling into what was left of the station cluster.

"Hah!" exclaimed Lee with such glee that his visor misted over. He tried hard to breathe again, but could not. Remembering the button on his helmet, he fumbled for it, pressed it, and felt the cool joy of sweet clear oxygen expanding in his lungs. Then he pressed the buttons on his control belt, firing little retro bursts that steered him down to the station cluster.

Ronald Carver was not slow to evaluate the danger of the situation he now found himself in. "There has to be some way out of this!" he shouted.

"There's no way," said the navigator. "Our control is

gone. We're spinning back into *Pacif* . . ."

"I mean out of this damn ship!" Carver struggled to keep himself from taking out his pulser and blasting this imbecilic officer all the way to Alpha Centauri. "Where are the EVA suits?" he demanded.

The navigator started to tell him, profusely, but that was not enough. "Show me!" yelled Carver.

Thirty seconds later the navigator slumped to the ground, his body riddled with pulses from Carver's gun. Within a minute, Carver and General Reeves had donned EVA suits and were standing in an airlock waiting for an opportune moment to abandon ship. Beyond the airlock they could hear the screams of the two crewmen trapped in the engineering section.

The moment for Carver and Reeves to make their escape came as the *Catalina* drifted back into the circumference of the spiraling cluster station, its fuselage passing within a hundred meters of Pod 17.

"Now!" said Carver, somewhat shrilly.

Reeves heard a faraway thump as detonators activated and blew the airlock bolts. Together with Carver, he bailed out. Using retro-packs, they steered toward the pod, pausing every now and then to look down on the crippled wombship.

Slowly it spiraled past the central section of the station cluster, decapitating booms and spars, taking gantries with it as it cartwheeled out of control. Within a minute, the wombship had drifted beyond the far end of *Pacifica*. It seemed to gather speed as it coasted out beyond the pods on the far side.

Carver lost interest in the departing wombship and maneuvered himself closer to Pod 17. Reeves remained stationary thirty meters away, addressing Carver on the headset.

"Sir, did you see anyone else bail out?"

Carver's reply was negative.

"I thought I saw someone in an EVA suit just below us—behind that angular walkway leading to the pod."

"Could be one of the *Catalina*'s engineers," said Carver. "Or a station workman."

"You go ahead, sir," said Reeves. "I'll take a closer look."

Carver retroed to within arm's reach of the pod-door. His outstretched hand pressed the entry button and he hauled himself aboard. Once inside he surveyed his surroundings. Station cluster pods were large enough for two. Though they lacked an oxygen supply and had none of the artificial gravity found elsewhere on *Pacifica*, being inside one was infinitely better than being lost in space. Carver took the pulse gun from his belt and waited for Reeves. He had no way of knowing how long his own oxygen supply might last—but with Reeves' EVA pack he could double his space-time, then take his chances with whoever was now in control of the cluster station. He held his handgun up close and examined it. It was small, he had fired it four times in dealing with the navigator, but there was surely enough pulse-power left to take care of the general.

One minute later a gloved hand drifted across the pod-door porthole and a white-suited arm stretched across the perspex toward the outer entry button.

The door opened. Carver waited for the general to enter before pulsing him—he did not want to risk losing that oxygen pack, or damaging it. For some peculiar reason known only to himself, Reeves backed in. Carver was so looking forward to seeing the general's expression that he could wait no longer. "Turn around, Reeves," he said.

Lee's headset was tuned to the same wavelength—he heard Carver's voice clearly as he turned.

Both men stared at each other for one crazy time-frozen moment. In that elongated instant, Lee said, "Hi, Ron."

Before a nonplussed Carver could react, Lee was on him, knocking the gun from his grasp, pinning him to the wall. The gun drifted slowly toward the open door as the two men grappled in a deadly hug. White-suited and white-helmeted in a white pod, their perspex visors rubbed and scraped together as if they were Eskimos embracing in a surreal metallic igloo.

Through the friction of visor on visor, Lee could see Carver's features. Teeth clenched, eyes wide with rage—or perhaps it was fear of the purple-wrinkled face that was so close, separated from him only by two thin layers of perspex.

Both men rolled slowly sideways. Carver's hands found Lee's neck.

Lee felt the pressure of the squeezing fingers and pushed hard.

Carver's face receded. His hands yanked at Lee's oxygen pack. Ungloved fingers would have pulled the lines out first time, but awkward EVA covers made it difficult.

Lee rolled over, instinctively protecting the lines. With his fist he thumped the side of Carver's helmet.

Carver turned away, carillons clanging in his head, then bounced his knee hard off Lee's testicles.

Lee gasped and spun away, throwing wild swipes that failed to register as pain ignited in his groin.

Carver brought up both arms and shoved Lee toward the door. He followed up with a clatter of punches that had Lee's helmet ringing.

Lee winced and lashed out, trying for Carver's head. He tried to twist away, but Carver was on him again. A quick one-two to the chest followed by a kick to the knee had Lee yelling in pain. His leg gave way. Had he been standing he would have collapsed, but zero gravity kept him upright long enough for Carver to push him through the door.

A blue planet swirled once again in Lee's vision. He grabbed the side of the pod and tried desperately to hold on. Carver had him pivoting on a knife-edge. Trying to maintain balance, Lee showed his back to Carver. Worse, his flailing arms led Carver's eyes to the pulse-gun floating so conveniently within reach. This time the gloved fingers were not so clumsy. But by the time Carver had grabbed the gun and raised it, Lee had succeeded in using the side of the door as a lever and was pushing himself back in over the edge.

Carver saw him coming and pulled the trigger. A solid pulse punched a neat hole in outer space, missing its target by inches. He had no time to fire again.

Lee headbutted Carver's visor so brutally that the perspex shattered into a thousand shards. Lee pulled back. Somehow his visor remained intact. A crisp downward parry knocked the gun from Carver's hand. Through a hovering veil of splintered glass, Lee watched the most powerful man in the world float up and back.

Carver turned, his face a screaming rage as he clawed for the oxygen lines on his back. The vacuum tasted bitter in his mouth. It burned up his nostrils. Breathless and panicky, his face ranged from pale through red, then purple, his skin creasing in oxygen-starved agony until his face matched Lee's both in texture and color.

Once again Carver saw the gun. It was in Lee's hands now and pointing straight at him. Carver felt a void expand like an inverted balloon in his lungs. His pulmonary artery pumped frantically. His two respiratory lobes—all light and spongy and full of craving air cells—came screaming up his trachea, crying out for the kiss of oxygen. His eyes bulged, their vision tunneled and blurred. He wanted to scream. His mouth contorted into a huge shriek, but he had no air to shout with. He saw the shadow of a gun-toting clandestitute. Beyond the gun, a doorway, stars and planets. Around and around the stars swirled; first in a slow dance, then faster and faster like silvery streaks growing ever thinner until they blended into a whirligig of dark, dark blue. Then the dark blue blackened, except for one small red planet beckoning like a beacon in the night. Carver's arms reached out for that planet, his heart and soul strived for it, his lungs collapsed for it, until it too, like all the planets and stars, winked into nothingness.

Death would have come quickly, more mercifully, had Lee pulled the trigger. But he did not want to let a pulse loose in such a confined area. More importantly, he wanted Carver to die slowly and agonizingly—for Haria, Raul, Zenga, Sharon, Hugo, Tamara, Mel and Max, and for the millions, born and unborn, who had died to support the crazed ego of the man writhing in the throes of death before him.

When there were no more spasms, when there were no more whimpers, when the purple wrinkles had subsided on Carver's face and the face itself began to turn pale, Lee yanked him toward the door. He removed Carver's oxygen pack to augment his own before jettisoning him to the all-embracing vastness of space. Just to make sure, he fired three pulses into Carver's corpse as it floated away. He watched the ragged body tumble slowly to a place among the stars where he hoped it would wither and shrivel. A place as far away as possible. No planet, no Earth, deserved to inherit the decomposing body of one so corrupt, to take it back into the soil, to recycle it. Then he remembered that in the vacuum of space it might never rot.

Though stars are innumerable beyond imagining, Lee doubted there would be enough energy between them to light a candle for each womb-banked fetus and activated child, each mown-down clandestitute and misguided militiaman, each wasted life and innocent victim. As he looked among the stars, he saw a Censurer standing off the far end of the cluster station. Then he saw another, its quantums and torpedo tubes pointed directly at the central core of *Pacifica*, demanding her surrender.

Chapter Twenty-Eight

Reporters were everywhere. Lucky ones with passes sat in the main chamber awaiting Xiao Qi Ching's press conference. Unaccredited ones stood outside hoping to get in.

Lee pushed his way down a corridor crammed with hopefuls. By the time he reached the security check, the conference had begun. He could have attended the press gathering but chose instead to watch it from behind the scenes. The off-limits area was less crowded as he made his way quickly to the transmission chamber at the rear of the conference hall.

Broadcasting was underway by the time Lee entered the studios. He stood behind an editing console and studied a bank of monitors all displaying Ching's great globe of a skull. Most screens showed it head-on; several concentrated on a side view; on every screen Lee heard the same words: a plea for understanding, for support, for peace and unity.

The last remaining womb-banked fetuses, Ching said, would be disconnected within days. Unfortunate perhaps, but the Association had decided that this was the unavoidable price that had to be paid. All currently activated twins would be allowed to live a full and, in so far as was possible, normal life. But fetuses were a different matter. There was no room for half measures. It was necessary to wipe all traces of Carver's legacy from the face of the Earth and to do so quickly.

Lee had heard this argument many times. As his eyes surveyed the array of screens before him, his thoughts drifted to the scenes outside the building.

Protests in the concourse were of riot proportions. The cut-off point for stored fetuses had been deemed to be August 20th.

Yesterday.

Support systems had been shut down worldwide and all womb-buildings and storage facilities were being destroyed. News of the mandatory cut-off date had leaked out prior to its announcement at the conference.

Lee sighed. Try justifying one date over another to those whose twins were due for Activation on August 21st. It wasn't just the centenarians who protested. People with ten, twenty, years left felt cheated out of their extra century. They did not want their twins terminated because they clung to the faint hope that perhaps one day Transposition might be re-introduced.

Then there were those who wanted Transposition continued until the current 'stock' of Activated children were 'processed' out of existence. There were also the traditional anti-abortionists who had taken to the streets advocating civil disobedience, labeling all Association members as baby-killers.

Lee scuffed his feet and looked up. Ching's globular head had disappeared as the cameras zoomed in on a journalist who asked why the fetuses could not be let come to term. For the umpteenth time Ching explained that according to all known psychological and behavioral research, there would be mental and emotional chaos if Geminizon-induced twins were let live contemporaneously. Their minds would seep into each other. There would be wide-spread mental aberration. There . . .

"That's just a scare tactic," shouted a hack from a tabloid vidmag that had sprouted up once freedom had been restored to the media. "Where's the evidence?" he demanded.

"Believe me," said Ching, "all scientific data points to mental problems on an epidemic scale."

"Prove it!" chorused the hacks at the back of the hall. The cameras swiveled. "How have you evidence," shrieked one of them, "when twins have never before lived contemporaneously?"

Lee shuffled uneasily out of the transmission chamber feeling sorry for Ching. So much for saving the world. He flashed his ID at the clearance desk, unhappy in the knowledge that security checks would be an everyday thing for a long time to come.

He needed room to think. A faraway place where burdens might drop from him like lead weights. For some reason he found himself hovering out to that thumb-shaped headland where he had first met Max. He parked the hover and walked to where the Bank Walk petered out into a small cove. On the other side the path puffed itself up into the Far Bank.

He came to a small grassy headland. There was a seat—a lovers' bench. He sat but did not want to sit, so he got to his feet again and stood at the grassy edge, staring out over the estuary. Endless mudflats glistened under a blue sky. The distant sea was flat calm. Larks hovered overhead.

Lee could never figure out how anyone, most of all poets, could be attracted to their noisy twittering. He shook his head. If Ching's conference had been anything to go by, press-curbs would be needed again. How strange to look at censorship from the other side and realize that it might have value.

He thought of all the capsules in all the womb-banks switched off and sucked dry; fetuses disposed of like rotting jelly. Mere cells, he told himself, though he knew that they were more than that. His own foster mother, Haria, had risked both their lives, and those of other Association members, to smuggle him out of Chicago Gemini Clinic when he was a twenty-week fetus—the same age as those destined to die on August 20th.

He looked out at the sea where offshore breezes whipped up the heads of faraway white horses. In a climate driven by moral dilemmas, there were no easy solutions. It was a question of balance—a balance the anti-abortionists did not want to see. To them the rights of the unborn were equal, if not superior, to the rights of the living. Lee could not sympathize with their stance, though he understood the frustration of the older generation who had just missed the last train to Transposition.

He kicked a stone down onto the foreshore. It half-buried itself in the mud with a sickening plop. People were so damned selfish. As soon as one war ends a new one germinates. Lee did not want to believe that it might come to that. All the old uncertainties had been blown away only to be replaced by a set of new ones. So many people had died, but for what? And what would he do now?

What does a guerrilla fighter do when his side wins, except defend the new order by becoming a mirror of his former enemy? Lee was standing on the other side of the scales. He saw clearly that, in the end, nothing changes. Everything remains the same. Ching was committed to establishing a new government, yet already Lee could feel a chasm growing between himself and the old man. Ching

311

was cut out for leadership, for steering the world, however perilously, onward through the storms to new crises. Lee could never be part of that. He had to get out, to get away, because whatever might happen in the wake of the August 20th decree, things were potent, to say the least.

The tide was coming in. Waves encroached on faraway sand, the monotony of the mudflats broken now by incoming streams. Like silver webs in the afternoon sun they glistened and weaved across drowning mud. Lee could not get Max out of his mind. This time his brother's presence was not a source of distress to him like the mental interference and loss of concentration he had experienced in Mississippi and Flok Island. Now it was more of a benign presence, a panacea to the turmoil going on around him.

Back in Mississippi, he and Max had figured out that their mental seepage was an unknown side effect of Geminizon. In the past week, Association doctors had confirmed it. They had described it as molecular fission that occurs naturally when Geminizon-induced twins are in close proximity. The minds produce some kind of strong force that binds the chemical activity in the brain, causing distortion and seepage. He put his hand to his face. In the two weeks since Carver's death his skin had lost its wrinkled, newborn aspect. Now he looked more than ever like Max. He ran his fingers along his forehead and wondered if more than mere chemical bonding had taken place. He put his hand down and looked out to sea.

All the people he had ever been close to were dead except Ching—and Mandy, but she was as much part of his past as Ching. She had escaped from Hokkaido and had made her way back to Longevity City. Lee sought her out ostensibly to tell her that her womb-banked twin had indeed been terminated under the old mental defective decree, but she already knew that. In reality he had come to tell her that he loved her. Again, he re-lived that moment in the lobby of Association HQ when she first glimpsed his reverted face. It drew a look of horror to her eyes, as if she had seen a ghost. Half turning from his fumbled embrace, she raised her hands to keep him at bay as though he had the plague. "Lee . . . I can't . . . How could you?"

He wanted to declare his love as he had been about to do in the sand dunes of Azing Baru on Hokkaido in the moments before the Bio Vindicator had swept in off the sea, but she stole a glimpse of him once more and wheeled sideways; revulsion etched on her every move. She, too, remembered liberating the children of the colony, and saw again his falling tears that night as he told her about Mel. To her that night now seemed long ago and far away. "How could you!" she shrieked, standing in the middle of the lobby. "How could you take his face!"

People all around stared briefly, then went about their business averting their eyes as though they, too, could not bear Lee's face. He followed her to the exit trying to explain that Bio had reverted it, not him; that it was his face, too, not just Max's. Before he could even suggest the possibility of getting another ethnic implant, she yelled, "You make me sick!" and turned, shielding her eyes, hurrying, tearful and distressed, down from the steps of the building. He stood forlornly on the topmost step, letting her spittle dry on his cheek, watching her walk briskly down what used to be Gemini Boulevard until he lost sight of her in the crowds thronging the sidewalk. Still shocked by her outburst, he turned away knowing she was gone from him forever. No matter what the surgeons might do, she would always know what lay beneath. It would be like living with an animated corpse. Later, over a farewell dinner with Ching, the Chinaman agreed that Mandy needed a stable relationship as much as Lee, but that it would probably be best for her to seek out someone who had not been through as much trauma as she had. "And likewise for you, my friend," Ching added.

Lee could understand that point of view, but it was little consolation to him now as he stood on the shoreline. Stars were coming out, hanging over the sea as if longing for a swim. He knew it was time for him to make a new start—preferably in some faraway place he knew not where, nor really cared. A place where his scars might heal in a new life away from the crazy destruction he had lived with all these years; where violence would not be like the incoming tide, unstoppable and irreversible, but where he might find gentleness and peace, and perhaps meet someone he could find happiness with.

There must be such a place, he hoped, though he knew it was not anywhere near Longevity City. And there must be such a person, though he did not know where she was. He made up his mind to search for both person and place. Where he found one, he might find the other.

He decided to go then. In the moment of his decision a current of air gushed from somewhere behind him. Like warm and tender breath it caressed the skin above his collar. He turned, startled, hairs bristling on the back of his neck.

There was no one behind him except more stars that seemed brighter against the darker sky above the shore. Lee looked at them for a minute. It was as if the stars were just hanging around above his head, waiting for someone to appear or for something to happen.

He considered straddling down the grassy slope and

stepping out along the shore, but it was muddy there. Turning from the grassy edge, he walked past the lovers' bench, away from the headland.

About the Author

Irish author **David Murphy** lives with his wife, son and daughter near Dublin where he writes, workshops, and publishes the magazine *Albedo One*, of which he is a founding editor. His first novel, *Arkon Chronicles*, appeared in 2003. After many years of magazine and chapbook appearances, his award-winning short stories were published in the collection *Lost Notes* (2004).